First published in the United States of America by Hydrangea Press.

WHEN HE WAS GONE. Copyright 2024 by Carla J Field.
All rights reserved. Printed in the United States of America.
For information, address Hydrangea Press, Boone, NC 28607.

www.hydrangeapress.com

Ordering Information:
Quantity sales. Special discounts are available on quantity purchases by corporations, associations, and others. For details, contact the publisher at the address above.

Printed in the United States of America

Publisher's Cataloging-in-Publication data
When He Was Gone. Carla J Field.
ISBN 979-8-9911193-0-6

Names: Field, Carla J, author.
Title: When He Was Gone : a novel / Carla J Field
Description: First edition. Hydrangea Press, 2024.

First Edition

HYDRANGEA
PRESS

WHEN HE WAS GONE

CARLA J FIELD

Part One

Chapter 1

ᑲ *September 1867* ᑲ

W hat have we done?" Frederick moaned, head in hands, his voice barely audible over the ship's creaking wood and the grinding of the paddlewheels.

He forced himself to look up and again saw the faces of his young sons in the flickering light of the oil lamp, the two of them, head on one pillow, sleeping under a thin blanket in the tiny berth across from him. The poor excuse for a bed was only slightly deeper than one of the shelves in the library he had built in the beautiful home they had left behind in their beloved Bern, Switzerland, just days before.

The past week had been torturous, but he had been buoyed above the stress and sadness by his wife's unrelenting energy and enthusiasm for what she kept calling their "great adventure." He knew Elizabeth chose the words carefully, hoping that her impetuous exuberance would spread to the eight children whose lives they had completely disrupted, and to him.

Now, with her sleeping in a nearby cabin with his youngest sons, one under each arm, and their four daughters, sleeping two-by-two in miserable berths identical to the horsehair-padded shelves his oldest boys slept on, the tears he had hidden as the massive gangplank was pulled back to the dock, began to course down his cheeks.

The ship's huge steam engine had come alive early that morning, the paddlewheels churning the harbor in Le Havre, France into roiling whirlpools as the *Arago* slowly moved away from the dock.

Dozens of family members, friends and gawkers on shore waved handkerchiefs that were answered by the hundreds of passengers aboard the big wooden ship, the waving and shouting continuing until those on shore slipped out of sight, enveloped in the thick, white fog.

Frederick knew in that moment he would never see his homeland—his aging parents, his sisters, his friends, all the precious places he knew since birth—ever again.

He laid back on the hard pad of his berth, barely wider than his shoulders, and his mind wandered back to how this had all begun. It was such a small thing, it seemed incomprehensible to him that it had now turned their lives completely upside down.

His father, Johan Christian, and his mother, Katharina, still lived in the Bern district of Malleray, about a half day's journey from central Bern, where he and Elizabeth were raising their children. Frederick tried to see his parents as often as possible, since his father was in his sixties, and though he still carried on the carpentry and cabinet-making business he had passed on to Frederick, he was definitely slowing down.

Before Elizabeth had gotten too uncomfortable to travel while awaiting the birth of their eighth child, they had taken the children to see grandpère Johan and grand-mère Katharina, who still spoke French, as did most of Malleray. Frederick was fortunate to be fluent in French and German, since Elizabeth had come from the German-speaking parish of Huttwill in Bern.

Though not as vigorous as he once was, Johan was a man of strong opinions, and for the last few years, he had been verbose about the economic challenges in Switzerland because of industrialization and its impact on employment.

"How can I make a living selling furniture when no one can afford to buy it?" Johan said.

"It is happening everywhere," Frederick said. "I am feeling it in the city as well."

Johan said, "I received another letter from my old friend, Jacob Fisher—you remember him? He moved to America about six years ago," Johan said. "He says it is a land of great opportunity, especially for hardworking men, since so many of the young men were lost in their terrible Civil War.

"Jacob said the young man who was a tenant on his property was killed in the War and his widow is moving back to her family. The home is free to someone who will clear the land and farm it. You are an excellent woodcrafter, Frederick, but you are also a great farmer," Johan said. "It is an opportunity I would take if I was a young man."

In retrospect, Frederick remembered how Elizabeth became extremely intrigued by what her father-in-law had said. Johan had given Frederick a small stack of letters from Fisher, and Elizabeth had read them over and over.

On their trip back to Bern, she said, "Frederick, maybe we should look into this possibility of a better life in America. We must make sure our children have opportunities."

And that was how it all began. Within weeks, Elizabeth had come home from the market holding a pamphlet with enchanting illustrations describing America's unlimited potential, free or nearly free land, and opportunities of all types in idyllically beautiful surroundings.

"I think we need to make the move to America, Frederick" she said. "We are not getting any younger. I will be forty years old in the coming year. Right now, we are still healthy and strong, and with our knowledge of farming and your cabinetmaking skills, we could have a wonderful life. If we don't do it soon, we will lose the opportunity."

"It seems somewhat intriguing, but so risky," Frederick said, knowing full well that if Elizabeth had decided they should move to America, that is what would happen. He adored her, and he had always loved her enthusiasm for life and her sometimes impulsive ways. And as long as he'd known her, Elizabeth always found a way to convince him of the next thing she wanted to do.

Elizabeth was clever in her own right, skilled with needlework and a gifted gardener. She managed their bustling family of ten with diligence and grace and seemed to be able to handle any challenge that came along.

Their mutual love of growing things, especially flowers, was something they had learned they shared early.

Frederick met Elizabeth when he was twenty-three and she was twenty-five. She was visiting a friend in the central part of Bern, and he had recently set up his cabinetry business there. He was a serious craftsman and a perfectionist. Sometimes he took his work so seriously that when creating a detailed piece, he would keep measuring and carving and fitting wood together for hours, forgetting to eat, and sometimes not realizing it was the wee hours of the morning.

The first time he saw Elizabeth, she was passing by his little shop and stopped to admire the geraniums growing in a window box. He looked up from his work, at first thinking she might be interested in a piece of furniture. He stepped out to speak to the little woman who was bending down to touch the geranium petals. When he said, "Hulloh," he startled her. She abruptly stood upright, smoothed down her dress, looked him straight in the eye, and said, "Did you plant these flowers?"

Frederick was struck, both by the sparkle in her intense blue eyes, and the strength and assurance in her voice. She was so tiny, that until she spoke, he could easily have mistaken her as being fragile.

It was not long before he was spending long hours visiting Elizabeth and talking about everything from growing flowers to their hopes and dreams for life.

Oh, how he now hoped this vision she had of life in America would become reality. He dried his tears on his shirt sleeve, and closed his eyes, determined to cast off the fears and doubts of their uncertain future.

In a nearby cabin, fatigue swept over Elizabeth as she cuddled her two youngest against her in the narrow berth, trying to adjust to the constant humming, creaking, and pounding of the ship, and the dank, acrid smell of the overused sleeping compartment.

The whirlwind of selling most of their worldly goods, emptying out and cleaning their big home before packing everything they could manage for themselves and their children—Frederick, eleven, Ernst, ten, Elise, nine, Marie, eight, Bertha, six, Rosalie, four, Franz, two, and eight-month-old Hans—had left Elizabeth exhausted. But she knew, though Frederick had complied with all the plans and had worked hard to make it come together, the move to America was largely her doing. Because of that, she felt that no matter what, she had to be energetic, positive, and ebullient as they plowed their way forward.

Frederick and his father and a few friends had built their big, beautiful home in Bern. It was three stories, counting the attic with its two gables. There were six windows across the front of the second story, making beautifully sunny bedrooms for them and the children. There was a large front porch, entirely covered by a trellis-style roof that during warm months was covered by flowering vines. The home was filled with so many lovely furnishings, some of them also designed and built by Frederick.

The large house had less land around it than the homes where Frederick and Elizabeth had grown up in more rural cantons outside the city, but even with their limited property, they had planted around the house love-ly small gardens that had flourished.

Elizabeth sold and gave away most of their household goods with her typical practical vigor, though she did feel twinges of sadness for the trees, vines, and flowers planted on their property that would be left be-hind. She, as always, took those feelings, put them on a high closet shelf in her heart and closed the door. Dwelling on what had been instead of what could be was something she simply would not do. Not ever.

Saying goodbye to their families in Switzerland before the train trip to Le Havre had been agonizing. Fortunately, at least Frederick's father saw merit in trying to make a better life, and Johan said the letters he had exchanged with his old friend, Jacob, made him feel confident Elizabeth and Frederick would have help getting started in their new life.

Elizabeth's parents and siblings were a combination of hurt, anger, and worry about what she was about to do. Her two younger brothers could not hide their concern about them getting on a ship with eight children to travel to a strange land from which they would likely never return.

Her brother, Johannes, was three years younger than Elizabeth. He held her close in heart and loved her like a best friend. Having been distressed and sleepless with worry as Elizabeth and Frederick sold their home and their goods, Johannes tried his best to dissuade his beloved sister from leaving Switzerland.

Johannes went into great detail about how the paddle steamer Pacific disappeared eleven years before on its way to America, with nearly two hundred aboard who were never found. As he talked, his voice became more and more intense. He went on to describe an English ship, the *Tempest*, that had disappeared just five years before while on its return trip from New York, with 150 lost.

"It's just plain foolhardy to drag your poor children onto a dangerous

7

wooden ship to cross the Atlantic! You just shouldn't do it, Elizabeth," Johannes said, before dissolving in tears.

She had thrown her arms around him and hugged him tightly. But she did not cry. Elizabeth, once her mind was made up, controlled her emotions like a strong horse with a tight bridle. They were going to America. She would not cry. She would not complain. She would not be weak. There was no turning back.

As she drifted toward troubled sleep, she thought of Frederick and her boys in the other cabin. She so relied on her husband's steadfast, unwavering work ethic. He was such a skilled craftsman. She thought of the trinket box he had made her while they were courting, one of the few nonpractical items she packed for this journey. It was an inlaid box made of more than a hundred individual pieces of carved and fitted wood that he had worked on for countless hours. It was a symbol of both his love for her and his general diligence in life.

When their relationship was new, there had been so much heat between them, he could not stay away from her ... and she did not want him to. Everything about Frederick charmed her. He was more than a foot taller than she, and slender, but muscular and sturdy. His work had made his hands exceptionally strong, but they were still graceful and gentle. Frederick had soulful, kind, brown eyes and, though he was generally a serious person, he had a quick wit, and she thought he had the loveliest laugh.

Life in Bern had been good, and they married in Interlaken near the banks of the beautiful River Aare in August 1855, when Frederick was twenty-four and she was twenty-six. Their son Frederick was born in February the next year. The following year Ernst was born, the year after, Elise, the year after, Marie, and by then, being parents became the dominating factor in their lives.

As she fought her way toward sleep on the first night on the steamer, Elizabeth kept trying to turn her anxious thoughts to hopeful daydreams about what their new home would be like, what they would accomplish in America, and what kind of lives their children would get to enjoy. As her mind wandered through their imagined farmland filled with an abundance of produce and beautiful flowers, the quiet warmth and comfort of her children's bodies finally lulled her to sleep.

Chapter 2

Frederick awoke to the dim morning light pouring in through the tiny cabin porthole. He felt like he hadn't actually slept but had more or less tussled and wrestled his way through the night. His joints ached from the hard pad. His brain ached from the stress. It took him a moment to resolve where he was. His sons, Frederick and Ernst, sat side by side on their berth a few feet across the wasy from him, silently staring at him, having done their best to keep from waking their father during the few minutes he remained asleep after they had awakened.

After an awkward moment of Frederick trying to gather his wits about him, his oldest son said quietly, "Father, can we go find mother and the other children?"

"No, you shouldn't be out amongst the strangers on this ship," Frederick answered. "I will dress, and we'll go to them. Put your shoes on."

After pulling themselves together and making their way to the shared bathroom, they went to the nearby section that housed women. There had been some cabins available for use by families, but nothing could accommodate a family of their size, so they had made the most feasible arrangement they could come up with.

As they headed toward the women's cabins, Elizabeth, with her little troop of six children, appeared, already headed their way. A look of relief and then a smile passed over her face when she saw Frederick, and he could not help but smile too, seeing his brave little wife. Her self-assurance and ability to always manage made him feel better and proud of her.

The ship was crowded, and with every passing minute, more people appeared, seemingly swarming through every door, generally headed to the common areas for dining, smoking, or getting out on the deck for fresh air.

There were more than 230 people on board, more than half of them men. Although Swiss men typically traveled with their families, there were some French and German men traveling alone, along with younger single Swiss men.

Much to the delight of the Garraux children, there were also dozens of other children on board, and they were already waving, smiling, and making faces at those who looked like potential playmates.

Conveniently for Frederick and Elizabeth, they had been told almost half of those traveling on the *Arago* were Swiss, and a majority of the rest spoke German.

The food provided in the dining area was adequate and tolerable. They were grateful not to be traveling below deck in steerage, where unventilated, ill-equipped, filthy space was shared by dozens or even hundreds of people who could not afford cabin tickets. The poor people in steerage had to prepare their own food from meager rations, and the stench and discomfort of their living conditions was entirely different than those in cabins. The cabins, however rudimentary and spartan, at least provided a modicum of privacy and minimal cleanliness.

Frederick thought back to when they had first arrived at the busy port at

Le Havre and saw the ship for the first time.

The *Arago* was a massive wooden-hulled ship, almost three hundred feet in length. When the children first laid eyes on the great steamer, they could hardly believe it. The older boys were beside themselves with excitement over the thought of boarding the big ship.

There were two huge iron paddlewheels on each side of the impressive steamer, along with two tall masts that would make it possible to continue with wind power if for any reason the steam engine failed.

While the family stayed in a boarding house filled with other immigrants also awaiting their time to board, Frederick had struck up a conversation with a man named Jurgen Huber, who knew all about the ships— especially the *Arago*—used to transport immigrants.

He was a large, strapping man, with a ruddy complexion, thick, sandy-colored hair and a big voice.

Huber, who lived in Le Havre and worked at the boarding house, had also worked aboard various ships. He spoke a good deal of French and English, but German was his native tongue, so he was enthused about sharing his extensive knowledge of the captain and his ship with Frederick.

Huber said the *Arago* had been launched several years before to carry mail back and forth across the Atlantic. But shortly after she started crossing the ocean, the U.S. Department of War had chartered the steamer as a transport ship for use by the Union army during America's great Civil War, he said.

With reverence in his voice, Huber said, "Captain Henry A. Gadsden was at the helm for the duration of the war. And lucky for you, he'll still be captain of the *Arago* for your crossing.

"Amazing captain, he is. Quite a man," Huber said. "Back in '63, the *Arago* was filled to overflowing with dead, wounded, and discharged soldiers from the battles at Fort Sumter and Fort Wagner when Gadsden spotted a suspicious ship in the waters out ahead of them. As the captain watched the ship, he saw her pick up speed as bales of cotton and other goods were being thrown overboard."

Speaking excitedly, Huber said, "Gadsden was not having it, and he gave chase. After seven hours—seven hours, mind ya—the *Arago* overtook the ship, and sure enough, it was the rebel blockade runner, the *Emma*!

"And you know, Gadsden had guns aboard the *Arago*, and the *Emma* had guns too, but not a shot was fired. I think the *Emma's* captain and crew were scared into surrender by Gadsden's determination. Gadsden never would have quit. He's one of the toughest captains on the Seven Seas, he is.

"You may know that war started when the Confederates fired a shell that exploded over Fort Sumter on the coast of the state of South Carolina. The poor outnumbered men in the fort tried to fight off the Confederates, but with the harbor blockaded by the rebel navy, they were on their own. More than four thousand of them died—God rest their souls—before they surrendered the fort, their flag was lowered, and the white flag raised."

Huber leaned in, looking Frederick intently in the eye, and said, "I tell you all this, because you ought to know what's happened in the country you want to make your new home, and because you should know about the captain and the great ship you'll be sailing on."

Frederick agreed, and he listened intently, nodding and trying to commit all the information to memory so he could later tell Elizabeth and the older children.

"When the bloody war ended, the tattered flag that had flown over Fort Sumter was retrieved from a vault in New York where it had been hidden for all the years since the horrible war. The precious flag was then loaded aboard none other than the *Arago* to be returned to Fort Sumter," Huber said.

"The general who had held the fort until it was no longer possible, as well as many other important people, boarded the ship along with the flag. Captain Gadsden then took them safely and smoothly down the American coast," he said.

"As they neared their destination, a guardship hailed them, and they were given the horrible news that their president, Abraham Lincoln, had just been assassinated."

Huber leaned back and took a deep breath, as though the weight of the information had fatigued him. Then he continued.

"Gadsden safely delivered them all along with the flag to Fort Sumter, where it was raised again, four years to the day when it had been lowered in surrender," he said.

"Are you hearing what I am saying?" Huber said intensely. "Captain Gadsden is a great man, and the *Arago*, she's a special ship."

The Garrauxs had seen little of the captain since he had formally greeted passengers just after boarding, but he was indeed an imposing man, serious of countenance, portly, with a thick black beard and a commanding presence. His self-assured manner conveyed a quiet confidence and helped to allay some of the travel fears felt by Frederick and Elizabeth, and the hundreds of others who relied on Gadsden to get them safely across an ocean that had taken so many lives.

Over the next couple of days, as they lost sight of land and entered open water, they spent their time managing the needs of the children. Frederick, Ernst, and Elise, being 11, 10 and 9, were assigned younger siblings for whom they were somewhat responsible, although Elizabeth rarely let any of them out of her sight. In the afternoons while the younger children napped, she would sometimes allow the older children brief playtimes with a few children they had known from Bern, along with some new friends.

The confines of the ship caused a strange, forced intimacy among its occupants. Within a short time, faces became familiar, and some connections were often made. There were also other passengers, based on behavior or appearance, that the family steered clear of.

Unavoidably, there were also many initial curiosities about the other passengers on board:

"Do you think that older man is her husband or her father?"

"Don't they seem more like siblings than a couple?"

And of the overdressed man who made pretentious entrances into the dining-saloon, "Do you think he's someone important, or does he just think he is?"

After the endless conjectures of the first few days, some genuine conversations sprang up between shipmates.

There were more than fifty women on the ship, a handful of them gray-haired and traveling with paid companions or elderly husbands, but most were younger than Elizabeth. Many of the younger women accompanied their husbands and had one or two children with them. There was only one family aboard the *Arago* with nearly as many children as the Garrauxs. The mother, Rosalie Isaac, was about Elizabeth's age. She had children similar in ages to the Garraux children, though none as young as Franz or baby Hans. But Rosalie was traveling by herself.

Rosalie was from France, and Elizabeth spoke just enough French to converse with her a bit, during those rare moments when the poor woman was not trying to locate her children, who seemed to be running wild on the ship. Elizabeth learned that Rosalie's husband had gone to America ahead of her and had made enough money in eighteen months to send for her and their children. Her story further encouraged Elizabeth that America was, in fact, the land of opportunity.

Elizabeth also befriended Maria Erric, a sad, frail young woman from Bern. At just twenty-six, Maria was traveling alone with her son, Carl

15

Albert, who was nine months old, almost the same age as Hans. Maria was also going to join her husband, who had moved to America months before and had taken a blacksmith position to try to help them escape the economic difficulties in Switzerland. Maria had wanted to go with him, but Carl was born early, and he was a sickly baby, and she wanted to wait until he was stronger. Maria had a sweet, quiet temperament, but her face looked much older than her age, as if life had already worn her out.

Elizabeth felt so sorry for Maria, who vacillated between hopefulness that America would offer a solution for her child's fragile health, and a desperate longing to be with her husband. She also struggled with despair and fear caused by what she could only see as a horrible journey to a strange place.

When Hans was napping in the afternoon, Elizabeth left him in the cabin with his siblings long enough for her to go hold Maria's pale, far-too-quiet child for a time so the tortured young woman could have a brief break.

Though Maria's baby was almost the same age as Elizabeth's youngest child, poor little Carl was so different from Hans. As she held him, he lay awake, but still, made no effort to move about. His breathing seemed shallow and labored, though he did not cough or make a sound. It was no wonder his poor young mother looked so completely exhausted and afraid.

While Elizabeth managed the children and made connections with a few passengers, Frederick spent much of his time in the smoking room, talking with other men, trying to glean as much information as possible about America. Some had family already in America who had arranged for their Swiss relatives to join them. Others were as unsure of their futures as Frederick remained.

In all the conversations, he had not met a single person with plans to live anywhere near where they were headed. Jacob Fisher was near Asheville, North Carolina, a place most people had not even heard of. Within a few days on the ship, Frederick wondered if they had chosen the wrong location. Many of the Switzers were going to existing Swiss colonies in Grundy County, Tennessee; New Bern, South Carolina; New Glarus, Wisconsin, and others.

"Do you think Asheville is the right place for us?" Frederick asked Elizabeth.

"Herr Fisher said it is beautiful land that reminds him of Malleray, and we have already committed to using the land grant," she said. "If we are unhappy, we only have to stay for five years before we can relocate. Five years is not very long."

As always, Elizabeth made a believer out of Frederick.

Her father-in-law's friend said he was living on a large parcel of land in the Bent Creek area of Buncombe County, North Carolina, just southwest of the town of Asheville. The whole area was often referred to as being Asheville, though Bent Creek was its own community.

Jacob Fisher was in his early sixties and had a bad knee and a wife in poor health. Losing the tenant that had been sharing and clearing his land left Fisher unable to accomplish all that would be needed to expand his farm.

Everything Frederick and Elizabeth had learned about the land grants made it appealing. Land-grant tenants were provided, free of charge, a good-sized garden, wood for burning, and sufficient pasture. Tenants were allowed to build a home and outbuildings, and they were allowed to keep all they could produce, in exchange for clearing the land they would cultivate. In this case, there was already a tenant house and barn on the property, so they would immediately have a place to live.

The typical tenant land grant arrangement was being used by North Carolina landowners to make their properties farmable. It was mutually beneficial to immigrants who needed a place to stay and a means to feed their families. It also provided them with the opportunity to become naturalized citizens with the right to vote in their new country.

The agreement between owner and tenant would continue for up to five years, at which point the Garrauxs would be required to begin giving Fisher, who would remain property owner, one third of whatever they produced going forward as payment for continued use of the property.

Frederick's misgivings once again assuaged, things aboard the ship continued to go along smoothly for the first few days. And then it was as though they had sailed into hell.

Chapter 3

After another taxing day of washing and dressing, feeding, and keeping track of the eight children, Elizabeth was sound asleep with the two youngest cuddled against her when a blood-curdling scream pierced the night. She shot upright in her berth, heart pounding, head swirling with imaginings, as the high-pitched shriek was repeated. Once fully, shakily awake, she realized the sound was the ship's steam whistle.

The children continued to sleep, but Elizabeth quickly realized, to her horror, the formerly mostly smooth, forward-pounding sensation of the ship's movement had been replaced with a lurching motion, and the ship was also beginning to be rocked from side to side.

A conversation she and Frederick had earlier that evening immediately came to mind. He had talked at length with a middle-aged German man aboard the ship, Heinrich Wagner, who had captained transatlantic ships for several years until he injured his back two years before and was forced to retire. Wagner still carried himself with the bearing of a man of importance, as did the brave ship captains of the day, but he would occasionally

19

grimace and reposition himself in his deck chair, obviously in pain from his lingering injury.

Wagner had recently decided to make the move to America, where he planned to work in his brother's tavern, believing he would find it less physical, or that at least it would provide him with an endless supply of ale and cheerful company in his later days. He had never married, a fact he blamed, somewhat grudgingly, on his life's time and attention having been spent on his first love, the sea.

Wagner, as is often the case with men of a certain age, chose not to talk to Frederick of his shipboard adventures or interesting people he met along the way. He instead spoke in dramatic detail of his numerous close encounters with death, and the horrible, weighty responsibility of holding the lives of all his passengers in his hands.

Wagner regaled Frederick with stories of a particularly awful week at sea during which he encountered a terrible storm that had blown down from the north, bringing high seas and fog so dense there would be no way to see another boat or ship on the water. He said they would have to blast the steam whistle regularly, and then stand silently and listen to see if another vessel whistled back so they could avoid a collision.

Lowering his voice, Muller said, "But that wouldn't save us if a breakaway iceberg was in our path," making the ordeal sound as terrifying as he possibly could.

Frederick had minimized Wagner's drama when he recounted the conversation to Elizabeth. It now felt to her like an omen of what would be, after being awakened by the high-pitched scream of the whistle, the one part of Wagner's tale-telling he had passed on.

"Oh, God help us," she said aloud, realizing that the lurching and the rolling of the ship was increasing, and the whistle meant that even their captain could not see what dangers lay ahead.

Franz and the baby continued to sleep in the pitch-dark cabin, but after the ship slammed and rolled over another large wave, throwing Elise and Marie against the wall of their berth, the girls awoke, screaming "Mama, Mama, help us, Mama!"

Their screams were joined by Bertha and Rosalie, who shouted, "What is happening, Mama? What do we do?" As the girls tried to clamber down from their upper berth, six-year-old Bertha was thrown to the floor as the ship slammed down over another wave, and she began to sob in the darkness.

Franz and baby Hans now awoke as well and added their wailing to the screams and sobs of their sisters.

"Children, children, hold on where you are and stay on your beds if you can. It will be all right," Elizabeth said, not believing her own words. She fumbled in the darkness, trying to strike a match to light the oil lamp. The ship's motion tossed her from one side of the tiny cabin to the other, bruising her arms and hips and legs, over and over.

She finally lit the lantern, and looked at the faces of her horrified children, five of them huddled together, sobbing and white-faced in the lower berth, while the baby screamed, head down on his hands and knees, in the opposite berth. She grabbed him up and wedged herself into the berth with her crying children. She pulled Bertha up from the floor as she shouted over Franz's wails and their crying, "It's a storm, children. It's just a storm. We will all be all right."

At that point, Rosalie, who was nine, said, "I feel sick, Mama. I feel very sick," right before she vomited on Bertha's feet and the floor. Almost immediately, without saying a word, six-year-old Marie also vomited.

Elizabeth had heard complaints from a few women on board the *Arago* the day before who said they had been feeling ill and that they or one of their children had vomited. They said they had been told it was sea sickness that some people experience from the movement of a ship over open water.

"Stay calm, children, and hold onto each other and the bed," Elizabeth said, as she attempted to use a wash rag and basin to clean up the mess on Bertha's feet and the floor.

Much to her horror, as she swayed and stumbled with the rolling and pounding of the ship, Elizabeth felt a terrible dizziness and an overwhelming rush of nausea. She tried to convince herself it was just the nastiness of the spew she was dealing with. Tried to tell herself that she had to take care of the children. Tried to take deep breaths while willing it away, until she found herself retching and vomiting into the basin she was using to try to clean up the mess.

The children clung to each other and cried quietly, but each time the ship would slam down into another trough, their cries would become high-pitched wails, combined with, "I want Father! Where is Father?"

Over the wailing, sobbing, and crying of the children, there was another long, screeching whistle and a sudden pounding on the cabin door.

"Elizabeth, let us in," Frederick shouted.

As she continued to hunch over the basin on the floor, heaving and trying to stay in one place on the floor as it seemed to roll from underneath her, Elizabeth said, "I can't, Frederick, just wait," followed by more heaving that drained every drop of strength from her ninety-eight-pound body.

"Elizabeth? Elizabeth! What is happening, Elizabeth? Are you hurt? What is happening? Open the door," Frederick shouted, sounding frantic.

The children continued to sob and cry out, as Elizabeth, too dizzy to stand, crawled the few feet to the door and unlocked it.

"Oh, my God," Frederick exclaimed, looking at his sobbing, red-nosed, pale-faced children, and his disheveled wife, sitting on the floor, looking far more battered than he had ever seen her, even having birthed eight children, and having lived through all the sleepless nights of childhood

22

illnesses and other motherly burdens.

Ernst and Frederick stood behind their father, suddenly looking much younger than their ages of ten and eleven. They had likewise been awakened by the whistle and the ship pounding through the tumultuous sea. And though they both attempted to take on the persona of the brave eldest sons, they were truly as terrified as their youngest sisters. Fortunately, neither of them had been sickened by the movement of the ship.

Frederick bent down to Elizabeth, and said, "Are you hurt? Let me help you up."

She was so nauseous she could not speak. She let him pull her to her feet, and then immediately turned away from him, grabbed the basin and heaved again. Fortunately, there was no more left in her system.

"Oh no, meine kleine maus," Frederick said, calling her his little mouse.

It was a term of endearment he had used since their courtship. He thought of her as so diminutive, her movements so fast, and her eyes so bright that she reminded him of a lively little field mouse. Right now, she looked like a sad little mouse that had been battered to bits.

The boat continued to roll and lurch for hours as Rosalie, Marie, and Elizabeth suffered bouts of nausea, vomiting and dizziness. Elise and Bertha both also complained of feeling dizzy and ill, but they did not experience the terrible sickness of their mother and sisters.

Frederick and the older boys went to find water and rags to clean up those who were ill, as well as the cabin. Dawn was breaking over the horizon, and it had begun to rain, washing away the heavy fog from overnight.

As they went from the aft deck to the kitchen area, they passed by dozens of similarly afflicted people, some moaning on chairs, huddled in covered nooks on the deck, some sitting on the wet deck, buckets between their legs, others hanging onto the railing in the rain, trying to spew in a direction unaffected by the wind.

The night of the storm, and the two days that followed, were a blur of sickness, fear, doubts, and exhaustion. Eventually, the rain stopped, and Elizabeth and the children who were suffering the sea sickness, were helped by being out on the deck in the open air.

As the turbulence of the storm passed, so did much of the sickness on board the ship, though Frederick believed he saw more than one woman who extended its effect to continue to enjoy the attention and assistance they were receiving. That was not Elizabeth. She was so independent that she resisted help, even when she truly needed it. He had to plead with her to let him handle the children so that she could sleep for a few hours in the afternoon. After those few hours with them, Frederick wondered how she managed to keep track of them all and accomplish everything she did every day.

On the fifth day of the journey, just as the sea sickness was becoming manageable and Elizabeth and the children were back to eating normally, tragedy struck the ship.

Chapter 4

Elizabeth was in the cabin reading a book to the younger children while Hans napped and the older children played with friends in the dining saloon, when there was a sharp knock on the door.

"Who is there?" she called out in German. A crewman answered in English, "It is the captain's mate, ma'am. I need to speak to you."

Elizabeth, not knowing what he had said, cautiously opened the door a small crack and looked at the young man.

"Ich spreche kein English," she said. "No English."

The children stared at their mother and the man at the door, their English language skills also too limited to be of help.

The young man looked both upset and frustrated. He started pointing at her, then pointing up the hallway.

"You come with me. Go to your friend," he stammered. Then he made the motion of holding a baby in his arms and rocking it back and forth.

"Your friend, the Swiss girl, she needs you to come. Your friend Maria."

She heard him say "Maria," and she turned and pointed questioningly at her daughter Maria behind her.

"Maria?" she said, quizzically.

"No, no. Maria with the baby. Young Swiss woman," he said, again acting out holding a baby, and then pointing up the hallway.

She suddenly realized what he was trying to say. He wanted her to go to Maria Erric for some reason. She nodded and said, "Ja. Ja. Yes," one of few English words she knew."

She picked up Hans and told the other children to stay in the cabin and she would send their father to them.

Elizabeth followed the young man, motioning to him that she needed to go into the dining saloon, where Frederick was talking with Heinrich Wagner. She handed Hans to him and explained that the ship's mate wanted her to go to Maria and she needed him to watch the children.

Elizabeth hurried behind the mate as he directed her to a cabin halfway down the ship's length. She reached the door and knocked lightly.

The door opened, and the ship's surgeon, a rather doddering and un-kempt man in his sixties, opened the door and stepped into the hallway, pulling the door closed behind him. Dr. David Bruckner spoke English and German, as well as a little French, and had obviously, at a younger age, been an educated and successful man. It was unclear if shipboard doctoring had worn him down, or if he became a ship's surgeon because of some other turn his life had taken.

Looking sadly at Elizabeth, Bruckner said quietly in German, "The child has died."

Elizabeth gasped involuntarily. "No," she said. "No, no, no."

"The mother knows no one," he said. "I asked if there was anyone onboard who could help her, and yours was the only name she said."

"Oh, the poor, poor thing," Elizabeth said, a hard lump forming in her throat.

Just months before, Elizabeth had sat with her cousin, Anna, as cholera took the life of her baby, Wilhelm. He was Anna's first and only child, and her devastation and grief nearly took her life as well. Anna was still no more than a dark shadow of the woman she had once been when Elizabeth went to say goodbye to her before leaving Switzerland.

There could be no greater pain than losing a child, Elizabeth thought, drawing in a deep breath and trying to muster strength as she nodded to the doctor and opened the door.

In the dimly lit cabin, Maria sat on the edge of the berth, still in her nightclothes, her hair unbound and streaming in long tendrils over her narrow shoulders, making her appear to be little more than a child herself.

Maria held the bundled body of her child tightly against her chest, and she rocked gently forward and back, humming and saying, "Sleep, sweet baby, sleep. Mama will keep you safe. Sleep, sweet Carl."

Elizabeth moved toward her, putting her hand on Maria's shoulder.

"Shhhh," Maria said. "He's sleeping now. He's not crying. Be quiet so my sweet baby can sleep."

She was not crying. Her eyes looked as though they saw another world before her, somewhere else, where her baby was still alive, resting safely in her arms.

The heavy grief filled the tiny cabin, and left Elizabeth without words. She quietly sat down next to Maria and put her arm around the young mother's waist. Maria continued to murmur softly to her baby, and she rocked and rocked and rocked.

Elizabeth remained silent for a long time, occasionally brushing Maria's hair back over her shoulder, patting her on the knee, looking into her face to see if she could see any recognition. There was none. No tears, only the continuous rocking and words of comfort to the child who would never respond again.

After what seemed like hours, Elizabeth finally said, "Maria, may I hold the baby?'

Maria looked at her, as though suddenly realizing she was even in the room.

"May I please hold him, Maria?" Elizabeth said again softly.

"I've just gotten him to sleep," Maria said. "But you can hold him. He liked it when you held him yesterday."

Elizabeth gathered the cold, still weight of the small body into her arms. She held him, as Maria looked at her, with a look of pride and terrifying calm.

"Isn't he such a sweet baby," she said. "My sweet little Carl."

Elizabeth said, "I am going to lay him on the bed now, Maria."

She laid the infant down, careful to keep the blanket he was wrapped in over his face—his face that had taken on the terrible pallor of a body whose spirit has departed.

Maria looked at the baby, and then Elizabeth. She looked back at the baby, laying there in such heartbreaking stillness. As she gazed at him, tears began to well up in her eyes. Her face contorted, and she suddenly wailed, "My baby is dead! My little baby is dead!" as she slid from the edge of the berth onto the floor.

Elizabeth got down on the floor next to her and pulled her into her arms.

"Poor, poor little girl. You poor, poor child," she said holding her tightly, as Maria sobbed, shaking, and weakening until it seemed her spirit might also leave her body.

Elizabeth stayed with Maria until she had cried herself to sleep. Then she went to the dining-saloon and found a small group of older women who were talking and doing needlework in a corner. They covered their mouths and gasped when they heard of the baby's death and agreed that since they had no children to care for, they would take turns sitting with Maria.

Elizabeth returned to her children and found all of them crammed into her cabin, six of the children sharing the three berths, and the two older boys and Frederick sleeping on the floor, their heads resting on balled-up clothing and wash rags.

Frederick heard her come in and sat up.

He whispered, "I was told Maria's baby died, and I knew you would stay with her."

Elizabeth shushed him, trying to keep the children asleep, and whispered, "We will talk in the morning."

She helped him rouse Frederick and Ernst, and they shuffled off to their cabin.

Without changing into her nightclothes, Elizabeth removed her shoes, gathered her skirts in, and climbed carefully into the bed with Franz and Hans, who were so exhausted by the disrupted day, they did not awaken.

Elizabeth pulled her eight-month-old and two-year-old sons against her, and under the secretive blanket of darkness, she finally allowed herself to weep.

Chapter 5

After a night of fitful sleep and troubled dreams, Elizabeth knew she had to go back to Maria. She hoped someone else had taken the responsibility of removing the poor deceased baby from the room.

She took care of the children's morning needs and left them in Frederick's care.

Not knowing what she would find in Maria's small cabin, she knocked on the door, and said, "Maria, it is Elizabeth. May I come in?"

The door opened, but it was not Maria. One of the plump, middle-aged needlework ladies, Emma Schmid, looked tired and frazzled as she stepped outside the room to speak to her.

"I've been here since the wee hours before dawn," Emma said. "She's nary spoken a word. She just sits and stares, then mutters about her baby and lays back down next to him. The baby, God rest his soul, he's still in there!"

Elizabeth thanked Emma and told her to thank the others who had spent the night with Maria. She then went inside, and sat on the edge of the berth, her back against Maria's, who lay facing her child's blanket-wrapped body.

Elizabeth waited, rehearsing in her mind what she would say and how she would say it. The doctor had left a note under her cabin door telling her that the baby's body would need to be removed from the cabin immediately, and that a ship's carpenter would be making a casket for the child's burial.

Elizabeth had realized, with horror, that they meant to throw the baby into the sea. She had heard of bodies being sent to watery graves after people passed onboard ships. It was both to protect other passengers, and to save poor immigrants the immediate cost of a burial or placement in a pauper's grave in their new country.

Trying to get Maria to release her hold on her deceased child would be hard enough. Elizabeth didn't know how she would help the poor grieving woman deliver her child into the sea.

When Maria finally awoke, she looked like a lost, heartbroken child, her puffy eyes rimmed in red, her hair tossed and wild from her night of heartbroken torture.

As gently as possible, Elizabeth tried to guide her toward the understanding that her child was gone. She held her tightly and reminded her over and over how well she had done to take care of the poor baby and how much love she had showered on him in his short life. She reminded Maria of her bravery and strength, for managing in the absence of her husband, with little help from her own family or his. And she told her again and again that her sweet little Carl would want her to go on to her new life in America, and that he would always be in her heart.

Finally, after much talking and sitting and hugging and sobbing, Maria allowed Elizabeth to pick up the baby to prepare to take him to the doctor's cabin. Maria buried her hand in her hands, but then she suddenly stood up.

"He's my baby. I should be the one to carry him. I am his mother. And I can be brave," she said in a shaky but loud voice. "I am brave. My baby wants me to be brave."

Elizabeth was overwhelmed with the grief of the moment, and maternal pride to see this young woman find the grain of strength left inside her.

She handed baby Carl to his mother, and watched Maria clutch him to her chest, tears beginning to stream down her face as she held her head up, as bravely as she knew how.

They walked slowly to the doctor's cabin, Elizabeth supporting Maria's elbow. Word of the tragedy had spread quickly through the passengers, and each person they passed bowed their head, touched their heart, or offered murmured words of condolence.

Elizabeth was glad that despite his appearance, Dr. Bruckner rose to the occasion. He was professional and matter of fact, but also kind. He took on a fatherly demeaner that made Elizabeth wonder again how he ended up as he was.

The sad reality of the immigrant ships was that most people never saw each other again, and those questions and musing about the lives of others would remain forever unanswered.

Frederick, without consulting Elizabeth, went to find the ship's carpenter.

"I in no way want to insult your work or abilities," Frederick said to the carpenter, "But I am, by trade, a cabinetmaker."

Elizabeth had told him that John Goff, the ship's carpenter, was designated to create coffins for anyone who passed away on the ship. After hearing from his wife about the life and loss and bravery of young Maria, he wanted very much to contribute something to honor the life of her baby.

Goff said, "But sir, I always make the coffins. It's part of my job. I am not sure the captain would like it if I let a passenger take on my responsibility."

"I don't wish to disrespect your position. I would just like to contribute," Frederick said. "I think it would be meaningful to the child's mother."

In a compromise, Goff agreed that he would construct the coffin box and would allow Frederick to build the cover.

Frederick had transported some of his tools since they were too specialized and too expensive to replace. He retrieved them from his luggage and had the older boys join Elizabeth and the other children in her cabin.

He laid out the wood Goff had given him for the cover and turned their cabin into a work area.

"Such very short pieces of wood," he thought sadly, as he began to work.

For Frederick, there was something honorable and noble about taking a piece of wood formed in the hearts of trees over years, sometimes decades, and crafting it into a thing of beauty. Even those pieces he created for practical purposes were given care of design, balance, and artistry.

As he worked to smooth and carve and join the wood for the tiny coffin cover, he hoped the lost baby's mother would see the respect for her and for the short life of her child in each chisel mark and groove.

The wood was of poor quality, but Frederick continued to work at it. He had not eaten breakfast, he had forgotten to eat lunch, and as it neared dinner time, he realized he was hungry. He was also nearly done with the coffin cover. He could have kept on finishing and working at tiny details, but he stood up and looked at it, and realized its simplicity suited an innocent life cut short.

He wrapped a light blanket around the cover, held it under his arm, and carried it to Goff's work room. The carpenter was not there, but the small casket was completed and was sitting on his work bench.

With deep sadness, Frederick noted the holes drilled in the sides of the box, and the bed of sand in the bottom, designed to help the coffin sink quickly, in hopes of causing less trauma to those who would watch the deceased child slip into the deep.

He laid the cover on top of the coffin. On it he had carved:

Carl Albert Ericc

Dec. 29, 1866 – Sept. 14, 1867

Beloved son of Carl and Maria Ericc

Frederick also carved a small single rose bud, to symbolize a life that ended too soon. As he often did, he silently thanked God for the chance to use his skills to honor another. And then he returned to his family.

The next morning, Frederick took Elizabeth to the carpenter's workroom to see the coffin.

"Oh Frederick, it is perfect" she said, placing her hand on the wooden box. "It's so small. It's so terribly sad."

He put his arm around her, and they stood quietly, looking at the carved cover and the small, simple coffin.

"I must help Maria get through this day," Elizabeth said. "She will have to somehow live through sending her only child into the depths of the ocean. It is just too horrible to imagine."

She spent the early part of the day talking with and listening to the grief of the poor young mother. Other women also came by to offer their help and condolences.

At one point, Maria was suddenly saddened by remembering she did not have any black clothing to wear to properly mourn her child. One of the older women happened to be there when she mentioned it and said she had packed a black cloak for the crossing because she expected to be attending the funeral of a sister in America who was very ill. She brought

Maria the cloak, so that she would at least have it to cover herself during the burial.

Oh, how Elizabeth dreaded telling Maria that her child's body would be committed to the sea. But strangely enough, the young woman immediately seemed at peace with it.

After Elizabeth explained what would happen, Maria seemed to take on an expression of calm resignation.

"I think freeing him into the ocean hurts me less than it would have to cover my beautiful boy with dirt," she said, in a calm and distant voice.

"I always knew he was sick, you know?" she said. "The doctors had told us there was nothing we could do except give him good food and fresh air and hope for the best. I think in my heart I knew I would not see him grow into a man. In my thoughts and dreams, I never let myself picture him as anything but a baby."

Maria began to sob quietly. "He will always be my baby," she said. "My little angel baby."

Dr. Buckner had moved the little body from his hospital room to the coffin in the carpenter's workspace. Goff had said a silent prayer as he nailed it shut.

"How lovely to see the child's name," Bruckner said, and the carpenter nodded his agreement.

The passengers, old and young, gathered on the deck of the ship. The sea was graciously calm and the winds light. It was cool, but the sun warmed those who stood quietly.

The engine was stopped, and the ship was stunningly quiet as the captain came up onto the deck, carrying the small coffin in his arms.

Maria was wrapped in the black cloak that was far too large for her, making her look even more vulnerable. She stood between Frederick and

Maria, shaky and wavering, but with a calm resignation.

There was no minister aboard, so the responsibility fell entirely to Captain Gadsden.

The large crowd of people was completely silent and motionless as he began, "There is no loss so deeply felt as that of a life ended too soon."

Gadsden talked about the strength of the child's mother in the face of such loss, and the importance that each person present live life fully, not knowing the day or hour of their passing. He spoke with strength and gentleness, and clearly as someone who had presided over more deaths than anyone should.

"We commit this child into the hands of God and the peace of the sea," he said.

Maria stepped forward, Elizabeth supporting her elbow as she leaned toward the casket. She looked at the cover, and then inquiringly at Elizabeth, who said, "Frederick did this for you," she said. "For baby Carl."

Maria placed her hand on the coffin cover, running her fingers over the carved letters and the rosebud.

She turned backed toward Frederick, tears welling in her eyes, and silently mouthed, "Thank you, thank you, thank you."

Frederick put his hand over his heart, bowed his head as tears burned in his eyes, feeling so humbled by the reaction of this poor, fragile, young woman.

Two shipmates, faces frozen in serious expressions, movements slow and deliberate, looped ropes around the small coffin to lower it over the side of the ship.

The crowd of passengers stood silently, a few women sniffling and dabbing tears, as the coffin was lowered slowly and respectfully the long, long distance to the water's surface.

Maria clutched the edges of the cloak, holding it over her face as quiet sobs racked her frail body.

The shipmates each then let go of one side of the looped ropes, allowing the wooden box with its precious contents to slip away, almost immediately dipping below the surface.

A moment later, it was gone from sight.

Chapter 6

The death and burial of the child left a cloud of sadness lingering over the ship into the next day. Many of the passengers, particularly the other Swiss travelers, rallied around Maria, trying to support the grieving mother in any way possible.

Finally, the day after the burial at sea, Maria was able to drink some water and eat a few bites of food. Elizabeth reminded her again that she was now being brave and would be carrying on with life in honor of the life of baby Carl.

In an attempt to further encourage her, Elizabeth said, "Your husband is waiting for you. You said he'll be in New York to gather you up, so you must think about the life you will be making with him."

That attempt at encouragement went very badly, with Maria suddenly wailing, "Oh my God, I am going to have to tell Carl his son is dead. Our son is dead, and he doesn't yet know!"

Elizabeth realized there was no way to help Maria get through all the grief she was experiencing. All she could do was to accept that the sad, young woman would eventually get past this. So many women had to grieve the loss of a child, and though there could be no deeper pain, there was no choice but to continue on.

The captain had announced that they were past the midpoint of their journey, and he said, barring any unforeseen problems, they would be in the harbor off Castle Garden, New York, within three days. He encouraged passengers to begin thinking about and preparing for their departure from the ship and the next stage of the journey to their new lives in America.

Elizabeth and Frederick had decided that before registering at Castle Garden, they would have the children take on American names. They did not wish to be Switzers living in America. They intended to be Americans.

They gathered the whole family in the larger cabin, and explained that it was an important day, a day of honor in which they would keep their surname, Garraux, but their German names would be replaced with appropriately English-sounding names.

Frederick and Elizabeth were common names in the states, but the children would start their new lives without the burden of being immediately known as immigrants upon introduction.

They tried to make the changes comfortable for the older children, choosing variants as close as possible to their given names.

Frederick, who was four months away from turning twelve, would keep his name, but would be called Fred. Ernst, ten years old, would now be Earnest. Rosalie, nine, would be Rosa, and eight-year-old Bertha would be called Bettie. Marie, six, would now be Mary, and four-year-old Elise would be renamed Lucy.

The youngest, two-year-old Franz would become Frank, and baby Hans, not yet a year old, would be called John.

The children took the changes in stride and actually seemed excited about it, as though it was the first step toward their big American adventure.

"I am so proud of you," Elizabeth said. "You are brave, strong children, and you are going to have wonderful lives in America."

Without saying so, she was also speaking to Frederick, who still lapsed into moments of anxiety that left him staring blankly, his brow furrowed, rubbing his hands together like a frightened child. She chose to not acknowledge his concerns and spent her time talking with him about opportunities and bits of good news she gleaned from other passengers who already had friends and family in the states.

Elizabeth deftly excised any negative stories she heard from her memory and their conversations. This would be a good move for her family. They would find success. They would make a good life. And she would never let the fears or the challenges they would encounter change her mind.

Frederick agreed that giving the children English names was important. Like Elizabeth, he wanted them to feel welcome in their new land. He was well-aware of the difficulty his family would face since German was their native tongue. Frederick had been born and raised in Malleray, the French-speaking area of Bernese Jura, so his first language was French. Because his father's carpentry work frequently took him into the center of Bern, he and Frederick had the advantage of also being fluent in German.

Elizabeth and the children both spoke rudimentary French in addition to German, but none of them spoke English, beyond "hello, yes, no, and thank you." The very least they could do for the children was to let their names be American, knowing that, as children, they would learn their new language much more quickly than their parents.

Frederick found it impossible to avoid worrying. They had left so much behind. The comforts of the lovely home that he and his father and some friends had built, with plenty of room and comfort for their family—the family that had grown larger about every other year.

But he did have to admit, since the economic difficulties began in Switzerland, fewer people were requesting new pieces of furniture. Hardly any new home construction was going on, so it had been months since anyone had ordered a mantel, newel post, entry door, or the other household accoutrements he enjoyed crafting. The family's vegetable garden provided well for them in the summer, but with winter just around the corner, their finances and general situation had begun to look bleak.

Elizabeth was so excited by the possibility of new opportunities and plentiful farmland in America that he tried to keep his concerns to himself. He knew that the tenant land-grant agreement guaranteed they would at least have a place to live that he would be able to add onto. But he did not like knowing that if they stayed longer than five years without acquiring their own property, he would be required to pay Fisher a third of whatever they earned from farming his land. Even though Fisher was his father's friend, he had made it clear to Frederick that this would be a strictly business arrangement.

Frederick enjoyed farming, and together, he and Elizabeth were skilled growers. But he also did not want to give up his cabinet making. He felt it was both a gift and his father's legacy, and he intended to find a way to continue it, even if much of his effort would have to be shifted to clearing land and growing crops.

He had heard from others on the ship that Americans were welcoming to immigrants, especially the Germans and Swiss who they saw as generally skilled and literate additions to their communities. But his oldest sons were already nearing their teenage years, and he worried about what skills they would have and what wives they would choose in this land he knew so little about.

Frederick did not want to tarnish the "streets-paved-with-gold" image of America that Elizabeth had developed from pamphlets describing nothing but positives. She seemed to overlook the fact that the pamphlets were created by ship operators who hoped to get rich by transporting immigrants. He felt Elizabeth was also overly influenced by Fisher's idealized letters. Besides needing help with his land, it was clear Jacob Fisher desperately wanted to have fellow Switzers join him in his new home in North Carolina.

The Bern they had left behind was the capitol city of the country, with a population of about 30,000 people. The train station in Bern had opened years before, and the city was a busy center of commerce, with many businesses and shops, numerous four- and five-story buildings, and some densely populated, sophisticated neighborhoods. The University of Bern had been founded more than three decades before and was attended by several hundred students a year.

The Garrauxs were moving to a North Carolina town they learned had a population of about the same as the number of students at university each year. There was no railroad, no library, no newspaper, no university.

Trying to remember positives about their potential future home, Frederick thought about having learned from Fisher's letters that many people were coming to believe the sulfur springs near Asheville and the mountain air were good for restoring health. People had actually begun traveling to the area for recovery from tuberculosis and other ills, rather than going into sanitariums. The wealthy from all over the southern states would travel by coach to the mountain town, either for health or to escape the oppressive summer heat of the Lowcountry. Though Asheville was small, there were already three good-size hotels available for lodging, one that was said to accommodate more than three hundred people.

Fisher also described an amazing roadway that he said ran right through the center of town. He said the highway went from Kentucky and Tennessee all the way to the coast of Carolina, and drovers—men and boys who herded the hogs, cattle, and turkeys—used the rambling road to take them to market.

Fisher said local farmers along the way would sell hay and grain to the drovers for their herds and flocks, and the men and boys also needed places to rest overnight for the arduous journey. He said inns and layover stands had sprung up along the highway, bringing new businesses and money to the area, including Asheville. Before the Civil War, the road had been a major source of income and development for much of Western North Carolina, with some loss of revenue from it during and after the War.

When their journey to America had just a couple days left, Elizabeth went to check on Maria as she had every day since the funeral. She encouraged her to prepare for arrival in New York, but Maria had terribly mixed feelings. She very much looked forward to seeing her beloved husband. She also very much dreaded telling him their child was gone.

"Carl will be waiting for you, waiting to start your new life together," Elizabeth said. "It will be difficult for him to learn of little Carl's passing, but you must remember, he is also waiting for you. The wife he chose. The wife he loves. The wife he sent for and has planned for. Try to think of that, Maria. You will finally be together again."

Maria seemed to summon some strength, and though her eyes frequently filled with tears, and she would become silent and distant, she was again properly dressed, her hair combed and pinned back, and she had begun to organize her clothing and items to leave the ship.

Back in the cabin with the children, Elizabeth said to her older sons, Fred and Earnest, "You may choose which set of clothing you wish to wear as we step off the ship into our new country." Her sons looked pleased and validated by the responsibility.

She then busied herself preparing clothing for the other children and sorting through which items she would return to their luggage for transportation to the mainland.

To the older boys and Lucy, Mary, and Bettie, she said, "Now, you will help me clean every inch of the cabins. The ship will be inspected, and we must do our part."

The ship had begun to buzz with a different kind of energy. Instead of minds being turned back to the families and homes left behind, the passengers' thoughts were now fixed on the new country that lay ahead, and all the hope and promise it held.

Off and on throughout the crossing, after the storms and the time of sickness had passed for most, there had been periods of time during which passengers would play games on deck, and sometimes sing and even dance. The music was provided by a handful of passengers who had brought along mandolins, a few harmonicas, and a violin. Two others had brought along accordions, and both were talented musicians with large repertoires of popular folk tunes.

Now, with anxious excitement over the impending landfall, there were multiple small groups here and there on the deck as well as in the saloon, dancing, clapping, and singing, giving the ship a festive atmosphere.

The conversations between passengers, many of whom had formed friendships and alliances over the week and two days spent in close quarters, took on a more cheerful tone, and there was much joy in realizing their time on the ship was nearly over.

The Garraux family was just finishing the evening meal in the dining saloon when there was a sudden commotion. A man burst through the door and shouted, "Land! We see land!" just as the steam-whistle began to sound repeatedly.

The passengers leaped up from their meal tables, flatware and a few dishes clattering to the floor and more than one chair knocked over backwards as they rushed toward the saloon door. Frederick picked up Frank as Elizabeth scooped up John, grabbed Rosa's hand and they quickly herded the children out onto the deck.

Along with dozens of other passengers and many of the crew, the family rushed toward the ship's railing. Seeing them trying to move all their children through the raucous crowd, several people stepped aside to let the little ones reach the rail.

The sound of the steam-whistle and shouts of "Land ho" by crewmembers mixed with screams and tears, backslapping laughter, shouts of "America, America!" and prayers of thanksgiving uttered out loud in multiple languages.

Frederick and Elizabeth were silent, their eyes transfixed on the thin dark line at the edge of the horizon. Their minds and hearts were flooded with every hope and fear, leaving them momentarily unable to speak.

Rosa broke the heaviness of the moment when she said seriously, "But Mama, America is so small."

Laughter took away the weight of the moment, and they went about explaining to the children that they were still miles away from land.

The captain had told the passengers the day before that if the ship arrived too late in the day, they would anchor and wait until the next morning for the inspection before passengers and their luggage would be transferred to Castle Garden, the center where immigrants were screened and registered, reunited with their belongings, and sent on their way into their strange new land.

The family, along with the dozens of others, remained on deck for the next hour looking westward as the ship churned toward land. The sun sank lower and twinkling lights and the vague shapes of some buildings became visible. By the time the *Arago* reached the docking area several miles south of the city, the six and eight-story buildings along the coast began to form the silhouette of a dark, odd-shaped wall, with gas lights in the streets and some windows.

It was nearly impossible to get the children to sleep, and after they did, Frederick and Elizabeth lay awake for hours, thoughts swirling in their heads. During their time on the ship, it had almost been as though they were separated from reality. Now there were arrangements to be made for the next several hundred miles of travel, that would prove to be more difficult than all the days spent at sea.

Chapter 7

Before dawn had fully illuminated the deck, a majority of the passengers, including the Garraux family, had gathered on deck, huddled in small, excited, talkative groups, awaiting the day that would finally put them back on dry land.

The Garrauxs had been warned that many immigrants arriving in America were overcharged, bilked, and sometimes even robbed of their possessions. Women and girls, especially those traveling without male companionship, were often victimized, sometimes by crewmembers, other times as soon as they arrived in the city. Many people were tricked out of whatever savings they had brought with them by unscrupulous shysters who sold them train and boat tickets they would later find to be worthless.

Now, passengers on the *Arago* waited, with varying degrees of patience, while the ship was inspected. Another agent then boarded the ship to inspect the luggage. Passengers were given brass tokens, with a letter A-F and a number 1-600, that were matched to the identifiers assigned to their luggage.

All of the warnings about potential mistreatment of immigrants had made Elizabeth concerned about the impending separation from all their worldly goods as the luggage was to be transported to shore and stored separately from the passengers.

"I questioned the landing agent," Frederick said. "He assured me that our luggage would be awaiting us in the section assigned to us. He said they have recently become more watchful after the luggage of several German passengers went missing. He says we have no need to be concerned."

Elizabeth still felt it uncomfortable to have all their carefully selected items out of their possession, but she set the feeling aside, and dealt with the more pressing task of managing their eight children, the youngest of whom were having a difficult time sitting or standing and waiting for the hours the process was taking.

Elizabeth had Maria join them during the inspection, and she was pleased to see her holding herself together well. Maria even spoke pleasantly with the children, and helped divert the attention of Frank and John, who were having the most difficult time tolerating the long wait.

Watching Maria with her sons, Elizabeth knew the young woman would eventually find her way past her grief, and likely to motherhood, and for that she was grateful. She did not, however, fool herself into thinking she would ever see Maria again after this day, or that she would ever know how her life turned out.

Finally, they all boarded the barge that would take them to the immigration depot.

Castle Garden was a large, round, sandstone fort, built in the early 1800s on a small manmade island. It was one of five forts planned and built to protect the southern side of New York from attacks by the British. But since the British chose to attack other ports, the fort was never used for defense. In the 1820s, it became an entertainment venue, renamed Castle Garden when it was being used as a beer garden. Twelve years before the Garrauxs' arrival, it had become New York's immigration registration depot, handling the arrival of more than 200,000 immigrants a year.

Once on land, legs wobbly and heads slightly dizzy from having spent more than a week at sea, the family was first taken to an exchange agent, who gave Frederick American currency for the Swiss bills he had brought along. He also had gold coins, but the agent told him to keep them because they were worth more than he could exchange them for.

Later, when in privacy, Frederick divided the currency three ways, between the leather satchel, a money belt he wore around his waist, and a secret pocket Elizabeth had sewn into the lining of his jacket.

Frederick had an immigrant's guidebook to help him understand the new currency, but it was so confusing, he just put the new bills in a small satchel that would never leave his possession. He planned to study the use of American money along the way as they traveled.

They were then confronted by one government official after another, all of whom scrutinized them, almost as though they were commodities that could be either purchased or rejected. After determining they spoke German, Frederick and Elizabeth were asked the same questions by multiple German-speaking agents:

"What is your name?"

"Where are you from?"

"Whither are you going?"

And to Frederick, "What is your trade?"

Jacob Fisher had convinced Frederick that being identified as a farmer would be to his advantage upon entering the country, so rather than cabinetmaker, he answered, "I am a farmer," each time.

The family was then herded into a large, open rotunda, already filled with hundreds of immigrants from the *Arago* and other ships. Many were dressed in clothing peculiar to their homelands. Mixed in the crowd were light-haired, Black Forest Germans with knee-high red stockings and carved wooden shoes and Scandinavians in homespun clothing with dirks in leather sheaths attached to their belts. There were many rosy-faced, red-haired Irish folk, who all seemed to be moving together in one large, talkative group.

But beyond the disturbing number of people, crowded and herded into the space much like sheep or cattle into feed troughs, what was most noticeable in the rotunda was the overwhelming stench. The huge space, nearly as wide as the *Arago* was long, was dimly lit by small windows fifty feet above through which clearly, no air moved.

There were three counters where food could be purchased, and the stagnant air was filled with the heavy, swirling stench of decaying bologna, unwashed bodies, sauerkraut, herring, rancid cheese, dirty feet, and boiled cabbage.

"Mama, it smells so terrible in here," Earnest said, before Elizabeth shushed him as they moved slowly into the crowded space. The throngs of people and the putrid air overwhelmed their senses. It was not the welcome change they had hoped for after their difficult days on the ship.

Frederick carried Frank, Elizabeth carried John, and Maria held Rosa and Bettie's hands as they guided the children through the crowd to a quieter location at the edge of the rotunda.

Those people in the crowd who were visibly sick were immediately being escorted out of the space to be taken to a nearby hospital. Fortunately, it appeared that no more than a dozen or two passengers were taken away.

An agent explained that there were bathing facilities available for men and boys on one side of the rotunda and women and girls on the other. Since the family had taken only the most minimal of sponge baths while on the ship, Elizabeth decided the younger children should be thoroughly bathed.

The large bath had a long trough of water running down one side of it and a screen separating the bathing area from the rest of the space.

A German-speaking woman who was attending to the bath area told Elizabeth that there was plenty of soap and towels and running Croton in the bath. When Elizabeth asked what Croton was, the woman gave her a brief history of the running water.

She said that in the early 1800s, fires destroyed many homes and buildings in New York City because there were no water sources adequate to extinguish them. The fire dangers, along with contaminated wells that sickened and even killed countless New Yorkers, made access to a reservoir a necessity.

An aqueduct, based on the same principles and design as the Roman aqueducts, was built by Irish immigrants in the 1830s to feed water from the Croton Reservoir to the city, she said, and many referred to water fed through the aqueduct simply as "Croton."

Elizabeth found that there was, in fact, plenty of soap, water, and towels in the bath. Though at home in Switzerland they had typically bathed once or twice a month, they usually changed undergarments frequently for hygiene's sake. She had dutifully washed and dried their undergarments during the crossing, but with the illness they experienced and the generally unclean interior of the ship, she was gratified to scrub the children clean in the fresh, cold water, and eventually herself as well.

For what seemed like endless hours, landing agents continuously called out the names of passengers who had letters or funds awaiting them. They would walk the perimeter of the rotunda, calling the names again and again until they got a response, or until they gave up after several attempts.

Then agents began the process again, now calling the names of passengers who had family, friends, or contacts who had registered and were there waiting for them.

Maria stood away from the family, listening intently for her name to be called. With each new name that was announced that was not hers, she looked increasingly anxious. Was her husband not there? Had something happened to him? Her concern over seeing him once again overrode all her fears about being there without their baby.

"Maria Ericc, Maria Ericc," the agent called out. "Carl Ericc here for Maria Ericc."

She nearly fainted when she heard his name. She rushed back to Elizabeth and said, "Mein Gott, he is here, Elizabeth. My Carl is here."

Elizabeth grabbed her and hugged her, saying, "Oh, Maria, your new life is about to begin."

She agreed to walk with Maria to the area outside the fort where her husband would be waiting, but Elizabeth would not be able to leave the building, because once passengers did, they were not allowed back in.

The two women gathered Maria's small bag and checked to be sure she had the token that would reunite her with her steamer chest. They walked together, hand in hand, through the door to the waiting area that was on the other side of a low fence.

Maria kissed Elizabeth's cheek. "Thank you for all you did for me," she said. "I don't know what I would have done without you."

Elizabeth looked the young woman straight in the eye and patted her cheek. She said, "You would have done what women do. You would have found a way to carry on. Now go, Maria. Go to your husband. Go to your new life."

Maria hurried through the door, across the walkway and through the gate. She spoke briefly to an agent, and then she suddenly dashed across the open area. Elizabeth saw a tall, young man grab her in his arms. He lifted her up and swung her around in a circle before he set her back on her feet, took her face in his hands, and kissed her.

Elizabeth's eyes brimmed with tears, for gladness that the young couple was now reunited, and for sadness, as she knew Carl would momentarily ask where their son was.

She said a silent prayer for the young couple and their future, before she waved at them and turned to walk back to her family, and whatever was next for them.

Elizabeth wove her way back through the crowd. She could see Frederick on the far side of the rotunda holding John, watching over the children who were playing with marbles and amusing themselves with playmates who had been on the *Arago* and who had found them in the swarming mass of people.

She passed by a room that appeared almost like a chapel, seats on either side of a long aisle, a man at a podium at the front of the room. When she peeked in the door, a police officer standing just inside said, "Looking for a position?" He spoke English, and when she said she spoke Swiss-German, he shuffled through papers in his hand, and pulled out one in German and handed it to her.

The flier explained the process of being hired as household help. The room was apparently filled with people who were looking to hire cooks, chambermaids and other types of helpers, and girls and women who wanted such employment.

"Oh, no thank you. No," Elizabeth said in her best English, feeling grateful that her life had never become that desperate.

She looked at all the sweet-faced girls in the room, and the tired-looking, mature women who wore expressions of desperation, and she felt sorry to know many of them had very difficult lives ahead. No matter how challenging hers and Frederick's journey was to be, she knew that they would succeed, and they would make good lives for their children. Of that, she was sure.

Frederick left Elizabeth with the children while he went to find railroad agents.

He quickly found a German-speaking railroad ticket agent.

"I need tickets for myself, my wife and our eight children, please," he said. "We need tickets from here to Asheville in the state of North Carolina."

"You need tickets to where?" the agent said gruffly.

Frederick repeated himself, and assuming there was a reason the agent seemed somewhat resistant, he added, "We have money for the tickets. It is not a problem."

The sale of their home in Bern along with most of their possessions made him feel assured that their trip arrangements would not be difficult. That was until the agent said, 'I've never heard of Asheville. And this railroad and our connector run to Virginia. We can't take you to North Carolina. You'll have to make a connection in Richmond. That's in Virginny. We go no farther than that. And you better check on this place you're talking about. Never heard of a place by that name."

Frederick's heart sank. If he didn't know for certain that Fisher was indeed living near Asheville, he would have once again wondered if it was all a mistake.

"We must go to North Carolina," he said. "We need to get as close as possible to Asheville. We have eight children. Eight of them," Frederick said, his voice growing intense. "We have eight children."

The agent told him to wait while he consulted with another train agent who had more knowledge of the Southern states.

After a few moments, as Frederick was left reeling in panic, the agent returned.

"Herr Gruber knows of this place you wish to go, but he said it is in the mountains, and I doubt you will find a train that will take you within 100 miles of it. It will probably take at least three or four rail lines to try to get to where you will be able to get a wagon or stagecoach to head west," the agent said. "And Gruber said there are barely even roads to get you there."

Shaking his head, the agent said, "We can get you as far as Richmond. That's it."

The agent's expression appeared to be largely one of irritation.

"You know we just got out of a war, right?" he said. "The damn rebels ruined tracks and destroyed the bridges of most of the southern railroads, and the ones they didn't get, we had to blow up to stop them. You're lucky if you can get anywhere near the state you want to go to. Eight children? You're doing this with eight children? Maybe you should have had a plan."

Frederick thought they did have a plan. Fisher had said they would have to travel by train until the tracks ran out, and then they'd have to travel by wagon. Frederick understood that. He knew where they were going was nothing like the city they had left behind. What he hadn't considered and what Fisher had not mentioned, was what the Civil War had done to the country. Even if his former tenant had died in the conflict, Fisher didn't travel, and his life in Asheville was one nearly sequestered in the mountains. Frederick wondered if that was why he had never described the disaster left behind by the conflict.

Frederick had planned and prepared for a long train trip, followed by a wagon trip. He was not ready to deal with multiple railroads, destroyed bridges and tracks, and a lack of dependable roads.

Once again, Frederick found himself thinking, "What have we done?"

He did not want to tell Elizabeth how bleak this travel plan appeared. There was no way out, and no turning back.

"All right," he said to the railroad agent, "I want tickets for my family to go to Richmond. We will figure out where to go from there."

A short time later, tickets in hand, he went back to his wife and children, three of whom had fallen asleep. As he approached her, Elizabeth, surrounded by their children, looked so small and so very tired. His family huddled together at the edge of the constantly moving, cacophonous crowd.

As he carved his way through the throng, his eyes caught hers, and he held up the tickets in his hand. She smiled, bowed her head, and mouthed, "Thank God."

The train agent had taken Frederick's brass luggage token in trade for a paper document that would give them claim to their possessions at their future destination. Their trunks and bags were to be moved to the train depot, and they would be able to catch the last train of the day out of New York, the agent said.

Elizabeth and the children were so excited, and anxious to leave Castle Garden, Frederick decided he would not tell her what the trip ahead would hold until after she was able to get some sleep on the train.

Chapter 8

A short time later, the family walked through Castle Garden's dimly lit, undulating, overwhelming crowd. They stepped out of the stench and into the street, passing aggressive vendors selling nearly rotten apples, salesmen shouting offers of other offensive food and drink, hawkers, some loudly pitching cheap rates at boarding homes and others offering questionable work opportunities. There were street waifs begging for handouts and women of questionable pursuits hoping to catch the eye of men exiting the depot.

They finally broke through the motley crowd surrounding Castle Garden and into the fresh, cool September day. As they walked along the bustling, sunlit sidewalks past colorful store fronts and successful looking businesses, it was hard for even Frederick to not to begin to feel hopeful.

They hailed a large coach and were taken crosstown through the busy streets of New York to the big, busy train depot. There would begin the American journey that would change their lives.

The sun was setting before they were able to ascertain that their possessions had been safely transferred and they were finally settled on the train.

They were in an open-seating car, with pairs of seats that faced each other on either side of an aisle. With the help of a porter, they converted the four pairs of seats they occupied into four lower berths with four upper berths above them, taking up a good portion of the car. There were curtains to screen the berths from the aisle, as well as a curtain that separated their half of the car from the other, in which another family and an older couple were seated.

Thankfully, the cushions were considerably wider and more comfortable than the berths on the ship, though they did carry some residual odors of previous passengers, food, tobacco and other less definable, unpleasant scents.

Frederick and Elizabeth, as well as all the children, were so exhausted that after eating some of the sausage and cheese they had purchased at Castle Garden, they all climbed into the shared berths, in much the same configuration as on the *Arago*.

Within moments, they were all asleep, the rhythmic rumbling of the train far less disturbing than the constant grinding groan of the steamship.

Just after midnight, the train whistled and stopped in Philadelphia, but other than Frederick and the two older boys, no one awoke to see the twinkling lights of the city.

The sun was coming up when the train slowed as it chugged its way along curved tracks in the nation's capital. This time, it was Elizabeth who awakened first, and after she peaked out the window, she leapt from her berth, rousing Frederick and the children, shaking them awake as she pulled back the curtains.

"It is Washington!" she exclaimed. "It is the Capitol of our new country."

They rushed to the right side of the train, all peering out the train windows as the huge dome of the Capitol came into view. They recognized it from pictures and could scarcely believe they were actually laying eyes on it. Elizabeth tried to explain its significance to the children, and she found herself getting choked up, overwhelmed that this brave young country was welcoming them, giving them the chance to create new lives and find new opportunity.

The train stopped at the station with the Capitol still in view as more passengers boarded.

As the train rumbled away from the station, the children rushed to the windows on the other side as they passed the Smithsonian and other impressive buildings. Bern was a beautiful city, but Elizabeth was quite struck by what she was seeing of Washington.

"What a beautiful capitol our new country has," she said to Frederick, her voice filled with pride and hopefulness.

"Yes, it is beautiful," he said. "But I am afraid we need to talk about our trip. I have learned about some things that we did not expect. I am afraid Jacob Fisher did not make it clear how difficult this is going to be."

Elizabeth's face went from one of sleepy excitement to concern.

"What's wrong with the trip, Father?" Fred said. "What did we not expect?"

"Your father was addressing me, not you," Elizabeth scolded. "It is none of your concern."

But as she guided Frederick away from the children, who were still ogling out the window, Elizabeth looked worried.

"Please tell me what you are talking about, Frederick," she said.

He explained what the Castle Garden train agent had told him, and that he had only been able to get them tickets to Richmond, Virginia. He said there was nothing they could do but forge ahead and try to acquire information about what to do next when they got to Richmond.

Elizabeth, still holding onto the glow she gained from the images of their new capitol city, said, "I am sure it will be all right. We will work it out, Frederick. There must be ways to get to North Carolina. The war has been over for almost two years. Repairs had to have been made, I am sure. It will be fine."

Frederick shared little of his wife's optimism. But since there really was no turning back, he kept his dark thoughts to himself. Her typically indomitable spirit filled the space, as she and the children looked excitedly out the windows while the train chugged on through Washington and continued south.

The day was spent quietly, the children playing together, while Elizabeth managed and entertained the youngest of them. Frederick read his emigrant guidebook, trying especially to gain an understanding of American currency. He then attempted to demonstrate his knowledge to Elizabeth, and they practiced together how to make purchases and count change.

Late that afternoon, they arrived in Richmond, where they would need to spend at least a night or two while arranging the next leg of their journey. But Richmond, having served as the capitol of the Confederacy, would also be where they would confront the harsh realities of what the Civil War had done to much of the South.

They disembarked the train, the porter having helped them arrange for a wagon to transport them and their bags and trunks to a local inn.

In the long shadows of the September afternoon, they were horrified to see what was left of the city.

The worn wagon, pulled by a plodding team of two tired, aging horses, slowly passed by block after block of nothing but piles of brick and stone that had once been stout commercial buildings. On one street, all that remained of a formerly substantial bank building were the front pillars holding up an impressive portico. The whole of the building, starting at the front door, had been reduced to a pile of bricks, a few feet deep, that covered nearly half a block.

Anything made of wood was burned. Anything made of brick was leveled. Taking a wider look at Richmond as they moved toward the outskirts, it appeared that as much as half of the large city had been destroyed.

The Garrauxs were shocked. They had never seen anything like this. And as Elizabeth thought back to the bleak conversation she'd had that morning with Frederick about travel conditions, she found it increasingly difficult to maintain her positive outlook.

The accommodations that awaited them would do nothing to help with their feelings.

The driver spoke no German, so when he pulled the wagon up in front of a rambling, old house that appeared to be in great disrepair, Frederick said in his best English, his German accent thick, "No. This place, no," and he pointed at the piece of paper on which the porter had written the address and name of the inn.

The driver continued to speak angrily in English as he began to haul their bags and trunks out of the wagon, slamming them onto the ground in front of the dilapidated wooden structure. As Frederick fumbled with the few English words he knew to try to explain that it was a mistake, the man dropped the last bag on the ground and held out his hand to be paid.

"No, no, no." Frederick said. "Not this place," he said, again pointing to the address on the paper.

The man became so agitated he appeared to be on the verge of violence as he demanded his payment.

At that moment, a short, round, aproned woman opened the door, and spoke to the driver, who gesticulated angrily while shouting and kicking one of their bags.

The woman, who appeared to be in her late fifties, turned to them, at first unsuccessfully speaking in English. Then she asked if they spoke any French.

Frederick was grateful to say that he did, and he explained to her that they were to have been taken to an inn, and a mistake had been made.

She told him, unapologetically, that the building she stood in front of was the inn, and they should be grateful for it because there were few places to stay in Richmond since the city had been burned.

Frederick unhappily paid the driver, who stomped off muttering under his breath. The woman told Frederick where to find a hand cart to move their luggage, and she directed Elizabeth and the children into the ramshackle building.

Chapter 9

It was already dark, and there was only one oil lamp in the front room and the woman clearly didn't intend to share it. She lit a candle, put it in a stand and handed it to Elizabeth, with directions to follow her upstairs.

With Fred carrying baby John, and Elizabeth carrying Frank, they, along with the other children, followed the woman up the creaking, narrow stairs to a dark hallway. They followed her into a room in which there was a small bed and three small dirty mats on the floor. The woman told Elizabeth it was the "family room," the only one with enough beds for them.

The room reeked of sweat, filth and mildew, and Elizabeth did not want to envision who had recently slept in the disgusting space. Trying her best to remain civil and courteous, she thanked the woman, who said she'd send Frederick up with another candle after their luggage was deposited in the barn.

Elizabeth spread her shawl over one of the thin mats, and laid Frank and John on it. She brushed off the other mats and the bed and laid the lap blankets they had used during the wagon ride on them. Tattered curtains on the window were blowing gently in a breeze that she determined was coming in through a broken pane. Elizabeth also quickly realized from the buzzing around her head that hungry mosquitos were being carried in on that breeze.

She told the children to be quiet, not knowing who else might be sleeping nearby, while she got out some cheese, a little bread, and a small bit of milk they had from the train. She gave each of them a few bites and a swallow of milk to keep their stomachs from gnawing them awake during the night.

Frederick finally creaked his way down the dilapidated hallway and joined them in the room. With few words spoken between them, they both forced down a bite of the bread and cheese with a gulp of milk as they swatted away the mosquitos swarming around their heads. Elizabeth wrapped the remaining small chunk of cheese and hunk of bread in a linen handker-chief, and set it on the rickety table, not knowing if it would be all they would have to eat in the morning in this dingy, ill-equipped place.

She left the bed to the older daughters, and joined the youngest sons, lying on the edge of one of the mats, as the other children spooned together on the remaining two wretched pads.

Frederick found a small pile of tattered, lightweight blankets on a rickety wooden stand that were just enough to cover the children and Elizabeth to help fend off the relentless mosquitos. He lay down on the floor, his head on a satchel, covered only by his long jacket, and placed his derby hat over his face.

They left one candle burning for comfort, and for anyone who needed to make way to the chamber pot during the night. The other they blew out, saving it in case they needed to move about during the night for any rea-son. In a few short minutes, despite the miserable conditions, they all fell into the deep sleep of exhaustion.

A short time later, a thump startled Elizabeth awake. She lay motionless while her mind sorted out where they were, as she tried to identify the sound that had awakened her. Besides the deep sleep-breathing of the children and Frederick's light snoring, she heard what sounded like something dragging across the floor.

When she sat upright, her eyes adjusting to the darkness in the room, she saw a movement in the corner. She grabbed the candle off the table in time to shine the light in a corner where a large, black rat was dragging away the remainder of the loaf of bread it had knocked to the floor. She gasped, and it scooted into a gaping hole in the baseboard, taking the bread with it.

Elizabeth grabbed her shoe, and flung it at the rodent, hoping to scare it deep into the wall, where she hoped it would stay. The sound of her shoe hitting the wall woke the baby, who immediately began to wail, awakening Frederick and most of the children.

"There was a rat in the room," she said quietly to Frederick, as she tried to soothe John back to sleep.

Unfortunately, nine-year-old Lucy, who had also awakened, heard what she said, and she began to cry. "I hate rats, Mama." Lucy said. "I don't want the rat to bite me!"

By then, nearly all the children were awake and weepy with fears over the invading rodent.

Frederick and Elizabeth consoled the children, assuring them they would keep watch for the rest of the night. They took turns sleeping briefly, while the one who was awake kept at bay the rats that continually tried to sneak back into the room.

As the light of dawn filled the room, Frederick and Elizabeth, stiff, bug-bitten, and exhausted, awakened the bleary-eyed children, and tried to prepare for the day.

As they dressed and attempted to get the day started, they felt hopeful about what seemed to be the smell of food cooking downstairs. They heard chairs being moved, and the sounds of pots and pans and plates echoing up through the open center-hall staircase, coming from the back of the building.

Frederick agreed to see if there was any food available, while Elizabeth nursed the baby and tended to the children.

He returned smiling, and cheerfully announced that the inn keeper had prepared a morning meal for them.

The kitchen was at the back of the house. In the center of the sparsely furnished room was a long plank table surrounded by mismatched rickety chairs and a bench. The bulk of the narrow table was filled with a platter of fried salted pork, a bowl of boiled potatoes, a plate of eggs and, to the children's delight, a couple of apple pies. The rich scents of brewing coffee and bread baking in the big, wood-burning stove added such a feeling of comfort that Frederick and Elizabeth immediately forgot the horrors of the night before.

Their inn keeper, Clotilde Le Blanc, who spoke both English and French, but no German, guided them to the table. She poured milk for the children and coffee for Frederick and Elizabeth, as she explained, with enthusiasm and brevity, her life since relocating from Quebec ten years ago. She and her husband and two children had moved to Virginia six years before her husband left her a widow, and three years before the war destroyed Richmond, the place they had moved to with the highest of hopes.

Her only son had fought and died in the first year of the War. Her only daughter then died of tuberculosis in the last year of the war.

Clotilde said, with a laugh, she was now doing her best to avoid dying too, as the inn fell down around her.

Clotilde told her story with resignation and a surprising lack of bitterness. It was as though all that could be done to her had been done, and she had found strength in her resiliency, if nothing else.

She said a man who brought her milk and cream before dawn most days also delivered dairy products to a German-speaking family who lived nearer to the city. She had explained the Garraux family's situation to the dairyman, and he said he would ask Hans Weber, the man of that house, to come to the inn to talk to Frederick to help him figure out the next part of their journey.

Frederick and Elizabeth knew more than a million German-born immigrants had already moved to America, so they knew relying on those who came before would be an important part of their new life.

They gratefully ate until they were full, as Clotilde regaled them with story after story of her family's immigration from Quebec and life in Virginia. Frederick translated the parts of her stories Elizabeth did not understand because of her limited French, but he often had to wait until he stopped laughing over Clotilde's amusing anecdotes to tell Elizabeth what she had said.

The round-faced woman's sense of humor along with the good food were a welcome respite in the middle of their wretched travels, and her spirit inspired and energized them as much as a good night's sleep would have.

They spent the day at the inn washing undergarments, socks, diapers, and some clothing and hanging the laundry to dry in the hot Virginia sun. The older children ran about the property, enjoying being free and outdoors for the first time in weeks, while the youngest played and napped on a blanket in the shade of a big oak tree.

Hans Weber joined them for the evening meal of boiled yams, beans cooked with molasses, cornbread, and roasted chicken. Weber was a tall, heavy-set man, humbly dressed, with an impressive moustache that covered his upper lip and a voice that filled the room.

He had also been in the country since before the war and was a wealth of information. He and Frederick spent more than an hour after the meal talking through the journey that would take the family across Virginia to Western North Carolina. Frederick scribbled notes in the back of his immigrant handbook, even attempting a rudimentary map.

The productive conversation, full bellies, and a real travel plan lifted their spirits, making the facing of another night of sleeping in a mosquito and rat-infested room seem slightly more tolerable.

Weber agreed to transport them several miles to a train station the following day, where they could head west to Danville, which was just north of the North Carolina border. There they would change rail lines and begin the final part of the trip to their new home.

From Weber's description, it sounded as though they could expect to reach Asheville within a week, which left them in a state of excitement that made staying awake all night to fend off visiting rodents much easier.

Chapter 10

Weber gathered them up at about 3 a.m., since they needed to be at the train stop by 4:30 a.m. His team of draft horses pulled an old cattle van in which he had thrown a few bales of hay to provide seating.

As the men loaded the trunks and bags, Clotilde insisted on packing a basket of provisions to sustain them during their travels. She filled it with apples, cornbread, salt pork, hardtack biscuits and farm cheese. Frederick and Elizabeth were overwhelmed by the kindness and generosity of these people they had only known for hours. Frederick insisted on paying her more than the basket of provisions was worth, knowing the hardships Clotilde was enduring. At first, she refused the amount he offered, but after his intense persuasion, she expressed appreciation for the kindness.

Loaded into the wagon, the family set off for the next leg of the journey, unsure of what each step would entail, but feeling assured that they would succeed, thanks to the kindness and encouragement of Clotilde and Hans Weber. Elizabeth was struck by the irony that two of the worst nights of their journey ended with great encouragement.

Weber dropped them off at a small train depot south of Richmond and said his farewell with good wishes and a prayer for their safe keeping. The train that was supposed to depart at 6 a.m. arrived at the depot just after noon. By the time the train took on more wood and water for the engine, and the small group of passengers waiting at the station had boarded and their goods were loaded, it was early evening. Frederick and Elizabeth were so thankful for the provisions Clotilde had given them, but already concerned that they would run out quickly if they kept finding themselves delayed or abandoned in unpopulated areas.

The lavatories on the train were Hooper toilets, a drop chute that emptied waste directly into the railbed as the train rumbled down the track. Among the many challenges of traveling with young children, Elizabeth had difficulty convincing four-year-old Bettie there was no possibility of falling through the commode.

The next couple of days became a blur of train stops at one small depot after another, constant delays while water and wood were loaded, and handfuls of passengers got on and off.

In some cases, changes in the gauge of the railroad tracks between rail lines meant the train had to be completely unloaded and all the passengers and their luggage moved to a new train on the next section of track.

In other cases, they would come to long sections of track destroyed in the War that had yet to be repaired. All the passengers and their possessions then had to be unloaded and transported by carriages and wagons that were all in various levels of disrepair, to the next available train on a functioning section of track.

One such transport they endured was in a broken-down, retired army ambulance with boards nailed across its width that served as seats. As the old wagon jiggled and slammed across the plank roads, it seemed their spines might break.

The plank roads, an attempt to improve on dirt roads that had often washed away in storms, were built by cutting down young trees that were then flattened on two sides and laid side-by-side to form a rigid surface for wagons, livestock, and foot traffic. Unfortunately, most of them had fallen into disrepair during the war, so they now made for a more jarring trip than a dirt road might have.

During another transport around broken tracks, the family of ten and four other people shared an old stagecoach that was built for six on a trip that took them almost half a day. The others did not speak their language, but their expressions clearly conveyed that they loathed traveling with a family of eight children, particularly one who was still in diapers.

By the time they reached Danville, a small city on the banks of the Dan River just a few miles from the North Carolina border, they were so sore, exhausted, and starved, they felt as though they might just give up and stay there forever.

"The children need time to rest, Frederick, and we need provisions," Elizabeth said. "I am as anxious to get to Asheville as you are, but we need to stop for a couple of days."

He agreed, and they sought out a hotel where they could rest and bathe and even eat in a dining room. Danville was in a remote location away from the major east coast cities, so it had been largely unscathed during the War. The Confederate army had set up hospitals for wounded soldiers and prisons for captured Federal soldiers in Danville. The city had even served briefly as the Confederate capitol at the end of the war after Richmond fell.

The children, only mildly distracted by their current location, continually asked questions about the future that Elizabeth and Frederick tried to answer, but often could not.

"How long will it take for us to get to our new home?"

"How will we go to school if we do not speak the language?"

"What will our house be like?"

"Will there be children nearby for us to have for friends?"

Danville was encouraging in that it hadn't been terribly affected by the war. There was clearly commerce and farming going on in the area, and it appeared that many people were living normal, if not prosperous, lives.

The hotel rooms were not luxurious, but they were clean, pest-free, and more comfortable than any place they had been since leaving Bern. Their slumber was so deep that not one of the children stirred during the night. The sun was well up and shining brightly before any of them, including Elizabeth and Frederick, opened their eyes.

Little did they know how very much they would need that rest to survive the last leg of their journey to their new home.

Chapter 11

After a morning meal, Frederick set out to try to make arrangements for the next part of the trip. He found the small railroad depot, and using the notes made during his conversations with Weber, he was able to explain where they wanted to go.

"We go Asheville," he told the train agent, pointing to the town on the map he had drawn in his guidebook. He was pleased when the agent clearly knew of the town and how to get them closer to it.

As would happen frequently during the course of the trip, the train agent went away briefly and returned with another employee who spoke both English and German. The man was of great assistance and translated Frederick's questions and needs to the train agent.

"You will be going from Danville to Salisbury, North Carolina, and on to Morganton. That'll take you about two days with connections and transfers, if all goes well," the man said. "Morganton's the end of the line. You'll have to take a stagecoach or buy a wagon and horses to go on from there."

"Is it more than one hundred miles by wagon?" Frederick asked, remembering what the harsh train agent at Castle Garden had said.

"No, no," the man said. "But it's a very rough and sometimes very steep road. It's fifty, maybe sixty miles from Morganton to Asheville. It's hard going. If you take your own wagon, it will likely take you several days, maybe a week. If you take the stagecoach, you could be in Asheville in two or three days. The coaches stop and trade out fresh teams of horses that are waiting at the staging sites. The teams are changed out quickly. If you take your own wagon and team, you will have to lay over at night to rest the horses, so the trip will be much longer."

Frederick's heart sank. He knew Elizabeth and the children were weary of travel, and they had been led to believe they were no more than four or five days from their destination. He was disappointed to have to tell them there was probably more than a week of travel left for them between Danville and Asheville.

Frederick purchased the tickets to Salisbury. Once there, they would get tickets for the last section of their train journey. The departure time was 4 a.m., though the man warned him, as they had already learned, the trains seldom ran on schedule.

The time at Clotilde's inn where the children had been able to run and play outside had been good for them. The Danville hotel was more confining, and Elizabeth was trying to manage their excess energy while opening luggage and sorting through clothing to get them into fresh travel clothes, sponge-bathing the youngest of them while supervising the washing up of the older ones and getting them all into clean underclothes and new sets of clothing.

"We're getting near to our new home, and we're going to arrive there clean," she said firmly, silencing their complaints.

Once the lengthy process of washing and dressing the eight children was completed, Elizabeth finally sat down, exhaling, feeling for a moment like

74

the trip would never end.

"Only a few more days," she told herself. "I can do it."

Frederick returned to the room and cheerfully told her he had purchased the tickets to Salisbury, and about the kind German-speaking man who had assisted him.

"We need to be at the depot before 4 a.m.," Frederick said, "so, we should go now and buy provisions. This city has some stores where we can get what we need. I am not so sure about Salisbury. The gentleman told me the Union army destroyed the city three years ago, and it has struggled to rebuild."

They gathered up the children and walked to the neighboring commercial district where they found a well-stocked general store. They bought sausages, cheese, bread, apples, and pears for their travels. Elizabeth bought thread she needed to mend a few items of clothing as well as a card of buttons to replace a couple lost during the journey and some extras for the future. She bought some ribbon and hairpins for the girls' braids, and after much begging and pleading by the children, they bought a small bag of candies for them to share. The children chose molasses taffy, licorice sticks, lemon drops, and Necco wafers, which were a northern candy unusual to find this far south.

Their spirits were high when they returned to the hotel to retire for an early bedtime in preparation for the predawn departure of the train.

After the children were all settled in bed, Frederick said hesitantly, "I am afraid we have more travel ahead than we expected, Elizabeth."

She closed her eyes, wishing she could forget what he had just said. She opened them and said, "How much more? It's already been so much longer than we expected."

Jacob Fisher's unrealistic, uninformative letters had made it sound like they would be able to travel from New York to Asheville in less than a week. They had already been traveling for six days since they got off the *Arago*.

"I think it will take us about another week. Maybe longer," Frederick said.

Elizabeth tossed her head back and looked up at the ceiling. Then she leveled her steely blue eyes, looked into Frederick's, and said, "Well, if that is what we need to do, that is what we shall do. There is nothing more we can do but to continue."

He leaned forward, took her face in his hands, and said, "Oh, mein klein maus, you are so strong."

She smiled, then laughed, and told him he should not remind her of the rodents they had left behind at Clotilde's.

"What an amazing woman she is," Frederick to himself, in awe of his wife's unstoppable, unflappable resilience and drive.

"We will be fine," Elizabeth said. "We have come this far. We will continue. Our new home awaits, and soon this will all become a fading memory."

They drifted off to sleep, Frederick only dozing intermittently, afraid they would not awaken in time to get themselves and all their worldly goods loaded onto the wagon arranged by the hotel and to the train that would finally carry them into North Carolina. Elizabeth also slept fitfully, thoughts of the rest of the journey and the future travel by stagecoach or wagon through a strange land keeping her in turmoil.

After what seemed like a few short hours later, they, their tired children, and their trunks, satchels, bags, and baskets were dropped at the train depot in the dark. The children piled onto their parents, leaned on each other, and sprawled across the bench, more asleep than awake, hoping the train would be ready to leave at 4 a.m. so they could allow themselves to fall truly asleep, once safely in their seats.

That would have been far too easy. The train apparently encountered some mechanical problems after its last stop, and word was passed along to them that it would not be leaving Danville for at least a few hours, maybe not until the next day.

Elizabeth had the passing thought that it seemed each time she would rally her spirits and look forward to the end of the journey, something would take all the wind out her sails.

The depot provided limited comfort with its hard benches and minimal facilities. At least there was a public outhouse behind the building, and a water pump where they could get clean water to drink.

They did their best to make themselves and the children comfortable as the hours passed and the sun began to set. They also began to debate whether they should return to the hotel or stay at the depot. Word finally came that the train was on its way and was expected to arrive before midnight. It should leave Danville a couple hours later, so they decided to continue the miserable wait at the train station.

At about 11 p.m., nineteen hours after they arrived at the depot, they and their possessions were finally loaded onto the train, and it pulled out of the depot. Within an hour, they had crossed the border into North Carolina, the state they would soon call home.

By the time the train crossed the state line, the whole family was asleep, unaware they had finally passed into the last state of this long journey. But, unbeknown to them at the time, Asheville was not to be the place they would live out their lives in America.

Chapter 12

Whatever mechanical trouble had befallen the engine delaying its arrival in Danville apparently recurred within a few hours of their departure. The train chugged slowly and then rolled to a stop.

The lack of movement and sudden quiet woke Elizabeth and Frederick. They thought perhaps they had reached Salisbury, but lifting the curtain and looking out the window, they realized they were surrounded by a dense forest silhouetted against the night sky.

Men with lanterns passed by their car, apparently coming from the crew car at the rear of the train. Fortunately, the children continued to sleep, as Frederick and Elizabeth grew concerned about the lack of forward movement.

Finally, a porter came into their car, and explained as best he could that there was some kind of trouble with the engine. He pointed to their sleeping berth and, acting out the motion of laying their heads down, he said, "Sleep. Just sleep."

They understood him enough to realize they might just as well get some rest. Without disturbing the children, they climbed back into the berths they shared with them, and after a time, they all fell back to sleep.

Hours later, John began fussing, so Elizabeth got up with him. Much to her dismay, she realized the train was still not moving, and the sun was up.

Soon, the whole family was awake, and Frederick left their car to try to find out what was going on. He was gone for some time, and when he returned, he said, "The news is not good. The engine will not function until a faulty part is replaced. A train will have to come from Salisbury to retrieve us and to deliver the part so this engine can be repaired. A train worker told me we will likely be here for a few hours."

"Oh, no," Earnest said. "We're to be left sitting in the train, Father?"

"A few hours?" Fred asked. "But we were supposed to be there yesterday."

"Whining will not change anything," Elizabeth said to her sons, though internally, she completely understood their feelings.

Trying to sound encouraging, Frederick said, "The good news is that once the new train reaches us, it will only take a few hours to get to Salisbury."

Elizabeth sighed. Thank God they had started out from Danville wearing clean clothes and carrying a sizeable basket of provisions. The trip, already so tedious, was beginning to feel interminable.

"So, we'll be in Salisbury before nightfall, children," she said determinedly. "All will be well. If you are patient and quiet, you will each get an extra piece of candy when we reach Salisbury."

That was a good enough incentive for the children, who were exceptionally patient during the three hours waiting for the new train, the additional hour moving of the goods from the disabled train, and the four-hour ride to Salisbury.

They crossed the impressive Yadkin River railroad bridge, one that had survived the Civil War, and arrived in Salisbury as the sun was setting. The city had been the site of a Confederate prison where more than a quarter of the prisoners, more than four thousand of them, had died.

Salisbury, like many southern cities, had also been badly damaged by the war, with nearly half of the city burned when General George Stoneman and his troops stormed the town near the end of the war.

But much of Salisbury was intact and being a destination for two railroads had led to the construction of a few hotels before and since the war. Frederick had found them a large room with several beds in one of the bigger establishments.

Their possessions were left in storage at the train depot in preparation for another early departure. They stopped at a market they passed by on the way to the hotel and restocked their provisions for the next day.

After a simple but generously portioned meal in the hotel dining room, the children were allowed two pieces of candy, as promised.

They all retired to bed immediately after, once again rising before 3 a.m. to be at the station to take the train to their last stop in Morganton.

Frederick did not admit to Elizabeth how terribly glad he was that the ordeal of the train travel was ending. But Elizabeth, likewise, did not admit to Frederick how very much she dreaded the wagon or coach travel they faced for the last leg of the journey.

Unlike their experience in Danville, the train was waiting at the station in Salisbury when they arrived at about 3:45 a.m.

The trunks and bags designated for the trip were already loaded on the train. As a train agent processed the family's tickets to Morganton, the last of the wood and water needed for the steam engine was being loaded onto the train.

A small group of passengers boarded the train: a few couples, a handful of single men, two small families, and the Garraux family of ten.

In the quiet, predawn darkness, the train pulled out of the station just before 4:30 a.m.

"It is the last train ride of our journey, Elizabeth," Frederick said, as he took her hand in his and squeezed it. "No more waiting for the repairs of machinery, or detours around broken tracks. We will soon be at our new home."

He then began talking cheerfully with the children about the next part of the journey. Earnest and Frederick, despite being the oldest, had become increasingly sullen over the past week, often squabbling with each other, and pouting after being reprimanded. The conversation about the trip actually coming to an end seemed to cheer all the children, the boys in particular.

Elizabeth nodded affirmatively to Frederick's positive statement, but with her typically realistic approach, she thought to herself, *Yes, it's the last train ride. But now we'll be relying on others to take us to a place we know little about, carrying along with us all of our worldly goods and our eight children.*

She hoped he didn't notice the long, stress-filled sigh she released.

As the train chugged toward Morganton, the sun was bright, the sky blue, and mountains soon surrounded them on both sides. The hills were not quite as impressive as what they were used to in Switzerland, but seeing the mountains brought them a tremendous feeling of comfort and familiarity.

The train depot was just east of town, and there were several men waiting in wagons that could be hired to take passengers and their luggage into Morganton. They found a driver who would load their goods and take them to a boarding house near the center of town.

The town was situated on a high plateau, with the Blue Ridge Mountains looming ahead and beside the wide valley. There were just a few large homes along the road into town, and several old-German-style chinked log homes, typical in the area.

Morganton was small, but orderly, with a few shops, a couple dining places and traveler accommodations lining the main street. That main street, Union Street, was lined with two and three-story brick and frame buildings, and though the town looked a bit tired around the edges from having weathered the War, it suffered little apparent damage.

The boarding house proprietor, John Markham, appeared to be rather tired and frail to be operating a boarding house. His posture was slightly hunched over, and his face had an unhealthy pallor. He conveyed what seemed to be a mild irritation upon their arrival, making them at first feel unwelcomed. They later learned that the death of his only son in the War had taken the joy from his life, and he was just going through the motions of maintaining his household's only means of livelihood.

Markham was English-speaking, which combined with his dour attitude, was making for an awkward check-in. The process greatly improved when he called on Freida Braun, a chambermaid at the boarding house, who spoke both English and German. She appeared to be about fourteen or fifteen, and she proved to be very helpful until her endless chatter became quite tedious.

Freida was a slender, plain-faced, bright-eyed girl, already several inches taller than Elizabeth, who was just five feet tall in her stocking feet. Freida's long blonde hair was braided and pinned up on her head, and her starched and ironed apron gave her an exceptionally tidy appearance.

After helping arrange their stay at the boarding house, Freida bragged that she knew all about the stagecoach service through the mountains. Her oldest brother had become a driver for the mail coach service after they relocated to Morganton from Frankfurt when she was about ten. She was anxious to share all she knew with Frederick and Elizabeth, and she clearly enjoyed a chance to speak in the language of her homeland.

Freida explained that the first coach service would take them from Morganton to Old Fort, the last stop before the most difficult part of the journey to Asheville.

She said Old Fort was the site of Davidson's Fort, colonial America's westernmost outpost when it was built in 1776 as a defense against the Cherokee as more settlers began their incursion into tribal lands.

"From here to Old Fort, it's not too bad, just a long, slow uphill until you make the gradual descent into Old Fort. But after Old Fort, it's so very steep and slick. It's deadly dangerous up through the Swannanoa Pass," she said. "But you will have a driver who's a legend. He's the very best in all the Blue Ridge."

Elizabeth expected the driver she would brag about to be her brother, but that was not the case.

"Jack Pence has been driving Old Fort to Asheville since before the War. He came down here from Salisbury in '59," she said. "He drives a team of six to get the coach up those steep parts. They say one part of the road goes up a thousand feet in just four miles. And you're practically on the cliff's edge the whole way," she exclaimed.

"My brother, he says Pence is not afraid of anything. And he said Pence has never had a single wreck in all these years." The girl's voice was filled with awe and respect.

After hearing the description of the mountain pass, and the accolades of the driver, Frederick and Elizabeth immediately agreed that they would no longer consider attempting the mountain pass on their own in a wagon. They would definitely make the trip through the mountains with the stagecoach lines.

Frieda explained that a four-horse coach would take them from Morganton to Henry's station near Old Fort, stopping only once about halfway for a fresh team. She said that would take them about half a day. Then they'd have to wait overnight for Pence's coach, which would leave before

dawn the next morning. She said their luggage and steamer trunks
would be carried by a freight wagon driven behind the coach.

"You're lucky," Freida said. "There are so many of you, you can book the
whole inside of the coach. The three seats can handle nine people—you'll
be holding your baby, of course. But that middle seat is rough. If you're in
the middle, there's no back on your seat, and you have to hold the leather
straps attached to the ceiling to keep from getting tossed about on the
rocky roads."

"So, no one else will travel with us?" Elizabeth asked.

"Oh, I didn't mean that," Frieda said. "I just meant you can fill the inside
of the coach. But there will be others sitting on the roof, or up there on
the driver's seat with Pence. They take a full load. And some people like
being on the roof since it seems you're less likely to get sick from the
bumping and swaying if you're up on top in the open air."

Elizabeth felt a rush of anxiety at the thought of illness caused by movement. The time on the ship was still a very vivid memory.

"The coaches do stop along the way, though, correct?" Frederick said.

"Oh, yes sir, they do," Freida said. "The mountain pass is hard on the
horses, so a stage is only about eight to ten miles before they have to get
changed out. At each stage, you get to leave the coach. Some places will
have food and, ah," fumbling for words, "even a place where you can, ah,
where if you need to, well, relieve yourself."

Freida said. "The first run through the Swannanoa Gap and then along
the narrow cliff up to Ridgecrest is only six miles, but even on the best of
days, it will take at least three hours, and the horses will get changed out
two miles after that. My brother says it's terrifying and only brave men
can make that drive."

Elizabeth glanced at Frederick, and she could see concern in his eyes and
his jaw muscles tensing.

"So, this is a hard journey," Elizabeth said, "But we will have a capable driver who has never had an accident. All will be well. It will be exciting for the children to see mountains once again. It will be a wonderful trip, I am sure."

As much as she was trying to encourage Frederick and the children, Elizabeth was also trying to convince herself.

Freida clearly enjoyed having an audience for all the information she had worked so hard to remember. She had listened to her brother, Anders, repeat his stories of the journey through the Swannanoa gap many times to anyone new who would listen. Anders fancied himself quite special and very brave because of being a gap driver. The young chambermaid also felt elevated by association.

"Oh, and Pence always stops to pay his respects at the mystery grave," she said, especially liking the dramatic detail. "No one knows for sure who's in the grave. Probably a Yankee soldier, but it could be a Confederate."

"So, the way it happened was the Union army tried to come through the Gap, but our Home Guard felled big trees across the roads, so the Yankee brigade never got here. They gave up and ended up going up to Asheville, just as Lee surrendered and the War ended."

"Some people say it was a deserter they shot. Other people say it was a Rebel picked off by a Yankee. Some say the body was later dug up and moved to a cemetery and the grave's empty. So, there's a grave up there in the Gap that we know is from the War, but no one really knows whose it is."

She looked intently at Frederick and Elizabeth as though expecting a reaction. They were so far removed from the drama of the War, so tired of traveling, so weary of keeping bored children under control while Freida talked on and on, they didn't respond, in hopes it might end the enthusiastic girl's unrelenting chatter.

After an awkward moment, Freida said, "Well, all right. I will be here until nightfall if you want to know anything else."

"Thank you. You've been very helpful," Frederick said, as they tried to inch toward the staircase that would lead them to their rooms.

The boarding house was clean and comfortable, and though the bedrooms were small, there was a second adjoining room, so the family was fully accommodated, with three beds in one room and two in the other.

With their luggage and trunks safely in a storage room at the back of the building, they settled into their rooms, glad to be able to move about without constraint. Freida brought up a pitcher of warm water for their basin so they could wash before dinner. Elizabeth was grateful the loquacious child was too busy to begin another conversation.

Frederick found the coach agency just down the street and arranged for the family to be taken to Old Fort the next afternoon, and on to Asheville the following day. He was pleased that they were, in fact, able to book inside seating on both coaches as well as a freight wagon to bring along their goods. Each time a travel arrangement came together, Frederick experienced a great sense of relief.

The evening meal was chicken made in a rich gravy with thick dumpling noodles that reminded them of the Knoepfle egg noodles back home in Switzerland.

They had been traveling since before dawn, and Elizabeth was grateful to learn the coach to Old Forte did not leave until midday.

Even with all the tumultuous thoughts about the impending mountain trek, they, and the children, were asleep shortly after the sun went down.

The next morning, the family enjoyed sleeping until everyone was rested. Even baby John slept until after seven.

The dining tables were in a cozy room off the kitchen. There was one long table and three smaller ones where two couples and a family of three were seated by the time the Garraux family made its way into the room.

They had a simple breakfast of eggs and cracklin cornbread, a rich, moist bread, cooked in an iron skillet with bits of rendered, fried pork rind added to it. There was no coffee available, but Mrs. Markham had brewed them a strong pot of tea. Mrs. Markham wore the grief of loss differently than her husband, staying distant and silent as she moved from table to table, only nodding when asked a question by one of the other couples.

As Freida cleared off the table when breakfast was done, she told them dinner would be served at 1 p.m., the traditional time in the South for the big meal of the day. Less talkative than the night before due to her many daytime responsibilities, she gave them brief, helpful answers and directions when they inquired about shopping for travel provisions. They would need to be ready to go to the coach stop immediately after dinner, so she recommended the transfer of their luggage before they ate.

Frederick and Elizabeth took John and Frank with them, leaving the rest of the children playing in their rooms. After arranging for the transport of their goods by freight wagon, they found shops within a short walking distance that had all they needed to prepare for the trip through the mountains. They had learned from the earlier parts of the trip not to be reliant on food or drink being provided.

They also bought licorice sticks for the children and several special glass marbles to add to their collections, rewards for their tolerance of the seemingly unending journey.

When they returned to the boarding house, it was filled with the rich smell of apples and cinnamon. Freida was coming down the stairs as they were going up, and she said as she passed, "Mr. Markham's wife is a very good cook. You will like your dinner."

The children were excited about the candy and marbles, and everyone looked forward to their last big meal before heading into the mountains.

One of the couples had departed, but the family of three and the other couple were seated by the time the Garraux family made its way into the room.

There was already a large soup tureen on the long table filled with thick potato and leek soup accompanied by a pewter platter with a freshly baked loaf of bread and a pot of newly churned butter. Elizabeth served the soup to the family, noting the other tables also had soup and the guests were already eating.

Frederick blessed the meal, and they began to eat, the children exclaiming how delicious it was, and all of them enjoying it very much.

After soup, a young woman, who they assumed by appearance might be the Markhams' daughter, appeared carrying a steaming platter of cabbage, onions, carrots, and potatoes stewed with salted pork. The sight of the heaping pile of food delighted the children, despite the dish being unfamiliar to them. Several of them said, in their best English, "Oh, thank you! Thank you!"

"Yes, thank you," Frederick said, also speaking English. The hardy, simple cooking was just what they needed to prepare for the next arduous leg of their journey.

As if the bounty of fresh seasonal vegetables wasn't enough, once the table was cleared, Mrs. Markham set a large pan of apple cobbler on the table. Looking at the dessert, Earnest excitedly clapped his hands as the other children murmured excitedly. Mrs. Markham smiled weakly and patted Earnest on the top of his head as she left the room.

Somehow, they all made room in their full bellies for the delicious, fresh-from-the-oven dessert.

When it was time to leave, Freida helped them get their travel bags and all the children down the stairs and onto the front porch. The Markhams stepped outside, Mrs. Markham drying her hands on a dish towel. As the family walked away up the street, Freida called out, "Goodbye and good luck."

As they turned to walk back into the boarding house, Mrs. Markham shouted, "God bless you." Even with their limited knowledge of the language, Frederick and Elizabeth knew what she had said. And they also prayed that their family would soon be safely in their new home.

Chapter 13

The worn and tattered stagecoach was large enough for the family, but Elizabeth wondered what it would have been like to share the cramped space with strangers. She sat on the backwards-facing seat with John on her lap and Bettie and Rosa on either side.

Frederick sat on the center seat with Frank on his lap and Fred and Earnest on either side of him. If needed, they would be able to reach the leather loops over their heads to stabilize themselves. They faced toward Elizabeth, away from the sisters, Mary and Lucy, who were in the only forward-facing seat.

The strangeness of this new situation left the children quiet and wide-eyed as several men climbed up onto the roof of the coach. The driver sat quietly, only speaking when directing the men where to position themselves on top of the coach.

Elizabeth looked at her children, marveling at their resilience and overall cooperation with this difficult journey.

Fred and Earnest had seemed to come out of their sullen moods of the preceding weeks. They were actually being patient and encouraging to each other and their siblings.

Lucy was, as usual, helping her year-younger sister, Mary, who had a difficult time managing new situations. Lucy was a cheerful, easy-going child, and she generally had more patience with Mary's slowness and limitations than the other siblings did.

Betty and Rosa, who were used to getting more attention at home than they had on most days of the trip, remained obedient and easy to manage. That delighted their mother, who had her hands full with two-year-old Frank and eight-month-old John.

Elizabeth worried for her children's safety, hoped constantly for their futures to be good, and thanked God for blessing Frederick and her with their beautiful offspring. No matter what life in America would hold, it was for their children that they were doing this—for the lives and opportunities they hoped and prayed they would have.

The horses stepped forward and the stagecoach lurched and pulled away a few minutes after 2 p.m. The trip to Old Fort should take less than five hours, even with the team change at midpoint, according to their stagecoach expert, Frieda. Elizabeth hoped she was correct, because that would put them at their overnight destination as the sun set.

The old coach moved along quite well, even while fording a small creek west of the town. Several miles from Old Fort, the coach crested a low hill, and during the long, slow descent, they could see the mountains ahead of them.

At least four mountain ranges were visible ahead, piled up one after another against the sky, forming a beautiful but imposing wall in shades of blueish purple. The view of the mountains was breathtaking. But knowing they would travel through them on narrow roads along the steep cliffs that edged the peaks was intimidating.

After a few hours of bouncing and jolting over the rocky road, they stopped briefly while the team of horses was changed out. They were able to relieve themselves, wash their hands under a water pump and get a drink of cold, mountain spring water.

After winding through the heavily wooded land for another hour, they began a long, gradual descent, allowing them to again see the imposing wall of the Blue Ridge Mountains.

"I am glad—we get to stop and rest again—before we start over those—big mountains," Elizabeth said. Her words were spoken in stops and starts as the coach bumped and bounced down the dirt road that much of the time seemed more like a washed-out riverbed.

The road was just as rough but at least more level, as they descended to the area along the Catawba River. The shadows were growing long, and the temperature was dropping. They had retrieved their lap blankets at the last stop, and now Elizabeth covered the children and herself. Thankfully, even with the rocky road, John and Frank had slept much of the afternoon.

Frederick was weary from trying to hold his sleeping son while also trying to steady himself with the leather strap attached to the ceiling. He had to let go regularly to reposition the child and let the blood return to his hand, but it seemed each time he let go, the coach would hit a bone-jarring bump.

Frederick was grateful the day had started after a good night's sleep and a wonderful meal. If this was the easier section of the mountain trek, he feared just how rough the leg from Old Fort to Asheville would be.

By the time they reached the station near Old Fort, they were all tired of being banged and bumped around. The night chill made them glad to get into the rudimentary accommodations of the station. It was more of a barracks than a hotel room, but at this point, they were just relieved to stop moving.

The station had a public room in which there was beer, coffee, a pot of beans cooked with molasses, some cold biscuits, and freshly harvested apples. They ate a quick and meager dinner, rewarding the children with licorice sticks, before quickly getting them to bed on several cots with thin mattresses.

They could see that the coach for the trip to Asheville was already parked at the station. The horses that would pull them on the first stage of the trip through the Blue Ridge were eating hay and resting in a corral nearby, having just made the last leg of a return trip from Asheville.

They did not see Jack Pence, the elusive driver they had heard so much about, but knew they would be meeting him before the sun was up.

The dormitory-style accommodations grew chilly after nightfall, and Elizabeth hunted down extra blankets she found in a small storage room. She then lay awake for the last few hours of the night, worrying about the remainder of the journey, and wondering what the arrival in their new home would be like.

So much of what Jacob Fisher had said in his letters and what she had read in the brochures about America seemed far removed from the reality they had been experiencing. Elizabeth was not a worrier. She tended to look past any problems she ever faced and toward solutions. But in this case, she felt she didn't even yet know what problems might be, so she had no way to plan for solutions.

She had just finally started to doze off when Frederick touched her and said, "It's three o'clock, Elizabeth. We are to leave at four. We need to get the children ready."

Without opening her eyes, she said, "One moment. I am coming."

She longed to allow her body to relax into sleep, but instead, she briefly prayed for strength and safety for the family for this the last part of the journey into their new life. She reached under the cot, grabbed her shoes, yanked them on and laced them up.

93

Right now, their impending new life loomed over her with the same weight and darkness as the unyielding mountains that stood between them and their destination.

After a night of fitful sleep and unremembered but disturbing dreams, Frederick had checked his pocket watch before he woke his poor exhausted wife. As she began to rouse and dress the children, he went looking for coffee and a chance to perhaps meet their driver.

Their fellow travelers to Asheville would apparently be the same group of people, with no additional passengers—just their family and five men, two young and three who appeared Frederick's age or older. The men were already up, gathered around a wood-burning Franklin stove in the public room, drinking coffee.

"Good morning," Frederick said, using one of the few English phrases he felt he had mastered. It was apparently too effective, because one of the men immediately started speaking to him in English.

"Sorry, no English," Frederick said, using the first phrase he had taught himself, knowing he would make good use of it.

He then said, "Sprichst du Deutsch?" to which all five men shook their heads and said, "No."

He saw mugs on a shelf and got two of them. He pointed at the coffee pot, and said, "Please?"

The men responded affirmatively, and one grabbed a towel, wrapped it around the coffee pot's handle, and filled both mugs.

"Thank you," Frederick said, feeling like he was already making progress with the language they would have to master in their new home.

As he walked back to the room where his family was getting ready for the day, he passed by the coach and the six stout horses that were being harnessed.

94

This is it, Frederick thought, his head swirling with excitement and trep- idation. *We're going to our new home. This is the day we will see Asheville. This is the day our lives change forever.*

Still in the predawn darkness, Elizabeth and Frederick gathered up their small bags, lap blankets, the basket of provisions, and herded the children toward the coach.

Elizabeth expected this day's journey to be even rougher. Her bottom and thighs were already bruised from the first, easier leg of the journey. She knew the children were likely in the same condition, though none of them had complained.

The first coach had been a bit worn and tired looking. This coach was tall, impressive, and finely crafted. Freida had told them the coach from Old Fort to Asheville would be one owned by Edwin T. Clemmons. He and his brother, John, ran several coach lines in the south. Clemmons had also bought the Eagle Hotel in Asheville where they would be staying.

The coach was ornately painted and looked much newer than the last coach. Elizabeth was especially delighted to see it had substantial-looking velvet seat cushions.

Jack Pence moved with purpose as he prepared the coach and horses in silence. He was not the stout coachman in a fancy waistcoat and breeches Elizabeth had envisioned. His skin was tanned and leathery, his clothing homespun, his hat soft and dirty with a floppy brim. He was slender, but wiry, and watching him adjust the harnesses and handle the baggage made it clear that he was strong and capable.

Pence climbed up into the driver's seat, reins held high above the big horses, who stomped and shuffled as if anxious to get underway. The driver's box, as it was called, was nearly as high up as the men who had climbed into their positions on the roof of the coach.

The impressive team of horses, lined up in pairs, was so long that Pence's whip, used to urge them up the steepest parts of the road, could not reach the lead horses. He kept a bag of small rocks near his feet that he could toss at them if he needed to get their attention or spur them onward.

Once their small bags had been secured in the luggage boot on the back of the coach, Elizabeth and Frederick loaded the children inside.

Before he got in, Frederick walked to the front of the coach and said, "Good morning," to Pence.

Pence nodded, touched the brim of his hat, and said, "Mornin'." That was all. Freida had said he was a quiet man who did not like to talk. That would be evident throughout the long day of travel.

The coach lurched forward into the darkness, only Pence's familiarity with the road and the lanterns attached to the front of the coach lighting the way.

They were off, a seemingly inglorious moment for the beginning of a life-altering event.

The horses moved at a slow but steady pace. They were used to regularly making a round trip on this leg of the route, so the horses plodded along, knowing the road almost as well as Pence.

The challenges of the mountain road were far too great to risk tiring the team on the easy stretches of road. Normally, a coach would move at a higher rate of speed on less hilly sections of road, but not on this trip.

Almost immediately, the ascent began, and they found themselves at the base of the high mountains within a couple of miles. The rocky, rutted road narrowed, and within a short time, the coach felt as though it was creeping steeply upwards along the edge of a very high cliff.

The view of the surrounding mountains as the sun came up was breath-taking. The height and steepness of the trail were absolutely terrifying. The coach crept along a narrow ledge, the sheer, towering cliffside of the mountain just feet to the right of the coach.

Just feet to the coach's left, the immediate drop-off into the deep valley below made Elizabeth feel as though she should lean toward the mountainside, feeling that at any moment, they could tumble off into the bottomless crevice.

Up and up the coach crawled. The men on the roof who had been talking and laughing loudly for most of the trip from Morganton to Old Fort were completely silent.

Fortunately, the children, being children, were for the most part thrilled with what they were seeing. When the stiff wooden wheels of the coach would occasionally slam down over a larger than average rock, Bettie and Lucy would shriek, a combination of fear and excitement. But overall, with Elizabeth and Frederick's encouragement, the children spent their time marveling at the views and the power of the big team of horses hauling them up the steep grade.

Occasionally, there would be a break in the trees next to the stagecoach road, and with the sun now up, they looked out across the cloud-filled valley below them. The low bank of frothing clouds filled the spaces between the layers of mountains like thick cream in a bowl. The beauty of the mountains was awe-inspiring, and despite the intensity of the journey, both Elizabeth and Frederick were thrilled with what they saw.

They were forced to cross through narrow streams and washouts about every half mile during the entire climb up the steep mountain. Pence used reins and whips and commands to keep the six powerful horses moving steadily upward. Despite the occasional obstacles of small limbs across the roadway or streams cutting their way through the trail, he kept the big team calm and controlled, and they continued without hesitation.

As predicted, one of the few stops in their day's journey happened when Pence reined in the horses. He locked the long wooden brake against the coach wheel, and he climbed down, spoke briefly to the passengers, saying something neither Elizabeth nor Frederick understood. The men climbed down from atop the coach and motioned for Elizabeth and Frederick to join them as they left the stagecoach road and followed a small footpath into the woods near the Catawba River.

Elizabeth told Frederick she would stay in the coach with the children, so he followed the men alone. When he caught up with them, they were standing quietly in the dappled sunlight, hats in hands, in a semicircle around a small gravestone. Frederick realized it was the soldier's grave the young chambermaid had told them about. He also took off his hat and said a brief prayer for the unknown victim in the grave, and for the other young men who had lost their lives in the terrible war.

He later explained to Elizabeth that they had stopped to honor the grave of the unknown soldier before their journey continued. They did not stop again until they reached the top of the Swannanoa trail. There they were able to take a brief break while Pence changed out the horses for a new team.

Shortly after that stop, they could sense that they were no longer traveling upward. There was no doubt they were on the slow and gradual descent into the high-mountain basin in which they would find Asheville. The plan was to overnight there until they could get word to Jacob Fisher to come fetch them. He had said in his last correspondence that he would come with a wagon large enough to fetch them and their goods, and he would deliver them to their new home in Bent Creek. The farming community was about ten miles southwest of Asheville.

There were a few spots where the descent was so steep that Pence asked all the men to get off the roof and out of the coach to lighten the load. The men walked along behind the coach until the steep grade became more gradual. That process was repeated a few times as they continued the gradual descent into a wide valley.

Chapter 14

It was still daylight when the road became less frightening, the path between the trees widened, and they were able to see the increasingly beautiful countryside. Between the majestic mountains and rich green forests were rolling fields of springlike green, much like those they had left behind in Switzerland.

"Oh, Frederick," Elizabeth said. "It is so beautiful. The worst of our travels is over. And this is the place where our new life awaits us."

He squeezed her hand, as they and the children were transfixed by the beauty they saw through the coach windows. The craggy mountain peaks were silhouetted against a sky tinged with the orange and pink of a hopeful sunset. As they continued on, here and there they could see lights in the windows of distant cabins and farmhouses along the way. Their hearts were almost bursting with the joy of having survived the journey and seeing the beauty of their new home.

It was well after dark before the coach rolled into Asheville. Even in the darkness, they could see the city, though sparsely built-up with wide spaces between homes and building, was substantial enough to meet their needs.

The road leveled, and ahead they could see a developed street with multi-storied buildings. Buggies and carriages moved along the streets, and they could see people walking past storefronts. The town was very tiny, compared to the Swiss cities they were used to, but there was enough substance for them to feel like they were reentering civilization.

Pence drove them slowly down a couple of the main streets of Asheville to the Eagle Hotel, considered to be Asheville's luxury hotel.

James Patton, an Irish immigrant who found his way to wealth, had built the brick hotel in 1814, the first three-story building in the town. Patton was one of several major slaveholders in Buncombe County. Slaves built the hotel and had comprised most of its staff. Patton's sons inherited his father's slaves. A couple dozen of them also staffed the Patton mansion, The Henrietta.

In April 1865, after the end of the war, more than 2,700 Union soldiers, including Negro troops, passed through Asheville. Crowds of emancipated slaves, whole families in many cases, bundled up a handful of their possessions and left the city in the safety of the troops, hopeful for opportunities and freedom in the mountains and towns to the west.

Hundreds of the emancipated slaves left, though a small number stayed in Asheville. Some others, disappointed by the lack of opportunities, eventually returned and were hired back at the hotel and other businesses in town.

The Garrauxs had seen black people during their journey, but as they pulled up in front of the Eagle, they found themselves for the first time face-to-face in close proximity with a black man. He was working as a porter and helped them out of the coach before unloading their luggage. While still in Switzerland, they had seen drawings and had read about slaves and freemen in Swiss newspapers, but they had never directly interacted with a dark-skinned person.

"Children, do not stare at the man," Elizabeth whispered, interrupting the children as they looked at the porter wide-eyed and whispered together. "It is we who are the strangers here," she said. "He has probably never met a Swiss family with so many children."

Frederick smiled at her. The practical but openhearted way Elizabeth saw the world always amazed him.

As they faced this great unknown, he thought again as he did so often, *I could not manage my life without her.*

Their baggage and trunks were expected to arrive the next morning, so they easily moved into their rooms on the second floor of the hotel. They once again had adjoining rooms, and this time the luxury of a private commode and washroom. The rooms were quite charming, and the long windows provided a view of the Main Street.

It was late, and there were few people left on the street, so they looked forward to morning and seeing what the town would look like in daylight. There was a man working at the desk who understood German, so Frederick was able to arrange to have a message sent to Jacob Fisher's farm at daybreak to let him know they awaited him.

They were long past supper time, but a porter kindly brought them a tray with sweet biscuits and a pitcher of milk. After the children were washed and sent to bed, Frederick and Elizabeth stepped out on the long narrow balcony over the main street.

"We have done it, Elizabeth. We have made our way to America, and will start a new life, just as you hoped," Frederick said, pulling her against him as they looked at the strangely unfamiliar town.

"I could never do something like this without you, meine kleine maus," he said. You are the strongest woman I have ever known."

Uncomfortable with praise, even from the man she loved, Elizabeth chuckled and said, "I may be strong, but your little mouse is also tired and smells of road grime. Let's wash and go to bed before one of the children wakes up."

At first light, Frederick went to the hotel desk and ascertained that a messenger had been sent on horseback to Bent Creek to let Jacob Fisher know of their arrival. The messenger would be able to travel the ten miles to Bent Creek in less than two hours. The wagon coming that distance would take at least twice as long, so they would have time to have break-fast and walk about in their new surroundings.

After a light meal, the children could not wait to get out into the streets of Asheville. They were over-excited, and had to be reined in repeatedly, especially Fred and Earnest. The girls, particularly Bettie and Lucy, were fascinated by the different styles of clothing, and especially by again see-ing an occasional person with dark skin.

Once when two black workers passed them going the opposite direction on the street, Elizabeth had to physically push the two girls to make them resume walking.

Knowing how small Asheville was had not prepared them for what the town was actually like. There were some beautiful large homes they would later learn were summer homes of very wealthy people who would travel up from the Lowcountry to avoid the heat and humidity. There were tidy businesses, shops, and official offices.

They could not help but be reminded of the Swiss villages outside Bern. In every direction, there were homes set on green hilltops with imposing mountains as their backdrop. The sky was the particular shade of nearly cobalt blue that comes with cool, crisp fall air, and there was not a cloud to be seen. Their spirits could not have soared much higher.

The streets were wide, and the distances between homes and buildings such that it was clear the town expected to one day be a city with all these spaces between filled in.

The Eagle Hotel was a short walk from the main city square where the famous Buncombe Turnpike passed through the town.

Although Asheville's population was fewer than 1,400 people, Jacob Fisher had said the Turnpike, most commonly called the Drovers Road, was a major money maker for the town. The road was named for those who drove herds of livestock through Asheville on the way to coastal South Carolina, where they would be moved by ships and railway to cities in the North and further south.

The family walked into the square, which was a large open area that seemed fairly unremarkable. There were a few gentlemen seated on a nearby bench, so Frederick walked over and asked if any of them spoke German. One man did, and he stood up and shook hands with Frederick and doffed his hat toward Elizabeth and the children.

"What is this place for?" Frederick inquired. "I have heard about the turnpike from my father's friend. He said this is an amazing highway."

"Oh, you are lucky you are here now and not later this month or in November. This place gets filled up with animals and filth!" the man exclaimed. "It's down to a trickle now compared to what it used to be before the war. Back then as many as sixty thousand hogs were moved right through here in just a month's time."

"Sixty thousand?" Frederick said. "That doesn't seem possible."

"It's not just hogs that come through," the man said. "Drovers from Kentucky and Tennessee and farms west of here bring their cattle and turkeys too. They fatten them up all through the summer, and then they take them to the coast to sell them for the best prices. The more tracks they lay in for trains, the fewer animals get walked to market. But there's still whole big herds that get brought through here."

The image of animals being moved through the town square was amazing to them. Elizabeth explained to the older children what the men were talking about, and they tried to imagine what it would be like to see.

"Oh, Mama, can we come back to see it?" Earnest said, as the other children said, "Yes, yes, please, can we?"

As was the case with so many of the children's requests, Elizabeth said, "We'll see," while she stored it on her list of things they should try to do.

Much of the economy of the area had been built around the Drovers Road. Besides animal feed, the drovers and the crackers—the young boys who earned their nickname by using long whips with pieces of flannel tied to the ends they would snap and crack to drive the animals—needed places to stay along the way. Since the herds were stopped every several miles so the animals would not lose too much weight before reaching the coast, inns, boarding houses, and hostels were built along the route.

The businesses along the road were a huge part of the prewar economy, but so many drovers were killed in the War and so many farms had suffered, that though the road still played an important role, it had been greatly diminished.

The Garrauxs couldn't know it at the time, but beyond just giving them a potential marketplace for the corn and hay they could grow, the Drovers Road would one day play a crucial and guiding role in the family's future.

The family returned to the Eagle in time for midday dinner, just as the wagon hauling their trunks and baggage pulled up to the hotel. Frederick was relieved that the day seemed to be falling into place.

The meal was adequate, though unimpressive. While they ate, a scene played out in the dining room that disturbed Elizabeth. She saw a young negro woman, clearly employed by the hotel, using a large feather duster to swat flies away from an overdressed, pretentious-looking white woman who busied herself with paper and pen. She was seated at a table near an open window, and she acted as if the dark-skinned girl was invisible, and her assistance expected. The younger woman looked tattered and fatigued, while the restaurant patron looked bored and bothered.

"I thought there were no more slaves in America," Elizabeth whispered to Frederick. "That woman looks as though she thinks the girl is a servant."

They watched the interaction with irritation, the scene the first of many times they would be confronted with some of the ugly realities of life in America after the Civil War.

Just after they finished dinner, they looked through the wide doors into the dining room and saw that Jacob Fisher had walked into the lobby and was inquiring for them. Frederick remembered him from years ago, though Jacob was now a thinner, much older-looking version of the man he remembered.

"Herr Fisher," Frederick called out, as Fisher turned and then walked quickly toward him.

"Call me Jacob," Fisher said curtly. "You are a grown man."

Staring at Frederick's face as though he was an apparition, Fisher said, "You look so much like your father did when we were young."

Jacob and his father had been close friends as young men, but they had been mostly out of touch over the last decade or more, other than his letters from America.

Frederick's childhood memories of Jacob recalled a person who seemed far happier than this stern, gray-haired man whose bearded face seemed frozen in a permanent scowl.

Elizabeth and the children stepped up next to them, and Frederick introduced each of them, starting with his wife, and then down the list, from youngest to oldest children.

Jacob's only response was to say, "The two boys look as though they can work. Are either of them clever with equipment?"

Frederick, caught slightly off-guard by Jacob's demeaner and his question, said, "The boys are strong and willing workers. But we mostly concern ourselves with their learning. They will hopefully learn their new language quickly. Hopefully, we will too."

"Hmph," Jacob said, then muttering something unintelligible. "Let's get your things loaded. Can they at least help with that?"

Again, put off by Jacob's attitude, he said, "Yes, they will help. They are good boys, and they are always helpful."

"We should get moving," Jacob said. "It will be a slow trip with all these goods and people."

Jacob and Frederick, with the help of the boys, loaded the trunks and luggage into Jacob's large buckboard wagon, pulled by two hefty oxen. Frederick climbed up into the seat next to Jacob, and Elizabeth passed Frank up to him.

Elizabeth, carrying John, climbed up into the wagon with the other children. They clamored over the trunks and bags, sitting behind the driver's seat at the front of the wagon. They sat on the lap blankets and shawls they had thrown down to try to soften the ten-mile rough and rocky ride to Bent Creek.

As they jostled and bumped along in the wagon, Elizabeth eavesdropped as Jacob filled Frederick in on the history of their new community.

The six-thousand-acre Bent Creek area had been divided up into more than seventy tracts of various sizes under state land grants in the 1790s. There were already dozens of homes in Bent Creek and hundreds of acres had been cleared for cultivation. But much of the land still needed to be cleared to be productive, Jacob stressed.

Jacob said the tract on which they would be living and working was already producing crops on several plowable acres, and there was a good size pasture as well as a small apple orchard. But he said there were several more acres of trees he had girdled three years before that were now ready to be taken down, as well as small trees that needed cutting and stumps that needed removal in order to expand the farm.

In the old days, they used to burn the felled trees, Jacob said, but now logs were either dragged to the lumber mill on the creek where they were cut into boards, or rafted down the French Broad River to Asheville, where demand for lumber was rapidly increasing.

As they headed toward their new home, the rutted dirt road took them over rolling hills, past open, verdant farmland and through deep, high-canopy forests, all with the backdrop of the majestic Blue Ridge Mountains. Elizabeth was greatly cheered by the clear mountain air, the warm sun, and the familiar beauty of high-slope farmland.

Chapter 15

The road took a turn into a forested area so dense it blocked the sun, making it suddenly look like nightfall. Frederick said, "Are there any Indians near the community?"

There were colorful and frightening stories told in Switzerland about the savages who terrorized America's settlers.

Jacob explained there were no Indians left in the area, except the few who had married into the white community.

He said the horrible stories they had heard in Switzerland remained true in other places, but none were true of Bent Creek. He said in the 1700s, the area was the site of a large, highly productive, and peaceful community of Cherokee.

For more than forty years, until most Cherokee were forced out of North Carolina at gunpoint in 1838, white settlers who moved into the area and its original residents lived side-by-side without conflict. Settlers farmed and Cherokee hunted and fished, and there was no friction between them in Bent Creek, Jacob said.

He said the Cherokee of Bent Creek avoided the deadly and tragic Trail of Tears in '38 because Colonel William Holland Thomas persuaded them to move to land he purchased in the Smoky Mountains.

Thomas was a hero to the Cherokee and to the people of Bent Creek, Jacob said.

Thomas had learned the Cherokee language when he worked at a trading post as a teen. Thomas's father had died before he was born, and the teen was befriended by the Cherokee chief. He was later adopted into the tribe and became a lifelong friend and champion of the Cherokee, officially representing them after he became a lawyer.

Jacob said that Thomas even led a Confederate legion made up of Cherokee and Scots-Irish in the Civil War and was credited with having been a clever and successful leader.

"We don't really understand what happened to him," Jacob said. "We all thought he'd be going to Washington after President Johnson pardoned him last year for all his Confederate activities. But he was having some money trouble, and the War left him not quite right in the head."

"We were sad to hear he got put into a mental hospital in Raleigh last March. He's a year younger than me—sixty-two years old—and the damn War stole the rest of his life," Jacob said, shaking his head.

The oxen plodded along at so much slower rate than the stagecoach had traveled that it sometimes seemed they were nearly stationary. Jacob said the trip would take the goodly portion of the day, but they would certainly be there before sundown.

They stopped after a couple hours so Elizabeth could tend to the baby and the children could run about and use up some energy. Fisher had brought them a jug of fresh milk, which they thoroughly enjoyed.

The children were terribly anxious for the trip to be over, and Elizabeth and Frederick were filled with both excitement and some apprehension, since so much of their living situation remained unknown.

It had begun to seem to Frederick that Jacob talked a bit too much about all the work that he looked forward to having him perform. In conversation, it now seemed to Frederick it was more that Jacob wanted help with his farm, than that he was providing a friend's son with an opportunity.

Neither Frederick nor Elizabeth was afraid of hard work. And no matter Jacob's motivation, they would now have a place to stay while trying to begin building their life in this new country. Though, admittedly, Fisher's general attitude toward them was already creating some discomfort.

Frederick had briefly told Jacob that their trip south from New York had been extremely difficult due to the damage from the war and the remoteness of Asheville. Now, besides beginning to question Fisher's motivation for his insistent invite, he also was curious as to why he had not forewarned them about what they would face on their travels.

As their trek resumed, Frederick said, "So, in your letters, you did not say what the war had done to this country, or that so many of the tracks and roads and bridges had been destroyed."

"The war is over. It's been over for two years," Jacob said. "And I keep to myself. I am not a young man, so I could not fight. I wouldn't have wanted to anyway. I had no kin in the war and no good reason to fight.

"Hardly anyone I know had slaves, and not everyone here wanted to fight over whether they should be free. But none of us wanted to lose the business we all need from the marketplace in Charleston. So, most were in favor of standing against the Union to keep the South Carolina trade going.

"I heard some about the fighting and battles from people who like to talk, but I did not think any of it would make much difference to you."

In remembering the destruction of the war and having read enough about it to have known how traumatic it was for the country, Frederick found Jacob's attitude off-putting. While living in Switzerland, they had also been disturbed that anyone would fight for the right to own another human being.

"So, men from here fought for the South? It seems you would have known of their successes or failures."

Jacob said defensively, "I know plenty. Doesn't mean I care about it. Many of the young men from here fought for the Confederacy. One company called themselves the Buncombe Rifles. They went as soon as they were called for. They marched under a flag made of silk taken from the dresses of Asheville women," he said.

"Right before the end of the war, there was one battle up here near Bent Creek, a ways up the French Broad. The Yankees ended up giving up before they could take Asheville. That happened just before word came that Lee had surrendered. And that was the end.

"A few weeks after that, in May two years back, we found out our tenant, Elias Tucker, wasn't coming back because he got killed. We couldn't just have his widow living in our tenant house like a charity case, so we sent her back to her family."

He spoke dismissively—as though Tucker's life and the more than 600,000 other lives lost, as well as many millions of dollars of damage done, was not important.

Jacob's views on the war, slavery, and even on the history of Buncombe County were all founded on inaccurate representations that Frederick and Elizabeth would learn many residents of the area chose to perpetuate.

Western Carolina preferred its image of not being involved in slavery, unlike coastal areas where plantation owners saw slave ownership as a necessary right. But in truth, during the war years, Buncombe County had a population of more than twelve thousand people, fifteen percent of whom were slaves. Slave labor made many of Asheville's richest citizens richer.

"You're here now. The war is past, and slavery is done. Winter is coming and we have much work to do."

So began a tenuous relationship that would one day determine the direction of Frederick and Elizabeth's lives, leading them ultimately to both great successes and terrible tragedy.

Chapter 16

As the afternoon shadows grew longer, their sense of anticipation also grew. The wagon rolled slowly into the Bent Creek community, gradually descending through a combination of large and small farms and still heavily forested areas.

The wooded areas were densely shaded by a towering canopy of massive trees, with little undergrowth. There were huge oaks, chestnuts, and yellow poplars, some up to five feet in diameter, creating a nearly solid roof far above the forest floor.

Jacob said that once a year, each winter, they burned the rhododendron and laurel as the Cherokee had done before them. Keeping the undergrowth controlled made it easier to hunt for the plentiful game in the area, and it allowed their stock free range from May to October.

"We have deer, rabbits, and bear, like in Switzerland, and we also have many wild turkeys and woodchucks. There are wild boar too, like those in the northern plateau.

"There are also troublesome animals called raccoons that steal my corn and get into any food stuff they find. They are as big as medium-sized dogs, with sharp teeth and claws. They are clever. Their markings make them look like they're wearing masks, and they can use their hands like a human. We trap and shoot them as often as we can."

Frederick realized he had much to learn about the animals of this new country. Somehow, he had believed he would encounter the same creatures in the woods as he had known in the Swiss mountains.

Life in America, they would quickly learn, would be an unending string of surprises, disappointments, delights, and defeats.

Homes, large and small, overlooked quilt-like squares of farmland cut into coves and hollows along the forested road. Elizabeth could not help but wonder what their home would be like. She knew it would be smaller than their big house in Bern, but she was still excited to finally settle their family into a place where they could be safe, and the unrelenting fatigue and challenges of the journey would be over.

"I shot four rabbits this morning, so my wife, Greta, will have hassenpfeffer waiting for us," Jacob said. "You can unload your things later. I am hungry."

Elizabeth thought, "We are all hungry," nearly saying it out loud. She was quickly becoming aware that Jacob appeared focused solely on himself. She knew that he had two grown sons, one who lived in Switzerland and the other who lived in Germany, but he never mentioned them in his letters, nor had he mentioned them during this day. He had told them little about his wife, except dismissively saying that she was "weak and unhealthy."

"We're around the next bend," Jacob said.

As butterflies filled Elizabeth's whole being, Frederick turned and reached back to take her hand.

114

He leaned toward her and the children, smiled, and said quietly, "We're almost home, meine liebsten. We have made it, my brave loved ones."

Tears glinted in his eyes, only a hint of the overwhelming relief he felt. His family was safe in America. In North Carolina. In their new home. Elizabeth's dream for them was coming true.

The carriage turned off the main road onto a smaller roadway barely as wide as the wagon wheels. The oxen slowly plodded along, straining as the narrow road grew steeper.

"My farm is at the top of the next hill," Jacob said. "Your house is on the right behind the barn. Mine is on the left. You will eat dinner in my house."

His tone continued to put a damper on what was an exciting, exhilarating moment for the family. They brushed it off, and the older children, so excited they could not stay seated, stood up and held onto the back of the wagon seat, straining and looking ahead in the dimming daylight to try see their new home.

"There it is!" Fred suddenly shouted.

"I see it!" Earnest chimed in.

"It's our farm, Mama!" Lucy called out.

"That's my house," Jacob said, gruffly. "You can't see yours yet."

It was a plain, white box of a house—a two-story, unassuming home with a small porch. There was visible smoke coming from the chimney, giving the nondescript home a cozy appearance. It looked pleasant enough, Frederick thought.

The wagon made a slow turn to the right, and they could now see a large barn straight ahead. Behind it was a log cabin. A very small log cabin.

That can't be the house of which Jacob was speaking, Frederick thought. It looked not much larger than a hen house.

"That's your place back there," Jacob said, pointing to the cabin and confirming his fears.

"It's small, but it will do until you can add onto it. You can store your trunks in the back of the barn. There won't be any room for them in there until you make it."

Frederick and Elizabeth's hearts sank, and the older children became quiet. They were all so very tired. The trip had been too long. And this so-called house was not what they expected.

"Look at the beautiful fields, children," Elizabeth said. "And look at those trees. I think I see red apples on the trees."

She did not look at Frederick. She could not look at Frederick. This was all her idea. They would not be here if not for her insistence.

Frederick stared ahead at the shabby little log-and-chink cabin with a small, covered porch, only slightly wider than the front door. It looked like the mountain hovels he and his father and uncles would stay in while hunting chamois in the Swiss mountains.

He did not look at Elizabeth. He could not look at her. If not for her, they would not be here in this strange place looking at this absurd cabin.

"There's a privy round back of the barn," Jacob said. "The Tuckers' washbasins and other things are still in the house. The well is in back of our house, up on the rise. There is a pump. You can wash there. I will tell Greta we will eat in a short time. So, hurry those children along."

As they climbed out of the wagon, Jacob unhitched the oxen and walked them away to the barn without saying another word.

The family stood huddled together, as if momentarily frozen in time. Even the children did not speak, seeming to sense the intensity of the disappointment their parents were feeling.

Finally, Earnest, their level-headed, persevering, second-oldest child said, "It will be exciting to live in a log cabin like the frontiersmen in my books. It will be an adventure—right, Mama?"

He broke the silence open, and the questions of the children began pouring out.

"Is that really where we are going to live? How will we fit?"

"Can we go pick the apples?"

"Are there wolves in the woods?"

"Are we going to eat soon?"

"Do we have to stay here forever?"

"I need to go to the privy."

"Yes," Elizabeth answered Earnest, "It will be an adventure if we make it one. And we will."

She still could not bring herself to look at Frederick, fearing the disappointment, and even anger she might see in his face.

"Children, we will put the small bags on the porch of our house. We will use the privy, we will wash, and we will join Herr Jacob and Frau Greta for dinner. Each get your own bag and we will leave the rest until tomorrow."

Elizabeth had shocked herself with the phrase "our house." She had shocked Frederick too.

He mustered up what resilience he had left, and said, "Do as your mother says."

As the children busied themselves pulling their carry bags out of the wagon, he turned to Elizabeth and said, "This is it. We must make this work. We have no other choice."

The children piled their bags on the porch of the little cabin, the boys and older girls trying to peek in the windows, though it was too dark to see anything inside. They washed their faces and hands in the ice cold well water they pumped into a bucket, drying themselves on a towel that had been left hanging on the pump.

Elizabeth thought the towel might be the first sign of kindness they had seen from Jacob. But then she thought it was more likely Jacob's wife who had left it for them.

Within a short time, they knocked on the door of the Fishers' home, and a small, rather pathetic-looking woman opened the door.

"Hello," she said, "I am Greta. Please come in. I have made a late dinner. You must be very tired."

She looked more tired than any of them. And with her pale face and disheveled gray-blond hair, she had a distinct air of sadness about her.

Greta repeatedly smoothed her apron, plucked her dress sleeves, and poked at her loosely pinned, partly fallen down hair, as though silently apologizing for her appearance.

The house was sparsely furnished, but reasonably comfortable. The table was not big enough for all of them, so Greta had set places for several of the children at a side table.

The big meal of the day was usually dinner, generally served before 3 o'clock in the afternoon. Supper was typically a light snack in the early evening, so the family greatly appreciated the exception made for their arrival.

She had made a meal of rabbit stew and rosti, traditional potato pancakes. The family had not eaten Swiss food since they left Bern, and the familiar tastes were welcome.

The children had been taught to be quiet at meals, but now Elizabeth wished they would speak. She wished anyone would speak. Greta scurried about in response to each of Jacob's barked demands, while he hunched over his bowl, shoveling in stew as though he was starving. Frederick and Elizabeth both tried to initiate conversation, only to get responses from both Jacob and Greta that clearly indicated they didn't intend to converse.

At one point, Elizabeth even asked Greta about her sons, assuming their shared motherhood might open the door for communication. Greta mumbled a few words about their sons doing well, but she cast a furtive glance at Jacob, and her words trailed off, seemingly shut down by his glare.

Frederick and Elizabeth appreciated the meal, but after expressing their gratitude and borrowing a lantern and a few candles, they departed quickly and hurried across the half-acre distance to the cabin.

Frederick opened the door, and Elizabeth hesitantly followed him inside. The children picked up their bags and burst into the dark room as though they were beginning that great adventure they hoped for.

The room they found themselves standing in did little to lift Elizabeth and Frederick's spirits. The cabin was about twenty feet by twenty feet, with a grimy plank floor and a few small, curtainless windows. There were rickety stairs off to the side of the room, leading to what they assumed was the sleeping area.

The first floor was one open room containing a table, a couple of benches and two chairs. There was a fireplace with an iron swing hook for hanging kettles and cookpots. A cupboard and shelves were in one corner of the room. There were some pots, plates, cups, a basin, and some forks and spoons visible on the shelves. In the other corner was a bed large enough for Frederick and Elizabeth, and a child or two if needed.

The upstairs was a slope-ceilinged room with a tiny window at either end.

Jacob had told them that he, at great personal expense, had purchased three trundle beds that would sleep two children each. He had also borrowed a large crib for the two youngest boys. The room was not much

119

larger than the ship's cabin Frederick and the boys had shared on the *Arago*.

The children each claimed which of the beds they wanted to sleep in, and dragged them about, making the room into a split dormitory, with the girls taking up most of the room. Fred and Earnest tucked themselves away in a corner, as far as they could get away from their sisters.

Frederick went back to the well and pumped a bucket of water he brought back to the cabin. He and Elizabeth were too tired and unfamiliar with their circumstances to consider trying to make a fire, so Elizabeth ended up washing a screaming baby in cold water to get him ready for bed. The children splashed water on their faces, dried off and got in their bed clothes.

A pile of linens had been left in the upstairs room, so after making up four beds and a crib, they finally got the children to bed.

Baby John would not settle in the new crib, so Elizabeth put him in the bed between Frederick and her. He finally dozed off, and the house was quiet.

For a long, dark time, the room lit only by the flicker of a single candle on a bedside table, Frederick and Elizabeth lay in stony silence.

Tears welled up in her eyes, overflowed and soaked her temples, then the sides of her head, then her pillow. She cried silently, but Frederick could feel the bed shaking with her sadness.

"It will all be all right, meine kleine maus," he finally said. "We will make this work. The land looks wonderful, and I can add onto this building immediately."

For some reason, his effort to be encouraging opened the floodgates on her grief.

"Oh, Frederick. I am so, so, sorry," she said, beginning to weep. "This is not as I thought it would be. Nothing about this is right. I thought we were making a dream come true, but it is a nightmare."

Hearing his normally strong, unflappable wife cry was unbearable to Frederick. She never wavered and she was never the one to give up. Her heartbreak called up courage inside him that he didn't know he had.

"I will make it good, Elizabeth. I have my tools. I have access to all the wood I could ever use. I will make us a good house. The end of season harvest is happening, and beef and venison will be put up for winter. We will not go without. And we have survived, Elizabeth. The ship, the trains, the carriages, the mountains—we have survived. And we will find our way. I promise you."

She lifted the sleeping baby, and set him behind her as she moved over, head against Frederick's chest.

"You are right, Frederick. We will make it good. I will work so hard. I will find every way there is to make our family good and give our children the opportunities we moved here for. I will never be deterred. I will never give up," she said, her voice changing from grief-filled to strong, to almost fierce.

"We will make this our home. We will be Americans."

Chapter 17

On the very first morning of the very first day in Bent Creek, Frederick determined that he would begin making them an appropriate home.

He was able to prevail upon Jacob to take him to a lumber mill he had told him about. The mill up the river was where he could buy lumber needed to expand the cabin. Most of the homes in Bent Creek up until the Civil War had been made of logs, but now there were two mills on the river where the huge trees were being cut into boards.

They took the empty wagon up the river to a mill run by a former Confederate colonel who had moved from Charleston to Bent Creek after the War.

Jacob said Colonel L. M. Hatch had brought a sizeable pile of money with him, some guessed it was as much as $90,000. In '65, he bought a mill that was the first built on Bent Creek, moved the dam, and rebuilt the whole enterprise.

"You're going to want to know Hatch," Jacob said. "He's got the lumber mill, but he's also got a lathe for making furniture."

"He makes furniture?" Frederick asked.

Being able to continue cabinet and furniture making was not something he expected to do immediately, especially after seeing the surroundings, but hearing there was a furniture maker in the community piqued his interest.

"Yes, most of the people around here have gotten beds, tables, chairs, pretty much anything they need from Hatch. He sells his goods all the way from Asheville to South Carolina and Georgia."

Hatch was indeed a man who Frederick would want to know. He was excited to learn that not only could he purchase the lumber he needed, some of the equipment required for furniture making might also be available to him.

"Not that those boys of your will have time for schooling with all the work that needs to be done, but Hatch also built a school in a church house where his daughter teaches."

"Is this school very expensive to attend?" Frederick asked.

"It's free," Jacob answered. "But like I said. They'll be working."

Frederick didn't hear anything Jacob said after "free." He suddenly felt his spirits rising. The possibility of making furniture, building his family an appropriate house, and Fred and Earnest being able to attend school made him feel more hopeful than he had in some time. He could not wait to get home later to tell Elizbeth.

Hatch's operation was impressive, especially in a small community. He had a big up-and-down, water-powered saw for cutting the huge trees, other ones for resawing the wide boards into smaller ones, a kiln for drying, a planing machine, the lathe that Jacob mentioned, and lots of other important pieces of wood-working equipment. He also had a grist mill and a blacksmith shop in the large building.

Hatch was intense and serious, but a pleasant man, and he was very welcoming to Frederick and happy to show him the furniture shop.

Jacob helped interpret for them since his English was quite advanced, and in short order Frederick had arranged to purchase lumber for the cabin addition.

By the end of October, Jacob, Frederick, Fred, and Earnest had harvested all the apples, many of which were sold to the traders who passed through the community on their way to South Carolina and Georgia. Jacob shared some of the profit with them, in his typically grudging fashion, and they added their share to the savings they had already set aside for future property of their own.

They also got a share of a healthy harvest of potatoes, squash, carrots, and onions, which, along with beef and fresh game, would help them get through the winter.

The children were adjusting well to their new environment. The community was close knit, and there were several families with children of similar age to the Garraux children, so they had already begun to make friends.

Colonel Hatch had shown a willingness to allow Frederick to use some of his furniture-making equipment in trade for creating a few pieces of furniture that Hatch could sell, if they met his standards.

The next few weeks became a blur of hauling lumber, stacking stones for the foundation, framing up the addition and meeting neighbors who were more than willing to help with the construction.

At a critical point in the project, several men volunteered to organize a family workday during which several households would all help get the addition built in trade for a social get-together and a shared meal provided by the Garrauxs. They said they did it all the time for neighbors, and Frederick would have his chance to pay the community back with family workdays in the future.

Dozens of men descended on the Fisher property, bringing with them hand tools and gifts of handmade nails and odds and ends of building products left over from other house and barn raisings. Some of the women came too, bearing pies, jars of preserved foods and even pillowcases they had made for the family.

The men swarmed like ants over the frame of the addition Frederick had begun, measuring, sawing, and pounding together the four-room addition to the little cabin. Over the course of just two days, it was closed in and functional.

Before leaving, the men and a few of their wives shared the huge meal of traditional Swiss dishes that Elizabeth had spent both workdays preparing for the crowd.

Frederick and Elizabeth were amazed by the welcoming and helpful attitude of their new community. The kindness of so many took some of the sting out of their initial disappointment with Bent Creek, and even with Jacob's ongoing gruffness.

Several of their neighbors spoke German, and every chance they had they would patiently teach Frederick and Elizabeth the beginnings of their new language. They quickly learned to understand and speak phrases that would help them manage their new situation, and they amused each other and the children by doing their best to speak English around the house.

Frederick and Elizabeth were pleased to make arrangements for Fred and Earnest to begin attending the free school where Hatch's adult daughter taught. The school was in a building that also housed the church. It was only about two miles away, so the boys would be able to go for lessons on most days, when they were not helping on the farm. There would be far fewer tasks for the boys during winter months, so they planned for them to begin school soon. Frederick intended to make sure there were many more school days than workdays for his sons.

Elizabeth was trying her best to break through the wall of silence and sadness Greta had built around herself. Each time she saw Jacob interact with his wife, it made her glad she did not have that type of man for a husband. He was hard, cold, and demanding, often speaking to her as though she was a servant, not a wife.

One afternoon in early November, as they sorted through vegetables that would go into the root cellar, Elizabeth decided she would speak more directly to Greta. There had been too many weeks spent talking around the edges of the tension that existed in the Fisher house. Jacob was away for the day, selling produce in Asheville, so she would have uninterrupted time to speak with his pale, frazzled, terribly sad wife.

"Greta, I don't wish to speak out of turn, but you seem so unhappy, I just wonder if there is something you would care to share," Elizabeth said.

Greta stopped ripping off the outer leaves of a cabbage and looked down at her hands. She did not speak for a moment, but when she looked up, there were tears already streaming down her cheeks.

"Oh, I cannot say," she sniffled. "I should not say. Jacob provides well for me. I am grateful he keeps me when I am too weak to help him on the farm. He does not mean to be cruel. He has just changed so much over the years."

Her words stopped as sobs took over. Elizabeth realized she was probably talking about something she had never spoken of before. Despite the kindness in the community, it was still easy to see that Greta lived a life of near isolation with a husband of difficult temperament.

Elizabeth moved her chair closer to her and put her hand on her arm.

"I am sorry, Greta," she said. She hoped that speaking her feelings might help the poor sad woman.

"What do you mean? How did he change?" Elizabeth asked.

She handed Greta a handkerchief, and as the frail woman wiped her eyes

126

and nose, she said, "He became more and more unhappy when we lived in Switzerland. He blamed industrialization for ruining life there, and each year he became more resentful of it. He made a plan to come to America, and he thought our sons and their families would also come.

"When our oldest boy, Andreas, told him he wanted to stay where he was, that he and his family were happy, Jacob was not pleased. Then when our younger son, Hans, also told him that he also wanted to stay where he was, Jacob was furious. And somehow, he blamed me, because I had told our sons I just wanted them to be happy."

She paused, crying again, the thought of her sons being left behind further adding to her grief.

"I am so sorry, Greta. Not having your family with you must be difficult. I miss my parents and my brothers all the time. But missing your own sons must be so painful," Elizabeth said.

Greta gathered herself up a bit, dried her eyes, and said, "I miss my sons, and my grandchildren. But I meant what I said. I want them to be happy.

"I thought that when they refused to leave, Jacob would get over his anger toward Switzerland and we would just stay. Instead, it was as though he now intended to prove to them that he didn't need them in his life. He tears up the letters they send without reading them or letting me see them. He hardened himself to them. To me. To everyone.

"He is such an angry man. Anything that does not meet his standards or fit his plans makes him angry. When our poor tenant was killed in the War, Jacob was not sad. He was angry. And not about the war or those who killed Elias. He was angry at Elias for abandoning him and the farm. He is always angry."

Then she suddenly sat upright and wiped her face dry, as though she had said far too much.

"Jacob is a good provider. For that I am grateful" she said. "We will never speak of this again."

Elizabeth knew that part of a woman's job was often hiding feelings. But this sad, lonely woman was having to tolerate far too much. Elizabeth had seen Greta cringe away from Jacob like a dog that was used to being kicked. She was quite sure he struck her on a regular basis. *No woman should be so dependent that she must live like this*, she thought.

"All right, we won't talk about it anymore, Greta, but I will be a friend to you. And you are free to tell me your feelings. You can always come to me, and I will help you however I can."

"You cannot help me," Greta said, going back to pulling cabbage leaves. "This is my life. I do not have any choice."

Elizabeth later told Frederick about what Greta had said, and why Jacob was angry all the time. He said he felt sorry for her, but sometimes it was just how life worked out. Elizabeth did not debate him, but she thought that was rather dismissive of the poor woman's plight.

She also decided that was not the right time to tell Frederick they had another child on the way.

Chapter 18

With the addition to their home finished, the original downstairs room of the cabin would now become a large kitchen that would hold a long table Frederick had built at Hatch's mill. He had also made Hatch some chairs to sell in trade for more lumber. Hatch was duly impressed with the quality of the work.

Looking at one of Frederick's chairs with admiration, he said, "You are a fine craftsman, sir." Frederick had to ask for a translation of Hatch's comment, and he was then flattered and pleased to learn his opinion.

Things were going along so well that he and Elizabeth agreed they should use some of their savings to go to Asheville to purchase a cast iron cookstove. With the size of their family, cooking in a stew pot on a hook in the fireplace hearth was just not practical.

"We promised the children we would take them to Asheville to see the herds come through on the drovers' road" Frederick said. "The timing is perfect. We can take the remainder of the feed corn to market, see the animals, and buy our cookstove, all in one trip."

The children were jubilant to hear that they would be going to Asheville, and Elizabeth was delighted at the thought of staying at the Eagle and eating in a restaurant.

Frederick asked Jacob if the drovers and their crews would be taking up all the accommodations in the town, making it impossible to spend the night. Jacob said if the men and boys stayed in Asheville, they typically slept in the stalls or wherever their herd was kept overnight, but they often preferred to stay outside the town at a drovers' stand. He said before the War, it might have been difficult to find a room, but now they should have no problem.

The drovers' stands were about every eight miles or so along the roadway, all the way from Tennessee to South Carolina. For about a dollar a day, the stands provided a meal for the drovers and corn for the animals that were penned nearby. The men were given space to lie down and sleep on the floor of a great room, shared by all who spent the night. The stands could accommodate hundreds of animals and dozens of drovers, some of them up to several hundred animals a night. Virtually all the stands had taverns, or at least a supply of whiskey.

If the drovers ran low on cash, some would give livestock in payment to inn keepers. Other times, inn keepers would allow them to stay with an agreement that the drovers would stop and pay them on their return trip.

The family was excited to make the trip back to Asheville and glad for an excuse to change out of farm clothes. Elizabeth added ribbons to the girls' braids, and she even ironed and put on a dress she hadn't worn since they left Switzerland.

The leaves on many of the trees on the open hillsides had turned beautiful fall shades of red, orange, and gold, and the sky was as blue as a robin's egg. As they rolled out of Bent Creek and onto the more open road, they were again struck by the beauty of Western North Carolina.

The children were in high spirits, and so were Frederick and Elizabeth.

130

The weeks in Bent Creek had been so busy and filled with so much work, it was almost as though they had stopped seeing the world around them. This was a chance to take a deep breath and realize that they had successfully begun their new life in America.

Frederick had mastered the driving of the oxen. Elizabeth sat up front with him, John on her lap and Frank next to her. The rest of the children sat on blankets thrown over the big pile of feed corn that filled the wagon.

It was the first time that Jacob would allow Frederick to make a transaction without him present. He had told him what price to ask and where to go to make the sale. Frederick looked forward to being out from under Jacob's thumb for a couple days.

The trip felt glorious to all of them. Frederick smiled and said proudly, "Our first trip to town as a family."

"It is lovely," Elizabeth said. "I feel so much more hopeful these days. The children love the new rooms in the house. They are very happy here. I am sure our new baby will be happy too."

"Our new baby," Frederick stammered. "A new baby. Oh, that is surprising. I just, well, I don't know. I guess I didn't expect it so soon."

"We've done this eight times, Frederick. I would think by now it would not be a surprise," Elizabeth said, with a laugh.

Though he had been momentarily caught off guard, Frederick said, "It is a good surprise. We are blessed. Our children are healthy and good. And now we will have a truly American child."

They told the children the news about another sibling on the way. The girls were excited, the boys disinterested. All they could talk about was seeing the city again, this time with herds of animals being driven through it.

By the time they reached the main road to town, there was a steady stream of animals, drovers, and crackers strung out along the twelve-foot-wide roadway along the river. Sometimes they would have to stop to let hogs, horses, mules, sheep, turkeys, and ducks pass in the opposite direction.

The herds were headed through the mountains and across South Carolina. Most would be loaded into trains in Columbia for shipment. Some would be driven on to Charleston and loaded onto ships and trains for transport to northern cities and as far south as New Orleans.

Each herd had a lead drover at the front and a follow drover in the back. Alongside, boys with their long flannel-tipped whips kept the herd from wandering off the roadside. There was a constant dusty shuffling, mooing, bleating, squawking stream of livestock and poultry along the road ahead. The road snaked along the French Broad River, the lowest terrain in the region.

The children were fascinated by the number of animals and drovers that passed them by. They could not imagine that before the Civil War, the herds were infinitely larger than what they were seeing. To the children, it seemed impossible that there could be so many animals in the world.

When they turned onto the main street in Asheville on their way to the Eagle, a stench drifted their way on the wind.

"Oh, it smells very strong, Mama," Lucy said, as the other children held their noses and murmured complaints.

"Herr Fisher said to be grateful for the smell of the herds," Frederick said. "He said it is the smell of money. After all the losses in the war, they have prayed for the return of drovers and animals. The sale of our corn to the herders should still provide well for our households."

The center of Asheville, within a block of their hotel, though a typical town filled with shops, hotels, and eateries, was now also strangely filled with animals standing about in the streets. It had rained days before, and the steady stomping and movement of hundreds of hogs, cattle, horses, and sheep had churned the town square into a deep mix of mud, urine and manure. Men stood nearly ankle-deep in the filth as they managed their herds and haggled over corn and feed brought into the town by the farmers from around the area.

The mud was too deep to drive the wagon through it, so they stopped at the edge of the square to sell the corn.

Frederick stepped into the slop, and he was quickly able to find a farmer who spoke both English and German. The farmer was in the process of selling his feed corn to a hog drover from Tennessee.

Fortunately for Frederick, he came late to a negotiation in which the drover wanted all the other farmer's corn and more. After a brief discussion, Frederick also sold the drover his load for a price better than what Jacob had told him he should get.

Frederick asked the farmer where the drovers were headed next. He said, after several stops at stands along the way, the herds would reach Greenville, South Carolina. The farmer said it was a fine city about sixty miles south of Asheville in the foothills of the Blue Ridge.

"It's got a lot better growing season than up here on the mountain. I am thinking of moving my family down there after the next drive," the farmer said.

"Why would you move there?" Frederick asked.

"Greenville's got twice as many people as Asheville," he said. "There's a railroad that runs down to Columbia from there. It's got the biggest coach factory in the South. The main street in town has a lot of stores and shops, and a lot of business is being done there. There's a real university, and believe or not, there's even a college for women."

Lowering his voice, he added on, "And not saying that I'm for it or anything, but they even have a school for Negro children."

The description of this nearby South Carolina town intrigued Frederick.

"Is land expensive there?" Frederick asked.

"There's still plenty of land available at good prices. I think you can probably get a better deal down there than you can up here in Asheville, ever since all the rich folks from the Lowcountry started building their fancy summer houses here."

Frederick would long remember that conversation about the city in South Carolina, but he could not have known that it would one day determine his family's future.

Frederick walked back to the wagon, money in his pocket, feeling very encouraged by his first real business transaction in America.

Elizabeth and the children stayed up in the wagon, even as the corn was being shoveled out, trying to avoid contact with the putrid mud.

With the wagon empty, the family took a roundabout route to get to the hotel from a small side street. The central square was the muddiest area, so it could be avoided, but animals and drovers lingered in every alley and side street in Asheville. Some even stood in the front yards of homes along the way.

Once checked into their rooms, they took the children out onto the hotel balcony to look at the messy, noisy, chaotic scene in the center of the town.

The deal that had been made for the corn cheered Elizabeth and Frederick, and they were excited the next morning to go shop for a stove that would greatly improve life in the coming winter. They had been in America for such a short time, but they already felt like they were making great strides in creating a successful life.

"This has been a good day, Elizabeth," Frederick said. "I have done business in our new country. We are well set up with our home, thanks to kind neighbors. We will have another child to join our family. We are very blessed."

Elizabeth agreed. She felt the difficult journey was already a fading memory, and their life left behind in Switzerland no longer tugged at Frederick the way it had.

"It is a good day," she said. "It is, as we were told, a country where there is opportunity. We will someday soon have our own land and make our own success. In the meantime, we can make a good life on Jacob's farm. He is a difficult man, but it is our chance to prepare for the life we will make for our children."

After an enjoyable dinner and overnight, they purchased a stove than was nicer and larger than what they had left behind in Bern, delighting Elizabeth.

The trip back to Bent Creek was slow, since they had to move at the speed of the animals being herded, stopping frequently as drovers, crackers, and herding dogs moved wayward stock back on track. The children were excited by the beautiful new stove in the wagon with them, and by all they had seen on their trip.

At about the midway point in the trip back, snow began to fall lightly—the first snowfall of winter. The light accumulation on the colorful trees looked magical. As the temperature dropped, they bundled up, and the mud in the rutted road stiffened and became harder and easier for the wagon to roll along.

The trip to Asheville would begin a winter in which the boys would start their schooling and the family would settle into life in America.

Over the next several months, Frederick would make several chairs for Hatch to sell in trade for having the use of his mill and lathe. He would also make several beautiful pieces of furniture for their home, including the bed where their next child would be born the following summer.

Sitting by the fireplace in the evenings as the children played nearby in the warmth, Elizabeth spent many hours working on a quilt she had started in Switzerland. As she pieced and stitched it together, she thought how much life is like a quilt. Sometimes quilt pieces were difficult to fit together, but with determination, something beautiful, useful, and lasting could come from the effort. Sometimes success came not from everything fitting perfectly or easily, but by making the most of what someone had to work with.

It was her vision of what life could be, and her boundless determination that would keep their lives and hopes for the future afloat over the next several years, no matter what they encountered.

Chapter 19

Frederick stayed very busy during the cold, wet, frequently snowy months felling trees that he either chopped for firewood, burned in large piles, or dragged to Hatch's mill. Little by little, the farmable acreage of the Fisher's plot began to expand.

Frederick also continued to build furniture whenever he could find the time. He bartered for and purchased a few pieces of wood-working equipment, including his own small hand-operated lathe. He then created a workspace in the back of a storage shed on the tenant portion of the property.

Before long, especially when Christmas was approaching, Frederick was getting requests from neighbors and community members for specific pieces of furniture, mantels, and stair rails. He was careful to only take on those requests that were items Hatch didn't want to produce. The colonel had been consistently generous in helping them get started, and Frederick was grateful and honored his kindness.

Though they were working at learning American customs and the language, the family decided to keep their first Christmas as much like it had been in Switzerland as possible. Frederick had traded a fine chair for candle wax and wicks, so at the end of November, Elizabeth and the children began Kerzenziehen, the making of special holiday candles.

It took a great deal of patience for the children to melt the wax and dip the candles over and over each day, letting them harden overnight, but in the end, they were pleased with their creations. They even made two special candles, one for Jacob and one for Greta.

The children were delighted that after they slept on the night of December 6, they awoke to evidence that Samichlaus, dressed in his robes, accompanied by his assistant Schmutzli and a donkey, had brought them treats of candies and cookies, just as he had in Switzerland. Then, on the twenty-fourth of December, they cut down and decorated a little evergreen tree with paper ornaments made by the children along with special small candles they had made for the tree. And they knew, if they were very good children, Christkind would bring them gifts that day.

On Christmas Eve, they trudged through the calf-deep snow to the little church they had begun to attend nearly every Sunday. The windows glowed with extra candles and lanterns and the little building that doubled as the school was soon filled with the joyful singing of Christmas hymns, most in English, but some in French and German for those who had left their countries behind.

Elizabeth and Frederick had invited Jacob and Greta to attend with them. He gruffly responded, "Thanks, anyway," and, as usual, she had an excuse, saying that she was too tired to walk through the snow.

After the service, the family returned home to a traditional meal of roasted ham, fresh from their smokehouse, and potatoes and fondue.

Elizabeth had the children bundle back up in their winter coats while she loaded an apple crate with a tin filled with ham and potatoes, another tin with two big pieces of strudel, the candles the children had made for the

Fishers and a handkerchief she had embroidered for Greta.

Elizabeth dressed the littlest children, wrapped the baby in a warm blanket, and the whole family walked quietly through the snow to the Fishers' front porch. She shushed the children until they were all assembled there, and then they began to sing Stille Nacht under the light of the lantern Frederick held above them.

After they had sung most of the first verse, the door slowly opened, and Greta's timid face appeared. They continued to sing, voices raised slightly louder, as Elizabeth held out the crate to her. Greta stood motionless, hand raised to her mouth, as if she did not know how to respond.

"What's going on, Greta?" Jacob barked from inside the house. He was suddenly behind her in the door, and leaned forward, saying, "What do you want? It's late."

A cloud of beer-scented breath accompanied his outburst.

Frederick said, "Frohe Weihnachten, Jacob." And in his best English, "Merry Christmas, to you and Greta."

Elizabeth and the children chimed in, proudly in English as well, "Merry Christmas!"

"We wanted to share our holiday dinner with you, and the children made you candles," Frederick said.

"And there's a small remembrance for you, Greta," Elizabeth said, as she handed her the crate.

Tears filled Greta's eyes, and she said, "Oh, thank you so much. We haven't celebrated Christmas since . . ." her words trailed off as she glanced toward Jacob.

"You didn't need to do that," he said gruffly. "We have nothing for you."

"We expected nothing, Jacob. We're just sharing our blessings. And we are grateful for this place we are able to live, thanks to you," Frederick said.

"As you should be," Jacob muttered.

And then he added grudgingly, "Well, thank you," before turning away from the door.

"Merry Christmas," Frederick and Elizabeth said again, as they returned to their home, casting a glance at each other, and shaking their heads as the excited children ran ahead to their home.

The exuberant joyfulness of the children immediately erased the interaction with Jacob and Greta.

The children were delighted with the nuts, candies, wooden toys, and books, some in German, but some in English, they found under the tree, each item labeled with a child's name. They squealed enthusiastically, showing each other their treasures.

"The Christkind brought us gifts, Mama," Lucy exclaimed. "How did he find us in America?" Somehow, Lucy always managed to bring laughter to every event.

Elizabeth explained to them that God always knows where his children are, no matter where they go. She smiled at Frederick, and he smiled back, in agreement, that God had in fact, found his little family here in America.

As they sipped hot chocolate by the fire, Elizabeth said, "Our first American Christmas. And we are all safe and well. We are blessed."

Looking at his content wife and his children gleefully enjoying their new toys and books, he said, "Yes, indeed we are. We are very blessed."

Elizabeth stayed healthy and energetic, once the early, queasy months of her ninth pregnancy had passed. She tended to the daily needs of the children, frequently making clothing for the older ones as they outgrew shirts and pants and dresses that were passed on to the younger children. Any denim from outgrown clothing would become shoes for the littlest feet.

Preparing and cooking food for their large family took up much of her days, when she wasn't continuing to care for the chickens and the livestock kept in the barn during the worst of the winter weather.

In midwinter, there was a slight thaw that took down some of the snow depth, leaving patches of ground clear and wet. Frederick and Jacob cut and raked all the brush and dead grass away from the fences and their homes and outbuildings, and as it dried, they burned the underbrush of the woodland on the property, as had been done since the Cherokees' time.

The dense smoke hung over the farmland for days in the heavy, still winter air, and their clothing smelled like a forest fire for weeks. But the forested land the brush fire left behind would now be easy to navigate on foot or horseback, making hunting, tracking livestock, and traveling less of a chore.

The community continued to be a source of enjoyment for the family, and they attended get-togethers that were nearly weekly, unless the snow was too deep.

The women gathered regularly to quilt and sew together. Elizabeth encouraged Greta to join them, but more often than not, Greta would agree to come, but then make last-minute excuses for why she could not. Elizabeth knew it was likely because Jacob did not want her to have a life outside their home.

Fred and Earnest were progressing well in their education at the community school. There were few books available, so much of the learning was done with singsongs and repetition. The boys would pass their lessons on to their parents and siblings, and the songs of the alphabet and word lessons were part of every day in the Garraux household.

Life fell into the rhythm typical of a large, hardworking family, and though Frederick was often pressured and sometimes even badgered by Jacob about things he wanted done, for the most part, they were able to get by with little strife.

They were used to winter weather in Switzerland, so they were pre-pared for the slow, quiet, endlessly gray, cold season. Elizabeth regularly thanked Frederick for enlarging their home, wondering aloud how they would have survived with eight children in the little cabin.

By March, winter was giving way to days that hinted at spring. There was still snow in the woods at the higher elevations, but it was melting off the lower slopes. Unfortunately, that led to a mud season that made any attempt at travel miserable, so they were still largely confined to their immediate community in Bent Creek. The work to clear, plow, and plant the new acreage would soon begin in earnest, so Frederick worked hard to finish the few furniture projects he could complete before Jacob and farming would fully occupy his time.

Elizabeth was at the midpoint of her pregnancy, and the nausea and fatigue of the first few months was replaced by high energy that made her anxious for warmer weather and drier ground. It also made her begin thinking ahead to summer and the birth of their next child. At the next quilting gathering, she inquired about how births were managed in Bent Creek.

"Who attends to births here?" she asked a German-speaking friend as they worked together stitching quilt pieces.

"We do not use the doctors who are in Asheville unless we suspect that something is wrong," Ingrid said. "They take so long to get here, they would never make it before the birth. There is a midwife who has watched over most of the births in Bent Creek as well as all across this county."

"Oh, I have never needed a physician for my births," Elizabeth said. "I much prefer a midwife. Who is the woman? How do I arrange for her presence?"

"Her name is Hattie May Burnham. She used to be owned by the Stead-man family, and she learned midwifery from her mother. She delivered all the slave babies, and then she got loaned out by the Steadmans to deliver their friends' babies. She's a kindhearted, God-fearing woman and she's caught dozens of babies and takes very good care of the mothers. She's never had a mother die."

"She is a Negro woman?" Elizabeth asked. The thought of a woman of color being a midwife had never crossed her mind.

"Yes, of course she is," Ingrid said, with the unspoken acknowledgment that it was a silly question to ask about someone who had been owned.

"We all know her as Aunt Hattie. She becomes like family to those whose babies she helps birth," Ingrid said. "She doesn't speak any German except 'hallo, danke, and auf wiedersehen,' but she knows all that needs to be known about mothers and births."

"Well, I shall need to be in touch with her before summer," Elizabeth said. "I could probably manage on my own, but Frederick will want someone to help me."

Elizabeth thought about how interesting it would be to have a Negro woman live with them, even briefly. Unlike Americans, the Swiss had no preconceived notions about those who have other skin colors or ethnicities, just curiosity caused by a lack of experiential knowledge.

She and Frederick had talked about how strange it was that they, as German-speaking Swiss immigrants, were generally readily accepted and treated well, while others, particularly the Irish, often received poor treatment. Beyond that, they did not like that there seemed to be an underlying feeling of superiority of many people with white skin regarding those with dark skin.

Even though the thought of Aunt Hattie attending her birth was unexpected, as she mulled it over, Elizabeth decided it would be a good thing for her and for her family. She and Frederick intended to be a part of the new America, not the one over which a war was fought, and that had left the country badly scarred and bruised.

Elizabeth was relieved that when she later explained the situation to Frederick, after a similar moment of surprise, he agreed it was a good thing for her to have knowledgeable and kind help during the birth.

When the spring thaw began to warm the fields and sunny days began to dry them out, Frederick set aside furniture making and began the arduous work of clearing and plowing fields. He and Jacob used hoes, mattocks, axes, and a oxen-drawn bull-tongue plow to break up the earth hardened by a season of rain and snow. They plowed along, slowly removing the remainder of the decomposing roots left behind by trees that had been cut down. The plow, dragged through the fields by an ox or the big mule Jacob owned, was made entirely of wood, except for the small metal point that they drove through the earth, rocks, and roots to clear the ground. One of them would drive the ox and the plow forward while the other dragged away the gnarly hunks and chunks of dead tree roots and rocks the plow churned to the surface.

The rocks would be piled in a cart and hauled to the edges of the fields where they were added to stone walls along the perimeter. Frederick and Jacob traded off who was driving and who was hauling. It was exhausting work.

The rotted wood would be left piled up to sun-dry until it could be burned.

Frederick would start each day dressed warmly for work in the still wintry temperatures. Within an hour, he would be working in shirt sleeves, drenched in sweat, despite the cold north wind. He loved to farm and took great pleasure in growing food and flowers, but this clearing of land was exhausting. He could not help but think regularly that he would not mind the work if the land was his own. Knowing it was always to be Jacob's property diminished his enthusiasm. He saw it only as a necessary evil that would allow his family to become established in their new country.

He and Jacob worked long days, and with planting due to start the last week in April, he felt it appropriate to shorten Fred and Earnest's school week to three days so they could help with the preparation for planting.

As Elizabeth's pregnancy advanced, the boys also took over some of the tending to chickens and livestock. Both boys were good about having less time learning and with their friends, though Fred spent far too much time thinking about and talking about Alice, a girl at school who he thought was the prettiest thing he'd ever seen.

He brought Alice up repeatedly in just a short time one afternoon, until Frederick finally said, "Fred, do I need to remind you that you are twelve years old? You do not need to be fussing about girls at this age. You need to get yourself educated and learn a trade and make your way in life before you can be thinking about girls."

Fred blushed and said, "Yes sir." But he absolutely did not intend to stop thinking about the girl with the beautiful golden braids.

Earnest, though younger, was the harder worker of the two boys. Even Jacob noticed the amount of work the boy with the wiry build and the quiet demeaner accomplished.

All in all, Frederick was pleased with his boys and the way they labored when given a task. And he was in awe of how quickly they were learning their new language. He would regularly ask them both how to say various words and phrases in English. Fred was even getting to the point where he would accompany him to Hatch's mill where he could interpret bits of conversation.

Fred was also quick to understand the workings of machinery and equip-ment, and he was always full of questions about how things worked. He would then surprise Frederick by remembering weeks later every detail he had been told about any piece of machinery that had been of interest to him.

Already, Frederick pondered what careers, trades, and opportunities would lay ahead for his sons. And because of Frederick's infatuation with girls, he could not help but wonder about what young woman would one day share their lives.

Chapter 20

Elizabeth learned that Aunt Hattie was coming to Bent Creek to visit to a woman whose baby was expected a month before Elizabeth's. Her friend, Ingrid, had a buggy, a carriage horse, and a teenage son who could drive, and she volunteered to take Elizabeth to the woman's home at the other end of the creek so she could meet Aunt Hattie.

Frederick arranged his workday so that he could look after the children while Elizabeth and Ingrid were gone. Elizabeth took baby John along, and the ride along the creek to the far end of the community was bumpy, but not unpleasant. Elizabeth was anxious to meet Aunt Hattie and settle the details of her impending birth.

When they pulled up to the cabin, they found the midwife on the porch with a very young woman, obviously the one whose birth she would be attending. Ingrid made introductions and was able to help interpret the conversations as needed. Elizabeth realized again how much she longed to speak English well enough to handle arrangements and business on her own.

Hattie May Burnham was tall and sinewy, with graceful movements and expressive hands. Her eyes conveyed warmth and friendliness, and her demeanor was cheerful and calm, immediately putting Elizabeth at ease.

The conversation was brief and efficient, and Hattie confirmed that she was available at the time Elizabeth was due. She said as soon as Elizabeth had the first signs of impending labor, she would come to their home and would stay with them until she and her new baby were ready for her to leave. Elizabeth assured her that she was very practiced with births. When she told her that this was her ninth birth, Hattie asked her how many of her babies had lived. When Elizabeth told her that all of them were alive, Hattie folded her hands, bowed her head, and said, "Thank you, Lord."

They agreed on how much Hattie would be compensated, and when Elizabeth was saying goodbye to her, Hattie suddenly grabbed her in her arms and squeezed her. She then stepped back, placed one hand on Elizabeth's round stomach, and her other hand over her heart as she spoke sincerely, looking deeply into Elizabeth's eyes. Ingrid translated her words.

"I will be praying for you and your baby," Hattie had said. "We will welcome your child into this world together."

Elizabeth then returned home, at peace with the plans, and pleased to know this strong, gentle woman would be with her.

Early summer was a whirlwind of activity, with long days of plowing and planting from sunrise to sunset. Two new calves and more than a dozen piglets were born on the farm, and the henhouse was full of fluffy chicks that had hatched out.

Frederick was still able to find time to make and sell an occasional piece of furniture, and after the sale of a particularly beautiful bed to a wealthy couple, they traveled to Asheville to buy nails, a new hammer, sewing supplies, and shoes for the older children.

Much to Elizabeth's delight, in addition to buying seeds needed for the vegetable garden of their own, they also bought seeds to plant a flower garden. There were so many new flowers to grow in America that she had never seen in Switzerland. She bought seeds for pansies, sweet William, morning glories, asters, and others.

As Elizabeth planned out and planted the flower garden behind their home, she realized that few things in the world were better reminders to never give up hope than placing a tiny, dry, brown bit of matter in the earth and seeing it become a thing of beauty. With her daughters laughing and playing and helping with the planting in the summer sun, and her baby inside bumping about inside the tight quarters of her belly, Elizabeth was filled with the joy of the moment and her hopes for the future.

The summer weather also led to more time socializing in the community. The families gathered nearly every week for a variety of activities, including ball games, quilting contests, dances, wrestling or shooting matches, and many family workdays for raising houses, barns, and outbuildings, as neighbors had done for their addition.

"The American people are so giving," Frederick said. "They treat us like we have lived here all our lives after less than a year."

Elizabeth agreed, realizing that in many ways, though they were without the family they had left behind, they were more welcomed than they had ever expected to be. It seemed, somehow, that since so many of the people in their small community were new to the country, they had an immediate bond.

The neighbors helped balance against the unpleasantness of dealing with Jacob's daily surliness and the awkward distance he forced between Greta and the rest of the world. The interaction with them was always strained, and at the late stage of pregnancy, Elizabeth had decided to keep her distance and focus on her home, her family, and the baby on the way.

On an unusually hot day in the second week in July, Elizabeth woke to find the tinged sign of early labor, and realized it was time to fetch Aunt Hattie. She sent Earnest out to the fields to find Frederick, who left in the wagon immediately to go to Hattie's.

Frederick passed by Ingrid's home on the way and seeing her hoeing in their garden by the side of the road, he shouted that the baby was coming, and he was going to get Hattie. Ingrid immediately laid down the hoe, saying she would come by to help with the children as soon as she was able.

By the time Frederick returned to the Garraux home with Hattie, Elizabeth was lying down, sensing that her labor was soon to begin. Hattie whisked into the house and motioned to Frederick to take the children to the front of the home away from the first-floor bedroom where Elizabeth was resting.

Hattie went to the bedroom, opened the door, and said, "I am here, Miss Elizabeth."

Elizabeth held her stomach and nodded to Hattie, who understood this experienced mother knew her baby was on the way.

Hattie returned to the kitchen, opened her satchel, and pulled out a long white apron she put on over her calico dress. She poured water from a bucket in the kitchen into a pot she could heat on the stove. Her mother had taught her that hot water and lye soap helped prevent the infections that so often took the lives of mothers after their infants were born.

Once she had thoroughly washed, Hattie went into the bedroom at the back of the addition. She helped Elizabeth remove her shoes, stockings, and long dress, replacing it with a short cotton gown she pulled on over her head. She spread clean cotton cloths on the bed where Elizabeth would labor, but first she encouraged her to walk about the room while she held her elbow. Hattie had learned that the longer women stayed upright, the quicker their babies would often make their way into the world.

They slowly paced around the room, standing by the window for a time before they would repeat their steps. Elizabeth felt comforted by Hattie's strong and capable presence.

As was the case with her previous deliveries, it was soon clear she needed to lie down because labor was beginning in earnest.

Aunt Hattie gently checked the progress of the baby's movement, and she exclaimed, "My, my, your baby is in a hurry!"

At that moment, there was a knock on the door, and Elizabeth heard Ingrid say in German, "I am here, Elizabeth. I will help Frederick with the children. God bless you and your baby."

Just a few hours after Hattie's arrival, it was clear the baby was coming. Between Hattie's presence and knowing Ingrid was there to help Frederick with the children, Elizabeth completely focused on pushing their next child into the world.

Hattie was amazed at the strength and quietness of this tiny woman. Even though Elizabeth had given birth so many times, Hattie had seldom seen a woman as calm and controlled as she was. She made almost no sounds, other than those accompanying the great effort to force the baby out of her body.

As is usual with births, after hours of intermittent straining and pushing, in a sudden flurry, the baby was in Hattie's strong hands, held upside down until he began to wail, the sound like a kitten's plaintive meowing filling the room.

"You have a son, Miss Elizabeth," Hattie said. "A handsome, healthy boy."

Elizabeth knew the word "son," and her heart soared. They loved their four beautiful daughters and four handsome sons, but now there was a fifth son, and she knew that would delight Frederick.

Hattie dealt with the cord and afterbirth and, after quickly cleansing the infant, she placed him on Elizabeth's chest. She then pulled a chair from the corner of the room, and finally sat down.

"You did good, Mama," she said, smiling at Elizabeth, feeling the enormous relief she experienced each time a healthy infant came into the world with a mother who would likely survive to raise him.

Elizabeth also recognized the word "good," and she smiled back.

"Thank you, Aunt Hattie," Elizabeth said, having carefully practiced the words in recent days. "Thank you."

"You rest," Hattie said, pantomiming laying her head down and closing her eyes. The newborn had quieted, and Elizabeth pulled the bed cover over her and the infant, as she nodded and closed her eyes.

Hattie went into the main part of the house. As she approached, Frederick, the children and Ingrid went silent with expectation.

"You have a new son, Mr. Frederick!" Hattie proclaimed. "He is healthy, and your wife is well."

In German, Ingrid shouted, "A boy, it's a boy! You have another son, Frederick! Hooray! Elizabeth is well, and you have another son!"

The children cheered and the older boys leaped about and shouted. They had hoped for another boy in the household. Now, five brothers outnumbered the four sisters.

Through Ingrid, Frederick told Hattie he wanted to see Elizabeth. Hattie cautioned him to wait an hour or more to let her rest. She had learned that too much activity immediately after birth could be disruptive to mothers and newborns. Frederick didn't particularly like being told to wait, but he did appreciate the care Hattie was giving his wife, so he agreed to be patient.

Ingrid had brought dinner for the family, and Frederick motioned to Hattie to join them. He pointed to Elizabeth's empty chair at the table and said, "Aunt Hattie, please."

The families of women Hattie helped give birth treated her in a variety of different ways. Sometimes she was fully welcomed. Other times she was given her compensation and hurried away. To be included at the family's table warmed her heart. Though the conversation was challenging, with the help of Ingrid's translation she was able to converse with Frederick, and even a little with the quiet, well-behaved children.

The children were sweet and polite, and she could tell there were no bad feelings toward her. The big Swiss family had made her feel more welcome than many people in Bent Creek who had known her for years.

As the sun was setting, Hattie took Frederick to see Elizabeth and to meet his new son. She left them alone, Frederick sitting in the chair Hattie had pulled up to the bedside. Elizabeth was nursing the baby, and she looked from the infant to Frederick and said proudly, "Meet your American son."

"Our American son," Frederick said, as he leaned in and kissed her forehead. "He is wonderful, Elizabeth. Thank you for another beautiful child."

Hattie stayed on a couple of days, until it was clear the birth and recovery were free of complications. She prayed over Elizabeth and the baby, and she gently kissed the infant on the cheek before saying goodbye to Elizabeth.

She thanked Frederick for his help and kindness.

"Danke, Herr Garraux," she said proudly in German.

Frederick smiled and said, "You are welcome," in his best English.

Elizabeth and Frederick named their fifth son Charles, but they would call him by the American nickname, Charley.

A few days later, Frederick came into her room and said, "Elizabeth, Greta is here, and she would like to see you."

Greta had not ever come into their home on her own, so Elizabeth was shocked and pleased by the visit.

"Hulloh, Elizabeth," Greta said hesitantly. "I wanted to come to see the baby. I made this for him," she said, as she held out a small, crocheted blanket.

"Oh, thank you, Greta," Elizabeth exclaimed. "It is so beautiful."

Greta stood still, quiet, and awkward, looking at the infant sleeping in Elizabeth's arms.

After a moment, Elizabeth said, "Would you like to hold him?"

"Oh, I, well, yes, I would love to hold him, if that is all right," she stammered.

"Pull the chair over," Elizabeth said. "Of course, you can hold him."

Greta pulled the chair over next to the bed, and Elizabeth gently laid Charley in her arms.

"Oh, he is so lovely," Greta said. "Such a pretty boy. He reminds me of my first grandchild. My son's oldest boy was round-faced and so pink, just like this when he was born. My little Heinrich, he was such a beautiful baby."

Tears welled up in Greta's eyes and spilled onto her cheeks.

"I am sorry," she said. "I do not mean to shed tears. Your baby is wonderful, and I am so glad you are both healthy."

"I understand your sadness, Greta. You must miss your children and grandchildren so much. How old is Heinrich now?"

"He is eleven—the same age as your Earnest," she said. "I miss them all so terribly. I know I will never see them again. When I see your children running and playing and growing, I cannot help but wonder how much like my own grandchildren they might be. It makes me so happy to see them. And so very sad," she said, tearing up again.

"Oh, Greta, I am so sorry for you missing them. Is there not a way for

154

you to return to Switzerland to see them and spend time with them?"

Greta passed Charley back to Elizabeth, pulled a handkerchief out of her sleeve, wiped her eyes, and stood up abruptly.

Taking a deep breath, she said, "I could never travel on my own, and Jacob would not hear of it. He has forbidden me to even speak of the children and grandchildren. I have not even spoken their names aloud in years."

Elizabeth said, "I would like to hear about them, Greta. About each of them. Please sit down and tell me all about them."

Hesitantly, Greta sat back down. Then she began to describe the births and childhoods of her two sons, haltingly and slowly at first, and then as though a flood gate had opened. She talked about their lives, their wives, her grandchildren, story after story pouring from her. It was as though years of having her feelings dammed up left her heart so full of memories, it was a wonder it had not burst.

Greta talked on and on, alternately smiling with the pleasantness of a passing memory, and tearing up at the life lost. Elizabeth listened quietly, until it seemed that the recounting of her past life had drained Greta of what little energy she had arrived with.

"Thank you for telling me about your family, Greta," Elizabeth said. "Your sons and their wives sound like accomplished people, and it seems your grandchildren are smart, healthy young people with good futures ahead."

Elizabeth said, "We don't ever have to speak of them in front of Jacob. But anytime you wish to talk about them, I am here to listen. And I thank you again for this lovely blanket. It will always remind me of the loving mother and grandmother you are."

Holding her clasped hands to her chest, Greta said, "Thank you, Elizabeth. Thank you so much."

Then Greta returned to the home where she merely survived her lonely life. Elizabeth was left feeling terribly sad for the poor, empty shell of a woman. But it also stirred strong feelings within her, and the realization she believed no one, not even a husband, could interfere with a mother's love for her children, or the maternal obligation to give children a better life than her own.

During the weeks following the birth of their son, many neighbors dropped by to bring meals for the family and occasionally gifts for the baby. Frederick and Elizabeth continued to be grateful for their new community.

Elizabeth, as always, returned to her household tasks and mothering quicker than most. Even with a new baby, she hated feeling unproductive. Within weeks, she was back to her daily routine of cooking, cleaning, sewing, sweeping, mending, baking, soap making, chicken tending, and garden weeding.

Having two babies in cloth napkins took an enormous amount of time all by itself. There was constantly a dozen or more nappies air-drying for reuse, and another soiled pile that needed to be scrubbed and washed in a big batch about twice a week. Elizabeth felt fortunate that she had accumulated enough nappy pins to use for both babies. She remembered that when Fred was born, many women were still tying cloths around babies' bottom the best they could.

Elizabeth would put Charley into a carry basket and set him in the garden next to her as she worked, while John, who was just a year and a half old, played on a blanket nearby.

The older children helped care for their younger siblings, while Frederick toiled long days in the fields and pursued his cabinetry business, often by lantern light after the family had gone to bed.

The summer brought successful crops and the fall an abundant harvest. Word of mouth about Frederick's wood-crafting brought him regular requests, some from as far away as Swannanoa and Black Mountain. Their first full year in their new country had been successful and bountiful, and they settled again into a productive, comfortable rhythm.

Life was generally so peaceful that Frederick was shocked by news that was brought back to the community by men who had gone into Asheville to cast votes in the first election held since the war ended.

Frederick was at Hatch's mill picking up some wood when he heard some men talking excitedly. As he watched, more men joined in the animated conversation.

Frederick had befriended a young man from Germany who worked in Hatch's blacksmith shop. Johann had moved to America just before the war, and he and his wife had both learned the language very quickly.

"Johann, something has happened that several men seem very excited and disturbed about," Frederick said. "Please come with me and find out what has happened."

They went to the front of the mill, where a small group had now gathered around the two men who continued to speak loudly and dramatically. Johann moved to the fringes of the crowd and listened, as more people gathered, drawn to the excitement.

After several moments, Johann stepped back to Frederick and said, "Oh, terrible things have happened in Asheville during the voting. A fight broke out, and several Negroes were shot. One of them died," he said.

"Why did they fight?" Frederick said. "Who shot them?"

"There's much dispute about exactly what happened," Johann said. "A Negro man wanted to vote, and the official said the man could not because he was a criminal who had been publicly whipped for his crime.

"The man was angry, and soon there was a group of Negroes in the streets along with a group of white men, some from the richest families in Asheville. They said the Negro who wasn't allowed to vote then threw a rock, and it turned into a riot. More than a dozen people were shot. The man who couldn't vote was killed."

"This is very bad," Frederick said. "This should not happen after the war has ended and slaves have been freed."

Johann said, "The men said there is still much political turmoil between Lincoln's Republicans and the Democrats who are angry about the war's outcome. They are saying this proves the war is not really over."

"But it is over," Frederick said. "There is a new government. The slaves have been freed. We have seen Negroes working and living in Asheville. Elizabeth's midwife was a Negro. How can this be?"

"There are people, even who live here in Bent Creek among us, who think slaves should still be allowed," Johann said. "They think the struggle will continue, and they believe they will undo what has happened."

"The two men who were in Asheville to cast their votes said they were also told that men who belong to a secret group were involved in the fight, but they said that will never be proved.

"The group is made up of former Confederate soldiers. They started the secret society in Tennessee. It has members all over now, even in our state," Johann said. "The men wear costumes to make themselves look like the ghosts of Confederates killed in the war. They ride at night and terrorize Negroes and people who support emancipation."

"This is terrible news," Frederick said. "We came to America because we believed the conflict was settled."

"Hopefully, once the election is over, everything will quiet down," Johann said. "But be careful what you say and who you say it to. Not everyone thinks as we do."

Frederick debated whether to even tell Elizabeth about what he had learned, and he decided against it. They would continue their peaceful and productive lives. They would teach their children well, and make sure this ugliness did not touch them.

Frederick remained determined that America would bring his family all they hoped for. He could not let the hatred left in dark corners of this new country diminish their dreams.

Chapter 21

As Frederick had hoped, life in their small community over the next few years remained largely peaceful, even as the country went through the pains and struggles of reconstruction.

He was able to build up a small furniture and wood-crafting business on the side, while he and Elizabeth continued to experiment with different crops and techniques of farming and gardening.

They were particularly interested in trying to grow grapes to make wine. Frederick's grandfather, Jean-Jacques Garraux, had been a grower and vintner in the lake region near Bern. Jean-Jacques was a patient teacher and he passed on his wealth of knowledge about grapes and wine to his son, Johann Christian, Frederick's father, who in turn, passed it on to Frederick.

Johann Garraux, in addition to being a gifted cabinet maker like his son, had become known as a very successful grape grower and wine maker. His success continued until the 1860s, when a terrible grape disease carried by vines imported from America destroyed grape crops all across

Europe, including his father's.

Growers had learned that even though the disease destroyed European grapevines, the vines grown in America had developed a resistance to the disease, phylloxera. Knowing this, as soon as he had the opportunity, Frederick bought a few dozen starter grape vines.

Frederick and Elizabeth were patient, persistent gardeners. Along with the other crops they tended, harvested, sold, and stored, they also cared for and pruned the grapevines for two seasons, keeping them unproductive so the vines could grow stronger.

In the second season of the vines, Elizabeth was once again expecting another baby. Reaching the point of harvest-ready grapes would take so long, that before they could pick the first grape, Elizabeth would give birth to their sixth son, William. Willie, like Charley, was born with Aunt Hattie in attendance. Once again, the birth was uncomplicated, and Elizabeth recovered quickly.

By the time they harvested their grapes and made the first batch of wine, Willie was one-year-old. The older children, Fred, now fifteen, Earnest, fourteen, and Lucy, thirteen, helped with every aspect of the farm, especially the grape harvest. The older boys continued with their lessons whenever the work on the farm allowed for it . . . and Frederick made sure that was very often.

Fred's interest in his female classmates had shifted away from Alice to another girl at school named Annamarie. He was always busy flirting with Annamarie, at least whenever he wasn't being enamored of his friend's sisters, or any other pretty girl he was exposed to.

Their daughter Mary, who was twelve, was a quiet child, inclined to spend more time on her own. She learned slowly, but she was just as sweet and hardworking as the other children and would help whenever she could. She especially enjoyed helping care for the livestock, and she had a special patience with animals that caused even the cattle and horses that

161

towered over her to return her gentleness.

Ten-year-old Bettie and her eight-year-old sister, Rosa, were like peas in a pod and they were virtually inseparable. They were often too distracted by whispering, giggling, and playing together to be very involved in the family's work, but they were never difficult and required little supervision.

Frank and John, now six and four, both well-behaved and content, also kept themselves busy and tended to play together in the apple orchard or barn.

Charley, at three, was a handful, and Elizabeth spent much of her time keeping him out of trouble, while toting around twelve-month-old William. She moved through each day operating like a foreman or supervisor, knowing that losing control of ten children for even a moment could prove disastrous.

Her neighbors took notice, and Elizabeth was respected and revered in the community for her ability to calmly manage such a number of children. The task became more visually impressive with every passing year, as four of the children were now taller than their diminutive mother, while one or two of them still had to be carried wherever they went.

The months passed, their day-to-day life a blur of hard work and teaching the children the skills they would need in life. Elizabeth taught the girls food preparation, cooking, and all the skills needed in the kitchen. They also learned sewing, darning, embroidery, and quilting from their mother's expertise with a needle and thread. But the girls also learned about growing crops and flowers and handling farm tools, and they regularly spent as much time working on the farm as the boys did.

The boys continued their schooling, and learned to read and write in English, passing their knowledge on in bits and pieces to their siblings and even their parents. Elizabeth was determined to be sure all the children would have the skills they would need in the future, and she even taught the boys to knit their own socks. They became as skilled with knitting needles and yarn as their sisters, though Earnest never quite seemed to get the turn of the socks' heels quite right.

By the time the second abundant crop of grapes was nearly ready for harvest, and just over a year since Willie's birth, much to her amazement, Elizabeth, now forty-five, found she was pregnant once again.

As always, she felt abundantly blessed to be expecting another child, but at her age, she knew this would likely be their last child, and, in truth, she had begun to pray that it would be. She had always wanted a large family but managing ten children while trying to maintain a home and farm was exhausting on many days. Elizabeth had never dreamed that she would end up a mother of eleven children, and on some days, she still found it hard to believe.

Their life continued on, organized, productive, and generally without conflict. But unfortunately, that changed about midway through her pregnancy.

Frederick had been spending a good bit of time at Hatch's place and in his workshop until late many evenings. Very often, Elizabeth would be asleep when he climbed into bed.

One night, Charley had a nightmare, and Elizabeth had just put him back down when Frederick came in the backdoor. She got into bed, and listened to him moving through the house, at one point stumbling into furniture and muttering something in the dark.

He came stealthily into the room, clearly trying to maintain silence, as Elizabeth sat up, and turned up the flame in the lantern she had left burning for him.

Frederick looked disheveled and shocked to see her looking at him.

"Why are you still awake?" he said, looking like a child who had been caught misbehaving.

"Why are you stumbling and bumping around in the dark?" she said tersely.

It immediately reminded her of a time early in their marriage when Frederick had begun to spend a great deal of time drinking far too much. They had begun to squabble about his tendency toward drunkenness, and she made it clear early on she would not tolerate something that she had seen render far too many men useless.

One of the many reasons she had been glad to make the move away from Bern was having her husband leave behind his group of heavy-drinking friends.

"I was talking with Johann and Henry and a few other men after working at the mill, and the time got away from me."

Then as he pulled off his jacket, he lost his balance, catching himself with a hand on the footboard.

She leaped from the bed, and in an instant, was standing in front of him in her bare feet. "Are you drunk, Frederick?" she snapped.

"I am not drunk. I just had a few drinks while talking with friends. I do get to talk with friends, don't I? Did I forget to ask your permission? I don't have to just work constantly and put up with Jacob and take care of children and try to meet your standards, do I?"

He spoke in a deep, harsh voice she remembered all too well from the times they had argued about his drinking in Switzerland. There was also a thick cloud that smelled of liquor surrounding him.

A fury rushed through every inch of Elizabeth's tiny body.

"Do you remember when you nearly ruined your cabinet business because you were so busy 'talking with friends?'" she snapped. "Do you remember when I debated whether I could even trust you to handle our funds? Do you remember when the friend you were 'just talking with' ended up falling in front of a carriage, leaving him a cripple? Now, with an eleventh child on the way, you're back to more just 'talking with friends?' I do not think so."

"Oh, you are so perfect, Elizabeth," he sneered sarcastically. "It's so easy for you to judge me. You know I treat you well and I work day and night to take care of everything to make a good life for you and the children."

"You insult me," he snapped.

Frederick was such a gentle, soft-spoken man, that this version of him shocked her every time it surfaced.

He was undressing, his movements sharp and angry, though he fumbled and fussed while trying to unbutton his shirt.

"Maybe I should treat you more like Jacob treats Greta," he grumbled, his back turned toward her. "Maybe I should teach you a lesson about how to respect your husband."

"Don't you ever threaten me, Frederick. Not ever. This is not like you. Do you see what being drunk does to you?"

Wheeling around and facing her, he snarled, "Yes, I see what drinking does to me. It makes me stand up to you and have thoughts of my own. It makes me realize I am still a man and I still run this household. It makes me wonder why I am here, working so hard with no appreciation. That's what it does, Elizabeth."

"Do not say another word," she said. "Not a word. Or we will both regret it."

She sat on her side of the bed, facing away from him as he climbed silently into his side, slamming his head onto the pillow, and jerking the bedcovers over him.

Elizabeth could not believe this was happening again.

She would not let drunkenness ruin their family like it had so many others. It would not happen. She would not allow it.

Elizabeth sat there, back ramrod straight, feeling her heart beating in her ears, making her temples throb. She felt Frederick toss around behind her and heard him grumble briefly before he began breathing quietly. He eventually began snoring loudly as the drink took him into deep sleep.

Everyone drank beer and wine in Switzerland. It was never an issue until Frederick began to spend time with a group of men who were basically known in the city as worthless drunks. He was defensive about enjoying the camaraderie and became angry when questioned. For some time, he had controlled the amount he drank. But eventually, it became a problem, as more and more often he would continue drinking with the men until he was also stumbling and slurring. He began sleeping too late into the day, and he had multiple furniture orders canceled by angry customers tired of waiting.

When Elizabeth, who was exceptionally good with figures, started looking at his business records, she realized how much money was being spent outside the household on his evening recreation, and how much business was being lost.

She had issued an ultimatum, threatening to take the children with her to stay at her parents' home. That had motivated Frederick to moderate his behavior. In the few years before they left Bern and ever since, he had been diligent to avoid any excessive drinking. Until now, she thought bitterly.

Americans were notorious drinkers, but she did not know spending time with neighbors could threaten to take him back to the dark, undependable, dangerous life he had leaned toward. By observation, she had learned Americans drank all the time—while celebrating, while mourning, while alone, and while together. Hard cider, whiskey, beer, wine, and moonshine poured like water in these mountains, especially among the traders and craftsmen in the area. As powerful as religion and churches were in the region, so was the commitment to drink.

She had suspected a few times that perhaps Frederick was drinking more again, but she attributed his evening absences to trying to run his furniture business in an addition to the farm work. She blamed the fatigue of overwork for the mornings he found it difficult to get out of bed. Now she realized she had actually been trying to avoid seeing the old pattern.

Elizabeth eventually fell into a light, disturbed sleep.

By the time Frederick awoke, the sun was well up, Elizabeth was through most of her morning chores, the children were dispersed into their daily activities, the babies were down for a morning nap, and she had brewed an extra strong pot of coffee.

Frederick, looking pale and rather sheepish, came into the kitchen and sat down.

He said, "Elizabeth, I was angry and tired last night, I should not have . . ."

She cut him off and quickly set a mug of coffee in front of him, saying, "I do not want to talk about it. I thought about it for hours last night. I do not like what drunkenness does to you or how I know it will affect our children. You will not be a drunk. There is no conversation to be had."

Frederick stared down into the steaming coffee. He exhaled, and his shoulders slumped.

"I will not be a drunk. I will be what you want me to be. I will work hard. I will be successful. I will take care of the children. I will do whatever you want."

True to her word, Elizabeth did not have any further conversation about it, but she never again went to sleep until he was in the bed next to her. There was tension between them for some time, but within weeks of carefully watching Frederick appear to keep his word, life began to return to normal. As always, Elizabeth wanted to believe the best of him. She put the incident out of her mind, and focused on the children, the work, and the impending birth.

Also, always in the backs of their minds, Frederick and Elizabeth knew that by the end of 1872, their tenancy agreement would require them to begin giving a large share of any profit from their efforts to Jacob. They had long decided that would be the time when they would acquire property of their own. The term of their tenancy would end shortly after the birth of the baby at the end of the summer.

They had been trying to save enough money to buy their own property, but they had not yet decided where they would live. They both also dreaded telling Jacob they were done being his tenants.

In August 1872, almost exactly two years after Willie was born, Elizabeth gave birth to their eleventh child—their fifth daughter, Fannie.

Fannie was smaller and a little earlier than expected, but Aunt Hattie said she was a "feisty little thing," and declared Elizabeth the best at birthing babies she had ever seen.

Greta once again crocheted a beautiful blanket for the new baby, as she had for Charley and Willie. She would frequently sneak over whenever Jacob was gone to Asheville or on some other business that would keep him away for hours. She cherished her time with the children, and she had come to admire and love Elizabeth.

On a regular basis, Elizabeth would encourage Greta to try to find her own way in the world, but then a thick, impenetrable door would slam closed between them. Elizabeth cared for her but knew there was little she could say or do that would change Greta's attitude and her resolve to just endure whatever life Jacob provided.

Frederick and Elizabeth had decided they would wait until she was recovered from the birth and Fannie a little older to determine where they would live next. By late fall, Frederick and the boys would have completed the harvesting of the crops and bringing the livestock back in from grazing in the unfenced wilderness. At least at that point in the year's work, letting Jacob know they were leaving his farm would be as easy as it ever could be. But they knew their news would not be received well.

In late October at the end of a workday, Frederick asked Jacob if they

168

could sit somewhere quiet to talk. He thought they might go into the house, but Jacob leaned his hoe against the barn wall and pointed at a nearby wooden bench. "Sit there," he said.

Then, in his typically gruff and suspicious manner, he said, "So, what do you want?"

Frederick drew in a deep breath as he sat down on the bench.

"We have had five good years here, Jacob, and we are grateful to have had the opportunity. As you had wanted, you now have much more acreage cleared than when we arrived. The orchard is mature, the grapes are producing, and the livestock are thriving. We have accomplished a lot together."

As he cleared his throat to continue, Jacob suddenly stood up, glared at him, and said loudly, "And now I suppose you think you are going to leave? After all you have gained from living off my land? After becoming an American citizen just for having lived here on my property all these years? Now, you are just going to leave? That's what you are telling me, isn't it? Isn't it?"

"We agreed to this length of tenancy, Jacob. We never talked about more than five years."

"You disrespect me," Jacob shouted. "You would not have survived without me, you and your ridiculous brood of children. You bring shame to your father and your family name."

The insult to his children and mention of his father proved too much for Frederick. His face reddened, and he felt the heat of anger stream through his body.

"We are done here," Frederick said sternly. "My father would never want me to stay on with a man who shows so little respect or kindness to others. You are not the friend he remembered from years ago. You have never been the man I thought you were. We will leave as soon as we find property."

"No," Jacob shouted. "You will leave now. I want you off my land. I want you out of my sight."

Jacob stormed out of the barn, leaving Frederick with his heart pounding and his thoughts swirling.

Frederick walked slowly to the house, and when he pulled open the door, Elizabeth was standing inside waiting, Fannie in one arm and Willie on her other hip.

"Did you talk to him, Frederick? What did he say?"

Frederick walked past her, wishing he didn't have to tell her what had been said. He walked into the room where most of the children were reading and playing.

"Lucy, take the baby," Frederick said. "You all take Fannie and Willie and go upstairs. I need to speak with your mother."

Elizabeth's eyes stayed riveted on his expressionless face as she handed off the babies to their siblings. Frederick, eyes dark and somber, sat down in a chair by the fireplace. He bent forward, leaning his head into his hands.

"What is it, Frederick," Elizabeth said as she sat down near him. "Was Jacob very angry?"

Without looking up, Frederick said, "He wants us to go now. Not next spring. He said he wants us to go now."

"He can't mean that," she said. "He's just angry. We haven't found another place to live yet. He can't expect us to just leave."

Elizabeth knew Jacob would be angry, but like Frederick, she thought they would have the winter months to work things out before moving in the spring.

"We must leave," Frederick said. "He has insulted our family. He is a cruel man who will make us suffer as long as we stay. I do not want the children around him. I do not want to be around him."

"Where will we go, Frederick? Winter is coming. We have the children. We have babies. Our food has been stored here for the season. The wood is chopped. We have not even decided where to go."

As the deadline had approached, Frederick had been constantly mulling over where to move the family. He had asked others for advice and had even looked into one piece of property he decided against because it would have taken every penny they had saved and then some.

As he had pondered what to do next, a conversation he had long ago came back to him. It was a conversation that had been reinforced many times since with traders and travelers passing through the region.

"I think we should leave Bent Creek," he said calmly. "We should leave Buncombe County. We agree the growing season for the grapes is not right here. And you said you worry about Fannie's fragile health with winter coming. Do you remember how often we have heard good things about Greenville, South Carolina? The weather is still cool there, but the season is much longer. And the city is more developed and there would be more opportunities for the children.

Over the years, Frederick had brought up Greenville several times. Traders on the drovers' road had told him many good things about the city. And Elizabeth agreed that she was worried about caring for tiny Fannie during the long, cold winter on the mountain.

Elizabeth was shocked by the sudden turn of events, but though she was never impulsive, she was always adaptable and nimble.

"Greenville. It does sound like a place with opportunities," she said. "But we don't know it. How could we buy property? We haven't even been there."

"We can relocate and lease a home for a time until we can buy our land. And we will build a house. A good house of our own. Not an addition to someone else's house. A home of our own on land of our own. If we must pay rent for a time, then so shall it be. We must leave this place. I do not

171

want to work with Jacob. I do not want to feel beholden to a man who insults my family. We will do better in a new place."

They talked long into the night, stopping only to get the children off to bed and the babies cared for. Both of them knew this day would come eventually, but not in this way, and not with this urgency. Besides Jacob's insistence, they also knew that winter, which could be vicious in the mountains, was just weeks away.

They finally agreed that Frederick would travel to Greenville on his own to try to secure a place where they could move immediately. Once he did, they would use some of their savings to buy a wagon and team to head down the drovers' road into the Piedmont, on to their new home.

Chapter 22

Frederick went to the mill the next day and told Hatch that he would no longer be taking orders for furniture because they were leaving Bent Creek. With his friend Johann assisting in the conversation, he explained what Jacob had said, and their intention to move to Greenville.

Hatch had dealt with Jacob enough over the years to know that he could be both miserable and intractable. He expressed his disappointment that the family would be leaving the community, but he also offered his support. He had connections to a wagonmaker in Asheville, and he even offered Frederick use of his own horse and buggy to make the preliminary trip to South Carolina.

As was common in the small, insular mountain communities, any news spread like wildfire. Word that the big Swiss family planned to relocate moved faster than most. A day later, before Frederick had even begun to arrange travel to Greenville, there was a knock on the door, and Elizabeth found Aunt Hattie standing on the porch.

The women had formed an affectionate and respectful bond during the labor and deliveries of the Garrauxs' last three children.

Hattie spoke slowly and carefully, knowing that Elizabeth's English was still weak.

"I hear you are going to Greenville," she said. "That's right? Greenville?"

Elizabeth nodded yes, and said, "Yes, we go Greenville," as she motioned her into the house.

She called to Fred who was upstairs in his room. His English-speaking was by far the most advanced of the family. The other older children were catching up, but Fred could not only speak the language well enough to understand most conversations, he could also read and write it quite well.

With Fred's help, she told Hattie about what had happened with Jacob, and she explained why they were leaving so much sooner than they had expected.

Hattie said she had come, not just to see if she could be of any help, but to also tell them about a connection she had to Greenville that she believed could be helpful.

Hattie said the son of a friend of hers had moved to Greenville after he married a South Carolina woman. She said the man, Porter Smith, was younger than Frederick, but he was also a carpenter.

Porter and his wife, Adeline, had seven children, she said. They made their home in a neighborhood in Greenville where they were able to rent a good house and where most of the residents were tradesman.

"I know it don't matter to you, but the folks that live in the neighborhood are for the most part Negroes or Mulattos," she said. "But Porter's mother tells me they are making a good life there, and they are saving money to buy their own land, just like I know you're wanting to do."

She said the Smiths lived in Brucknertown, a neighborhood of a few acres about a mile northwest of the center of Greenville.

174

Elizabeth asked her to explain the word "Mulatto." Hattie said if you had one drop of black blood in your family history, you were not considered to be white, no matter how you looked. She said the census takers labeled people Mulatto when they went door-to-door listing all the people in the community. You are either White or you're not, she said. If you're a Negro, you're either Black or Mulatto.

Hattie said a Mulatto named John Buckner was the husband of a slave who had been owned by Tom Gower, one of Greenville's successful businessmen. She said the Gower's slave, Harriet Buckner, was their cook. She was beloved by the family and was an endless source of love and support for their children. After Gower bought Harriet, he also bought John.

She explained that Gower was widowed twice, and Harriet faithfully saw the children through all the tragedy. She was much more like a mother than a slave or a servant, Hattie said.

Even after the slaves were freed and she no longer worked for the Gowers, the sons were still coming to the Buckners' home every Saturday for lunch.

"Everyone said there was never a cook as good as Harriet Buckner, and there never was a slave more loved by her owner," she said.

Harriet's husband, John, worked as a painter at Gower's company in the center of the town while he was a slave. He continued to work for Gower after he was freed. The Gower, Cox, and Markley Coach Factory was the biggest carriage maker south of the Potomac.

Hattie said the Gowers loved the Buckners so much that after the war ended four years ago and the slaves were emancipated, Mr. Gower helped John Buckner buy an acre of land. Buckner used the land to build a home and start a neighborhood.

"John Buckner bought a few more acres after that, and now there are nearly twenty homes there," Hattie said. "That's where Porter Smith and his family are living. And I asked his momma, and she said she thinks there may be a home or two for rent in Bucknertown, though most of them have been bought."

The possibility of quickly finding a home in Greenville was very encouraging to Elizabeth. She and Frederick had agreed they just needed a place for the family to stay while they established themselves on their own land. It seemed as though this Bucknertown neighborhood might be an answer to prayers.

The thought of relocating the family, finding a new home, arranging schooling for the children, learning to manage a new city in a new state all while finding land to purchase and some way to provide for their household felt daunting. The four older children were in their teens and capable and helpful. Even the middle children were able to handle themselves well at eleven, nine, and seven. But the youngest children were still a lot to manage.

No matter the challenges and no matter what it would take, Elizabeth was determined that this move would bring success to the family and would finally truly establish their lives in America. There would be no more working to keep Jacob happy while improving property that would have always been his.

Frederick brought Hatch's horse and buggy back to the house, and after Elizabeth gave him a bag filled with food for the trip, the whole family stood on the porch and waved him off as he headed to Greenville.

Without anyone seeing her, Greta also watched his departure from a window in her home, tears streaming down her face. She knew with Elizabeth's leaving, Jacob would once again drive her life into complete isolation.

The city was almost sixty miles away, most of the trip on the well-traveled Buncombe Turnpike, and Frederick hoped to reach Greenville in two days' travel.

The weather was cool and pleasant, and though parts of the journey were quite steep, the road was overall in good condition. At about the halfway point between Bent Creek and Greenville, the road was so steep and narrow that Frederick was glad to get through the pass without a wagon or carriage approaching from the opposite direction.

Hatch's young horse was spritely and kept a good pace. Frederick stayed the night at a midway point in Flat Rock at a charming two-story inn called the Farmers Hotel. He lay awake, cool mountain air drifting in the window, as thoughts, hopes, fears, and concerns about the next stage of life filled his head. Would they find success in Greenville? Would he be able to afford the life that Elizabeth hoped they could make for the children?

Back in Bent Creek, Elizabeth lay awake, having similar thoughts, though hers were always buoyed by her belief that if you worked hard enough, you could accomplish anything. She was sure this move would be the one to provide the children with all the future opportunities she hoped for.

Neither of them could have known that their future home would bring one of them great success, while the other would begin a road leading to terrible tragedy.

Frederick got an early start, hoping to reach Greenville by early afternoon. He had the name and address provided by Aunt Hattie, and he hoped to find someone in the community who could help him get his bearings.

The last ten to fifteen miles of Buncombe Road into Greenville were well maintained and easy to navigate, and there was a steady increase of passersby—congenial people on horseback, in carriages, and on foot, nodding and waving as they passed.

He stopped at a small roadside store, showed the clerk the address Fred had written down for him, and got simple directions to Bucknertown.

There had been only a handful of farms and homes along the highway, but soon he saw more homes clustered together, as well as a few businesses. His directions took him into a pleasant neighborhood of a few narrow streets lined by a collection of modest homes. He found the sign for Buckner Street, and located No. 161, Porter Smith's home. It was Saturday, so he was hoping he would find Smith at home.

He tied the horse at the curb and knocked on the door of the white clapboard house. He could hear children talking and playing inside, as a tall, thin black man cautiously opened the door.

In his most practiced English, Frederick said, "Hattie Burnham sent me to Porter Smith. You are Porter Smith?"

When he said Hattie's name, the man's face relaxed, though he still looked perplexed.

"Yes, I am Porter Smith. Why did Hattie send you here?"

"We move Greenville. Elizabeth, children. We move Greenville," Frederick said. "Someone speak German? Any German here?"

A young woman was now standing in the room behind Smith, and children huddled beside and behind her, curious about the bearded white man on their front step.

"So, you're gonna move here and Hattie sent you to me, so I guess you came from up in Asheville? You come down from Asheville?"

"Yes, Asheville," Frederick said. "Any German here?" he reiterated, suddenly realizing that without an interpreter, this could become very complicated. He wished that he had brought Fred along.

"There is a German who lives nearby," Smith said. "I will take you to him." He spoke to the woman, who Frederick assumed was his wife, put on his hat, and motioned to Frederick to go to the buggy as he followed.

Speaking slowly and deliberately as he climbed into the buggy next to

Frederick, Smith said, "I take you to the German. Arleto is his name, Arleto Brunges. He is German. He talks your language. I take you to Brunges."

A short distance away in the neighborhood of tidy homes and well-tended yards was a small cottage-style home. A young woman was sitting on the porch with a baby on her lap. Smith waved as they pulled up in front of the home, and the woman waved back.

"Hulloh," he shouted, "Is your husband at home?"

She responded that he was, and after tying the horse to a post, he and Frederick walked up to the cottage. Smith explained the situation to Brunges's wife, Mary, as she held the baby on her hip. She walked with them to the back of the home where there was a small barn. A few chickens that were pecking around in front of the little building scattered as they approached and Mary shouted, "Arleto, there is someone here to see you."

A young man with thick black hair and beard, an olive complexion, and dark-brown eyes stepped out of the barn. Frederick was surprised at his appearance, but later learned that although Arleto's father was German, he clearly took after his Italian mother.

Arleto was a robust, outgoing, cheerful man in his early thirties, and he was excited to meet another German-speaker. He had also been in America only about six years, but with an English-speaking wife from North Carolina who spoke only minimal German, he had mastered the new language quickly.

Arleto worked as a machinist in a shop that supplied the needs of local manufacturers, and he loved his new city, having moved to Greenville after living briefly in Charlotte.

He began to enthusiastically tell Frederick about Greenville and all it offered, speaking so fast in German that Frederick had to ask him to please slow down.

He agreed to go with Frederick into the town to show him around. They climbed into the buggy as Porter Smith waved them off, wishing them luck as he turned to walk back to his home.

Within a short time, the sparsely populated, narrow dirt road connected into a much wider one. The homes and buildings grew closer together, and it was clear they were entering the main business area of the town.

"This is Greenville," Arleto said, sweeping his arm in a broad gesture, beaming with pride as though he owned the town.

The buggy plodded down the wide, tree-lined, dusty Main Street, maneuvering around horses, wagons, coaches of all types, and occasionally odd lots of herd animals that milled and stomped about near water troughs.

There was heavy foot traffic on the street as well. Women with children in tow hurried along, carrying bags and boxes of groceries and goods as their floor-length dresses stirred up clouds of street dust. There were well-dressed professionals and businessmen, ragtag farmers and laborers, and handfuls of other men who appeared scruffy and perhaps indigent.

The downtown bustled and hummed with activity. There were a few large homes along the way in between wooden commercial buildings, along with short blocks of brick buildings. Some homes had large gardens and even cornfields behind them. The commercial properties were up to three stories tall and housed all types of shops and offices. Some buildings had apartments on the upper floors.

"Greenville has been growing fast since the war ended," Arleto said. "We were spared any battles, and the biggest business in town, the carriage factory, stayed busy even during the war years, making transport wagons and ambulances."

Remembering what Hattie had told Elizabeth about the town and its largest manufacturer, Frederick said, "The factory that is owned by Herr Gower?"

Arleto appeared impressed. "You know of Mr. Gower?"

"I know he helped Mr. Buckner buy land for the neighborhood you live in—the neighborhood we hope that we may live in. Aunt Hattie told us this. She also told us of his carriage-making business."

"I will show you the factory, and the bridge across the river. The bridge that was built thanks to Mr. Gower," Arleto said, as they rolled down the street. He continued to overload Frederick with information about the businesses and people of the city.

The city was geographically small, but Frederick was impressed by all it offered. A horse-drawn street railway ran the length of Main Street, connecting two railroad depots. Arleto said there were nearly a dozen physicians in town, along with several druggists. There were several hotels, the Mansion House being the most famous and opulent. People would go into the lobby just to ogle the cut-glass chandelier and the upholstered furniture. There were more than a dozen boot and shoe dealers and dozens of clothiers, dry goods, and grocery stores. You could send a telegraph from a downtown office, and there were more than ten attorneys to handle contracts and land sales. And, he said, smiling broadly, the city had nearly a dozen saloons.

"One of them is owned by Frank Hahn, who is also German. He and his brother, Christian, came to Greenville long before the war. Christian is a carpenter. You said you do carpentry, too?"

Frederick disliked the label of carpenter. He always felt the term was somewhat demeaning, though he respected the work of many carpenters he had known. He was determined that if this was to be their new home, he would be known as an artisan. Not just someone who sawed boards and hammered nails.

"I am a cabinet maker. I make fine furniture and home furnishings," he said. "I, too, can build a house, but I prefer to create lovely pieces that help make homes beautiful."

Arleto looked taken aback, and said, "I did not mean to offend. I will be anxious to see your craft. In any case, you will like the Hahn brothers. Christian is some older than you. His sons, who are in their twenties, both work with him in his carpentry business. He also makes furniture, so I guess I should call him a cabinet maker, too."

Information continued to gush from Arleto like a pot boiling over on a hot stove. It was fueled by his love for his new city and its people, and the joy of speaking his native tongue.

"Christian's brother, Frank, who is in his early fifties, has made a great life with his bar and billiard parlor. And he's done that despite being blind. Can you imagine? A blind bar owner. He has a wife who is quite a bit younger than him, and after the war and the freeing of the slaves, he hired back his cook and her son as house servants. So, I think that helps him get by without being able to see."

"They were his slaves, and now they are his servants?" Frederick said.

"Yes, that has happened in many households. The Freedman's Bureau helped sort it all out, though many slaves wanted nothing to do with owners who treated them badly. There were others who had kind treatment and they stayed on and are now paid a wage.

"Greenville is about half Negro and half White. For the most part, we live in peace. If you end up living in Bucknertown, you will be one of only a few white families in the neighborhood."

Then, sounding a bit defensive, Arleto said, "We are all decent people, hard-working tradesmen—family people. Mostly Black, but it doesn't matter. No one thinks they are better than anyone else. You better be good with that, or you should live somewhere else."

Sounding equally defensive, and somewhat surprised, Frederick said, "We have no problem with that. We do not care about the color of skin. There are good and bad of all kinds. Bucknertown will be a good place for us."

Before heading back, they crossed the Reedy River on a tall wooden bridge. The bridge was sturdy, but unimpressive compared to the stout, arched, stone bridges left behind in Bern. Frederick kept the comparison to himself, since Arleto was clearly quite proud of the wooden bridge.

"Mr. Tom Gower ran for mayor in '70, and he said if he won, he'd replace the little foot bridge with one big enough for carriages. He got elected and kept his promise. If not for him, we'd still be crossing the river in the shallows above the falls."

Gower's successful run for mayor had also been supported by the all-black, volunteer Neptune Fire Company, established just after the Civil War, and still active in Greenville.

Right in the middle of the city, next to Gower's impressive coach factory, the Reedy River tumbled over a series of large rocky falls. It was a beautiful sight, and the exhilarating sound of rushing water filled the air.

Unable to slow down his storytelling, tales continued to pour from Arleto, despite the distraction of the natural beauty. He said that back in 1856, a slave who had been rented from his owner to work in the coach factory was about to be sold to a Mississippi planter. The slave, Thomas Brier, begged Gower to buy him because he felt he would die if he was sent to Mississippi.

Thinking the young and capable Brier would be very expensive, and having no desire to purchase another slave, Gower refused the deal. Later on, Brier's owner again offered him to Gower, but at a price so low, Gower agreed to purchase him. Gower later learned that Brier had starved himself to convince his former owner he was sick with consumption so his price would be lowered.

"Gower went ahead and made Brier an apprentice at the factory, and he went on to become an expert tinsmith. He and Gower had quite a friendship. When some former slaves were angry and wanted to burn the factory and kill the owners, Thomas Brier stepped in and prevented it.

Gower felt that he owed him his life.

"You'll likely meet Thomas Brier," Arleto said. "He lives out near Buck-nertown."

After Arleto's detailed and talkative tour of the downtown, Frederick felt exhausted. He returned Arleto to his home, thanking him profusely for his time and information. Frederick arranged to return the next day to go with him to talk to John Buckner. Arleto had pointed out a good-sized vacant home in the neighborhood that Frederick hoped they could lease.

Frederick found a room in a boarding house on the edge of the downtown. After shaking the road dust out of his clothes and hair and washing his hands and face, he walked through the business district, back to one of the many saloons Arleto had pointed out. *Elizabeth doesn't have to know every detail of my visit*, he thought.

He had just the slightest glimmer of guilt, but he quickly cast it aside with one sip of Irish whiskey in the well-appointed bar.

Chapter 23

Frederick got a later start than intended the next day, blaming it on the fatigue of travel, not the extra glasses of whiskey purchased by a friendly, but loud man at the bar who wanted to welcome him to Greenville.

He drove the buggy back through the main part of town and into the Bucknertown neighborhood, going directly to Arleto's home. He invited Frederick inside and insisted that he have coffee and something to eat before they went to find John Buckner. It was Sunday, and he said the Buckners were likely still at church, so they could take their time.

Mary Brunges cooked some freshly collected eggs and made toast, for which Frederick's empty and gnawing stomach was grateful. The men left the buggy and walked the few blocks to Buckner's home on the street that bore his name.

Neighborhood founder, John Buckner, and his wife Harriet, lived at 172 Buckner Street. His son, named after him, lived next door with his wife and their three young children.

185

The home that was available for rent was at 177 Buckner Street. It was a simple home with straight lines and no adornment. It was two stories and had a porch that went across the entire front of the house. There was also an outbuilding that Frederick immediately sized-up as being large enough for his wood-crafting workshop.

Arleto explained that the family who had lived in the home had recently relocated to be near aging parents in Charleston. They had sold the home back to Buckner, and he was undecided whether he would lease it or sell it.

It was not a terribly large home, but the attic had been converted into sleeping space, and it had windows for light that added welcomed ventilation during the summer. There were three bedrooms on the second floor, so Frederick felt they could make do.

As they waited, the Buckners, dressed in their finest church clothes, came walking up the street, all six adults and three grandchildren.

Arleto approached the family, and spoke to the patriarch, a dignified man with a Bible in his hand, who cast a glance at Frederick as they all continued to walk toward their home.

Arleto returned to Frederick and said, "Mr. Buckner doesn't like doing business on the Lord's Day. He said you can come back in the morning, and he will talk with you. For now, he said the house is unlocked, and you can look in it."

Frederick was disappointed, but not surprised since most of the residents in Bent Creek also held the Sabbath as holy and did little but spend time with their families.

He checked out the house and found that it would be adequate for their needs, though acknowledging they would be crowded. He spent the rest of the day on his own. He observed life in the town and looked for potential property within a reasonable distance of the center of Greenville.

There was much land surrounding the town that appeared unclaimed or at least unfarmed. After hours of looking, he decided that a hilly area just north of town looked desirable for the grapes and other crops they hoped to grow. Beyond the north end of Main Street, there was a long, gradual slope that ran up toward the foothills. A small creek ran right through the area. The terrain was rocky, but he had learned from his grandfather that grapes favored rocky land. The slope of the land and proximity to the town also appealed to him.

Seeing a house that would be feasible for them to live in and so much potentially available land around the lovely city made him anxious to complete an agreement with Buckner and get back to Bent Creek to get his family moved.

Frederick was mentally fatigued from Arleto's unrelating chatter, and his mind was spinning with thoughts and muddled plans for the future. He decided to go back to the friendly saloon for another drink or two, feeling he deserved it after the overwhelming day.

The bar was far emptier than it had been the night before. The bar keeper said some people had begun to frown on drinking on Sundays since what he called "the God-damned temperance idiots" had become more active again.

Temperance societies had started decades before in the Northeast, but the Civil War had put a damper on the effort, especially in the South. With the war over, the temperance movement was seeing a resurgence all across the Carolinas, including in Greenville. In the small city, there was already an active Sons of Temperance group as well as a Grand Lodge of Good Templars, a group made up of mostly white men, but also some women, both black and white, all of whom thought of alcohol as the devil's drink.

"Bunch of crazy church fools need to mind their own damn business," he raged, in between pouring shots of whiskey for Frederick.

Frederick didn't understand all of the angry words spewing from the saloon keeper, but he gathered enough from his rant to realize he was connecting the empty seats in his bar to church people. That perplexed Frederick, who attended church, believed in God, and knew himself to be a person of good moral character. Elizabeth condemned drinking large quantities, but it was more that she thought it affected his work and bookkeeping than his religious standing.

The bar keeper eventually stopped complaining, went back to washing and drying glasses and the saloon grew quiet. A few drinks later, Frederick felt calmed and ready to try to get some rest.

The city was dark and asleep by the time Frederick shuffled back to his hotel, only a few random gas lamps feebly flickering light on his path. Without undressing, he flopped into the bed, pulling the covers over his shoulder as he kicked his boots off onto the floor.

He did not think, or dream, or stir until long after the first morning light. When he finally awoke, he sat on the edge of the bed, rumpled and bleary-eyed, thinking maybe Elizabeth was right about drinking. He would be careful and not overdo in the future, he told himself emphatically. He poured and drank a glass of water, trying to wash the stale cotton dryness out of his mouth.

He then poured a basin of water and attempted to wash the puffy-eyed fatigue from his face. He straightened his clothing, trying to look as orderly as possible before loading himself in the buggy for the stop at Bucknertown and the trip home.

John Buckner was a warm, soft-spoken, but direct businessman. Arleto came along and helped translate both sides of the conversation. Very shortly after, Buckner wrote up a simple lease that Frederick signed as he gave him a deposit. Frederick was relieved that the monthly payment seemed manageable, and that Buckner seemed content with the agreement. He committed to a year in the home, knowing they would likely be there longer as they tried to build a home and a life in this new city.

He shook hands with John Buckner, and as he walked back to the buggy, Arleto suddenly grabbed him, gave him an overly tight, back-slapping hug, as he exclaimed loudly, "We shall be neighbors, Frederick Garraux. Neighbors and friends! Get your family and hurry back. My new neighbor. My new friend!"

Frederick could not help but laugh at the young man's enthusiastic welcome. He imagined Arleto's personality came from the openness that would be typical of his Italian mother, since he seemed to have little of the reserve common among the Swiss and Germans.

"I will be back soon, my friend, and I will bring my family with me," Frederick said sincerely in German. He added in carefully articulated English, "Thank you for the help."

The return trip back to Flat Rock was graciously easy. Along the way, Frederick found his head pounding and his stomach growling, He was glad for an uncomplicated journey and a pleasant room waiting in the Farmers Inn. He had been starving all day, so he had a hearty and welcome dinner at the inn before falling deeply asleep not long after sunset.

He awoke the next morning feeling considerably better, filled with excitement over telling his family all about their new city, their new home, and all the people he had met. Elizabeth was already excited about the move, and he knew she would be pleased with all he had learned about Greenville. The children were ready for change, and the older ones ready for the new opportunities and friends a relocation would provide them.

Frederick was able to stay on the schedule they had planned. Anticipating his return home, the children spent much of the day lingering near the split in the road on the way to the Fisher property, each hoping to be the first to spot their father in Hatch's buggy.

As he made the final turn off the main road, he could hear Earnest shouting, "He's here. He's here. Father is here!"

The shouts echoed up the length of the roadway all the way to the house, child to child like a bucket brigade. Each of them then ran down the drive to meet the buggy. Mary, who was the last, closest to the house shouted, "Mama! He is back. Father is here!"

Elizabeth dried her hands, smoothed back her hair, and shook her skirts loose, as she rushed to the porch. She hoped to see a smile on her handsome husband's face and prayed he would be carrying good news about their new home.

The children ran alongside the buggy and then clamored around him, their questions filling the air.

"What was it like, Father? Is it a nice city?"

"Did you find us a new house?"

"Are there stores with pretty dresses?"

"What are the people like?"

"Did you see a school we can go to?"

"Is there land for farming? Can we buy our own farm?"

Frederick climbed down from the buggy, and said, "It is a good place, children. Yes, I have found us a house. I will answer all your questions after I talk to your mother."

He looked up at Elizabeth, her intense and hopeful gaze bringing a smile to his face that instantly put one on hers.

They talked long into the evening, letting the younger children stay up for hours past their bedtimes. When he and Elizabeth finally lay down in their bed, she said, "It is all such good news, Frederick. I so look forward to starting our lives over in a new place where we can make our own way and build our own home."

They both lay awake for some time, each lost in their own thoughts of what was next for the family. They could not hear the children's whispered conversations. They were so overwhelmed by the excitement of moving to a new place that their parents were asleep before most of them closed their eyes.

The next several days were a blur of travel to Asheville to acquire a large, covered wagon and a two-horse team, and to make arrangements for the transport a bit later of several large pieces of furniture by a company who handled the Asheville to Greenville route.

They spent hours sorting and packing the family's goods and giving away to neighbors and friends those things that were impractical to move. It was no small task to fit most of their worldly possessions into the covered wagon and a smaller one that Fred and Earnest would take turns driving behind them. Just the idea of getting thirteen of them more than sixty miles through the mountains was daunting.

Jacob, still furious that they were leaving, avoided them as best he could, glaring at them from a distance during any incidental contact. Elizabeth waited for Jacob to load up his wagon and leave one morning, and she went over to the Fisher home. She took Greta a lap quilt she had been working on for the last several weeks.

Greta, seeing her hold out the quilt, once again burst into tears.

"Oh, Elizabeth, I am so very sad to see you go," she said, while trying to compose herself.

"You have been a good friend to me," she sniffled. "I will miss you and your beautiful children. But I am glad you will make a life of your own. You both work so hard and should have your own land. I know you will find great success for your family."

She thanked Elizabeth for the quilt, acknowledging that another cold winter was on the way. Then she teared up again, saying, "It will be so quiet and lonely here without all of you."

Elizabeth took her hand and, looking hard into her eyes, said, "Greta, you do not have to be alone here. We will be a short journey away. You could take the stagecoach and come and stay with us. You will always be welcome."

For just the briefest moment, a glimmer of hope passed over Greta's face. But immediately, her expression darkened to that of a sad, resolute prisoner.

"That is very kind of you. I will always remember that offer," she said with staunch resignation.

In that one statement, Elizabeth knew once they departed Bent Creek, she would never see Greta again. It saddened her to think of the poor woman, trapped in another cold winter with her equally frigid and distant husband.

She gave Greta a gentle hug and a knowing squeeze of the hand before returning to the wildly gleeful house full of children about to start off on their new adventure.

PART TWO

Chapter 1

The whole community gathered to say goodbye to the big Swiss family that they were very fond of. The men helped move and load beds, chairs, disassembled tables, and they loaded Frederick's tools into the wagons. They tried to leave space for two adults, four teenagers, five children, a toddler, and a lap-held baby, but it was proving to be difficult. A few pieces of furniture Frederick and Elizabeth had thought they could take ended up being left behind for the transport company to handle.

Several women in the community had made food for those helping with the move, as well as to sustain the family through the next few days. Once again, as they had been over the years in Bent Creek, the Garrauxs were impressed with the kindness and generosity of their neighbors.

In the last hour, as they prepared to load themselves into the wagons, a familiar voice called out, "Hey, little Mama, you can't go without saying goodbye to me!" It was Aunt Hattie.

As always, Hattie felt especially connected to the women she helped give birth, and to the babies she helped deliver. She always referred to the family as "the children and my babies, Charlie, Willie, and Fannie."

Hattie had a special affinity for tiny Fannie, who at a few months old was still smaller than some newborns she had delivered. She loved that little baby, and Fannie delighted her with excessive smiles and cooing when she saw her.

"I know where you will be," Hattie said to Elizabeth, "And one day I just might come see you."

She held and hugged and kissed her three babies, patted and tousled the hair of some of the others, shook hands with the teens, showing them the same respect she would adults, and then she turned back to Elizabeth.

She was used to Fred, who was standing next to his mother, acting as an interpreter.

"You tell your mama I said she is one of the strongest, toughest little women I ever met. And you tell her I pray God's blessings on all of you. And you tell your daddy he better take good care of his wife, because she's something special."

Elizabeth smiled as Fred translated, looking slightly embarrassed by Hattie's effusive praise.

"Thank you, Aunt Hattie," she said in clear, practiced English. "Thank you for everything."

Colonel Hatch traveled over from the mill with a few of the workers, bringing with him a leather tool roll, that when opened, revealed a set of brand new finely crafted carving tools.

"These are for you, Frederick. You are an artist," he said, with a slight nod in respect of Frederick's work. "Goodbye and God's speed," Hatch said, stepping back, with a bow, still conveying the air of a military officer.

Frederick thanked him and shook hands with the mill workers and several of the other men in the crowd, thanking them for help with the move and their support through the years.

Jacob stayed off behind the barn, glowering in the direction of the crowd of people who waved and shouted well wishes as the two wagons began to pull away. His fury greatly increased when he saw Greta burst out of the house and run up to the covered wagon, reaching up to Elizabeth who was in the front seat.

"I baked this butterzopf for your trip," she said, as she handed her a bundle containing two beautiful loaves of Swiss braided bread and a jar of strawberry jam. "I will never forget you," Greta said. She felt Jacob's glare, but for the moment, she did not care.

"Auf Wiedersehen und Gottes segen," she said.

"Goodbye and God bless you, too," Elizabeth said back to her, but in English.

Then with a slap of the reins on the two big draft horses, they were on the road to their new home.

The weather was brisk, but they felt fortunate to be making the trip before winter set in. The trees in Bent Creek were nearly bare of leaves, but as they headed to lower elevation, there were more glimpses of colorful fall foliage.

Frederick had been so focused on his mission and getting to Greenville and then surviving a throbbing headache on the return trip, he had hardly noticed the beauty around him. Now, as Elizabeth pointed out crimson oaks and bright orange maples in dazzling contrast against the bright blue October sky, he realized how much he had missed.

They had talked about sleeping in a combination of tents and in and under the wagon that night, but agreed that for one night they would stay in the Flat Rock Hotel Frederick had found so agreeable.

Despite the lumbering, jerking, pounding, uncomfortable several-hour ride in the stiff-wheeled wagon, they made it through the day in good spirits. Trying to save where they could, they skipped the restaurant and made a meal of sausages, cheese, apples, milk, and bread that Greta and their neighbors had given them.

The older boys shared a bed, and seven-year-old Frank and five-year-old John slept end-to-end on a cot the innkeeper had graciously added to the small room.

Lucy and Mary were in a larger room where they shared their bed with two-year-old Willie. Bettie and Rosa slept end to end on a chaise lounge in that room.

The baby, Fannie, slept between Frederick and Elizabeth, and four-year-old Charlie slept against his mother's back.

The innkeeper, who was a ruddy-complexioned, rotund man, marveled that the big family could be accommodated in just three rooms. He laughed and said he was so large his wife could barely share his bed.

The children were accustomed to shared beds, and Elizabeth and Frederick frequently let Fannie sleep in their bed with them. Adding Charlie proved to be more of a challenge. With their sore joints from the wagon ride and Charlie's regular flailing in his sleep, their night was anything but restful.

Each time Elizabeth and Frederick were awakened, their minds would go racing toward their new home and all they would need to accomplish before winter. Thankfully, they had been very careful to save in every way possible, from making their own clothes, shoes, and furnishings, to holding on to some of the money they brought with them from Switzerland. In the quiet darkness of the sleepless night, both of them pondered all the ways they could invest in their future and build the life they had dreamed of. It was, for both, an exciting, hopeful, terrifying time.

After a fitful night and an early wake-up by excited children, the family gathered back up for a quick, simple breakfast before Frederick and the boys hitched up the wagons and they loaded up for the trip to their new

197

home. The children were beside themselves with excitement, and Elizabeth and Frederick found their enthusiasm both contagious and exhausting.

The children chattered endlessly and took turns running alongside the wagon. They would dash off to scare an occasional jackrabbit in the brush along the road, or to gather up bouquets of brightly colored fall leaves. At times, they would stop and stoop over to examine and collect particularly interesting rocks, and then they'd have to run at top speed to catch up with the wagons as they plodded forward.

Eventually, the youngest children fell asleep as the wagons bumped and thumped along the highway through the foothills. Frederick was so weary he turned the reins over to Elizabeth and climbed into the back of the wagon, clamoring over household goods and around children until he found a nook where he could lean back and close his eyes.

Before he dozed off, he looked forward at the silhouette of his tiny wife as she pulled and hauled on the reins, directing the big horses down the sloping road. He really believed there was nothing she couldn't do. Just as his mind drifted into exhausted sleep, he had the fleeting thought of wishing he had as much confidence in himself.

After Frederick's brief respite, they found themselves just hours away from Greenville, and they began to see more people passing by, and the farms becoming somewhat closer together. Elizabeth talked with the children, telling them what would be expected of them when they arrived at their new home. She knew their temptation would be to investigate their new surroundings, and not deal with the enormous amount of unpacking and moving that would have to happen before sundown.

Once they turned off the main highway and headed toward Bucknertown, the children grew quieter, suddenly confronted with the reality of an entirely new life in a completely strange place.

When they turned onto the street, Frederick said, "This is Buckner Street.

Ahead, on the right is our new home, the tall white one with the porch. It will be our home until we build our own on our own farm. We should all thank God for it."

As they pulled up the wagons in front of the house, several neighborhood children who had been watching them plod up the street scooted closer and began to peer curiously at them from behind nearby trees and around the corner of a neighbor's house. As Frederick and Elizabeth climbed stiffly down from the wagon and their children jumped and clamored down, one of the bolder boys ran up to them and said, "Are you the new family from Swissland?"

Frederick smiled at the lanky, dark-skinned boy, and said, showing off the language he was working to master, "Yes. We from Switzerland. We are Garraux family. We move to Greenville. We will now live in Greenville."

The Garraux children, who had frozen like statues when the teenaged boy approached them, immediately warmed to their surroundings, waving and smiling shyly at the gang of neighborhood children who stepped out from their observation posts.

As was typical of Elizabeth, she reined them in as they appeared to be ready to run off with the half dozen children of varying ages who had swarmed into the area.

In German, she instructed them in no uncertain terms that they were to unload the wagons. She said playing with the new children would wait until they were settled. She often heard herself sounding like a military officer as she barked commands at her children, but with the number of them and the ages they spanned, she felt she had no choice. There was always so much to do, and they had too much to accomplish for games and playing to take over. There would be time for fun when they were settled in this new home.

Some of the neighborhood children lingered, watching as furnishings and goods began to be unloaded and hauled into the house, while others ran back to their homes and yards with a "See you later." In short order, several neighbors appeared, offering a hand with the larger items, which Frederick gratefully accepted.

John Buckner's thirty-five-year-old son, named after him, came over to the Garraux house with his wife, Mariah. She brought along a freshly baked pie and warmly greeted Elizabeth, who was unloading pots and pans in the kitchen.

Mariah patiently and slowly explained that her father-in-law had told his family and others in the neighborhood about the big Swiss family who was moving in. The conversation was limited because of the existing language barrier, but Mariah was clearly a kind and welcoming person. Her husband, John, had immediately joined in with the other neighbor men who were helping with the move, making the unloading go very quickly.

John and Mariah lived just a few houses away, next door to her in-laws. Most of the neighbors who showed up to help were black, since most of Bucknertown's residents were, including Porter Smith, the first contact they had made in the city through Aunt Hattie.

The Garrauxs' new next-door neighbor, James Harrison, the rare white man to live in Bucknertown, also came over and introduced himself and helped finish the unloading. He commented several times on the quality of the furniture, and he went out of his way to tell Frederick how impressed he was after learning he had made the pieces.

Just as the last items were hauled out of the wagons, Arleto came rushing down the street shouting, "Frederick, Frederick! My friend, Frederick!"

He hugged Frederick, and enthusiastically shook the hands of the older boys and the men who were helping, while apologizing for not coming by in time to help. Frederick was relieved to have a German-speaking friend on hand to smooth over the conversations he was attempting to have.

Arleto clearly liked to talk about the neighbors. He told Frederick that his new next-door neighbor, James Harrison, was a thirty-year-old shoemaker, with a young wife and a baby. In his typically candid fashion, Arleto said, "You saw the Harrisons are one of the other white families in Bucknertown. There aren't many, but as you see, that is of no matter."

He went on to say, "Most of the people who live in Bucknertown are tradespeople. Buckner's namesake son, John, is a painter. His daughter is married to a carpenter. Even many of the women have trades. His daughter-in-law, Mariah, is a dressmaker.

"Become friends with your neighbors, and you will have shoes to wear and pretty dresses for your wife and daughters," Arleto said, followed by his booming laugh.

Frederick went back to moving goods and furniture into various rooms in the house, and Arleto pitched in along with the other men, who continued to work steadily, all of them diligent and pleasant. By nightfall, the wagons were empty, most of the furniture was in appropriate rooms, the beds were assembled and made up with fresh linens, and the children were chattering with new friends.

As they had been in North Carolina, Frederick and Elizabeth were amazed at and grateful for the acceptance and kindness of Americans. Just these several short years after a war that had torn the country apart, they found themselves in a neighborhood mostly made up of those who had once been slaves. And yet they were welcomed into this small community and made immediately to feel as though they belonged.

After all the children were settled into their new rooms, Elizabeth set the beautiful inlaid wooden box Frederick had given her on their bedroom dresser. She had carried it with her ever since he gave it to her while they were courting back in Bern. She ran her hand over the smooth, intricately inlaid surface, thinking of all that had happened in their lives since her handsome, dark-eyed husband has presented it to her.

"I think this a good place, Frederick," she said quietly. "I think we can make a good life here."

They climbed into their familiar bed with the oak headboard Frederick had built and carved, and they cuddled under the beautiful quilt she had started stitching in Bern and finished in North Carolina.

"We will make a good life here, Elizabeth. I am glad you were willing to make the move."

Despite the strange surroundings, they both fell asleep quickly. They were weighed down by exhaustion but comforted by the hope of beginning a new life. When the sun rose the next morning, they threw themselves into creating their new life in this new place with intensity and determination.

That intensity would serve one of them well but would leave the other's life in ruins.

Chapter 2

Frederick immediately threw himself into setting up his cabinet- and furniture-making equipment in the outbuilding behind the house. By the time the children woke up, he had nearly finished setting up his workshop. He felt driven to work quickly, since they had savings that would get them by in the short term, but their success in this new place hinged on his furniture and cabinet making.

His next-door neighbor, James Harrison, had admired the furniture he helped carry into the house. James was a quiet, ruddy-complexioned young man, with bright-blue eyes, sandy blond hair, and a ready smile.

James's son was about a year old, and he was outgrowing his crib, so James asked Frederick if he would make a child's bed for him.

"I'll pay you fairly," James said. "This is not a favor. I have seen your work, and I know it is your livelihood."

Frederick was pleased to think he had been in Greenville less than twenty-four hours before he had his first furniture order.

He and Elizabeth loaded the children into the smaller wagon, and he took them on a tour of their new city, showing them the highlights of what Arleto had pointed out, and recounting some of the many tales he had shared.

The fall weather was beautiful, and the city was lively and cheerful and felt welcoming to the family. The children peppered them with questions along the way, as they excitedly pointed out businesses and landmarks and impressive homes. They were all especially thrilled to see the waterfall in the middle of the city.

In short order, their lives fell into the organized rhythm needed to keep the chaos of a household of thirteen manageable. They enrolled the older boys in a small school that was within walking distance, and the girls continued learning to read and speak in English at home, along with their parents.

The children all made friends in the neighborhood, and the older boys also formed friendships at school. Fred, a self-assured seventeen-year-old, was now about the same height as his father. Within his first several months in Greenville, Fred fell in and out of love at least two or three times. Earnest, less than a year younger than Fred but about as tall, was almost like Fred's shadow—always near, but quiet, as though trying to be less noticeable.

Elizabeth schooled her daughters in needlecrafts and kitchen skills. Of the older girls, fifteen-year-old Lucy and fourteen-year-old Mary were willing to stay at home and enjoyed just being with their mother. Bettie, though not yet a teenager, was, like Elizabeth, always thinking of and talking about the next possible opportunity. Bettie was extremely close to Rosa, and the two of them spent virtually all of their free time together.

The younger children thrived in their new environment, and as each month passed, the youngest became easier to manage while the oldest became more self-sufficient and helpful.

Elizabeth quickly became known in the neighborhood for her good cooking. The tantalizing odors of freshly baked bread and meats cooked slowly in vinegar, brown sugar, and spices wafted from the home all through the chilly winter months. The bouquet was similar to that of the smoked pork common in the Carolinas, but the other spicy scents led to requests from the neighbors for recipes and tastings.

Elizabeth was also especially known for the chocolatier skills she had learned through generations of shared tradition in her homeland. At Christmas time, the Buckners, Harrisons, and Brunges, among others, were treated to beautifully crafted candies from Elizabeth's kitchen. Arleto may have been the first to suggest that she should find a way to turn her talents into a business, a seed that would one day germinate into a life-changer for her and her family.

Community connections and word of mouth also led to success for Frederick. He met and befriended Christian Hahn, the German cabinet maker, and his brother, Frank, who was the blind saloon owner. Christian referred several people to Frederick, since many people requested more ornate furnishings than he cared to be bothered with since he was now in his sixties. Fortunately for Frederick, that type of work had become his specialty.

Christian's ongoing friendship and referrals were pivotal to Frederick's cabinet-making success in Greenville. But it was his friendship with Christian's brother Frank, the blind bar owner, that would have the longest lasting effects on the family, both positive and negative.

In early spring, Christian arranged for Frederick to meet with George Heldman, one of Greenville's earliest German settlers who had found great success in the city.

Heldman, who had immigrated almost twenty years before the Civil War, was a prominent and respected businessman. He ran his harness and saddlery shop out of a handsome brick building on Main Street that also housed the residence he shared with his wife, Matilda, and their eleven-year-old daughter named Fannie, like the Garrauxs' youngest. Heldman was an imposing figure, with thick salt-and-pepper hair and beard, piercing blue eyes and a broad smile. Matilda was a delicate and graceful woman, who had passed on her good looks to their young daughter.

After seeing samples of Frederick's work, Heldman ordered several pieces for his showroom and for their home. He had great admiration for craftsmanship, but also a soft spot in his heart for those born in his homeland.

Besides being a respected business owner, Heldman, who was in his fifties, was an enthusiastic gardener. Since their move to Greenville, Elizabeth had been impressed with the extensive and luxurious flower gardens she had seen surrounding Heldman's home on Main Street in the center of town.

When she learned that Frederick was crafting furnishings for him, she insisted he introduce her to Heldman.

George Heldman was an affable man with a large personality and an unrelenting enthusiasm for life. His tidy beard, dark brown eyes and strong bone structure gave his appearance a sternness that completely disappeared when he began to speak. His engagement with the world around him and his insatiable curiosity made him a great conversationalist and a popular businessman.

He took an immediate liking to Elizabeth, and he was impressed with her knowledge of gardening. He spent a great deal of time showing her the extensive varieties he was growing on his large lot. He even gave her starter cuttings from several plants that she was excited to take home to root, picturing them one day growing on the property she hoped they would own.

Heldman also owned 160 acres outside of town on Paris Mountain, where he grew apples, pears, and other fruits, and, of greatest interest to the Garrauxs, he was also growing grapes.

The Garrauxs formed a warm relationship with the Heldmans, though

206

Frederick's connection was far more of a business relationship than the friendship that immediately formed between Elizabeth and George. The Heldman's daughter, Fannie, was close in age to Bettie and Rosa, who would often accompany Elizabeth when she visited Heldman's gardens.

Frederick soon had more furniture orders than he could handle, and he sometimes had to tell people they would have to wait for weeks or even months for the special pieces they wanted.

Elizabeth also put effort into planting a sizeable flower garden at their Bucknertown home that would produce bouquets of flowers all summer and into the fall. With the help of her daughters, she grew all she could fit in the small yard, utilizing the many seeds and cuttings George Heldman had shared with her, as well as seeds she had harvested from her garden in North Carolina. Soon neighbors were purchasing bouquets and arrangements for special occasions and graveside memorials.

Elizabeth's small successes just increased her desire for what she and Frederick had always wanted. At the end of their first year in Greenville, she said, "Frederick, it is time we should start seriously looking into buying land.

"We must have land of our own," she said. "We need to build our home and start our farm. We are fortunate to have a place to live while we do, but we must establish our own life here and build a legacy for the children."

Frederick agreed and said they could go over their savings and earnings ledgers, and he was sure they would be able to buy a decent piece of land to get started. He secretly hoped he could put her off for a bit. He told himself that he would stop spending any of his earnings in Frank Hahn's saloon or the couple of others he had come to enjoy in the town. If he could just set aside the full amount from the next few pieces of furniture, Elizabeth wouldn't notice any deficit. After all, he felt he worked so hard to take care of her and his large family that his occasional afternoon meetings with furniture clients and friends were really none of her concern. And really, he didn't spend all that much on his bit of well-deserved afternoon drinking, he told himself emphatically.

"I think there are many opportunities here, Frederick. We can grow grapes for sale and to make wine. I can have a floral business if I have enough growing space. With all the stores and businesses in this town, there is no winemaker and no florist. And there will be other opportunities for the children. We just need to buy our land and get started."

"Yes, we will. We will buy land. We will figure out the finances and choose land to purchase soon," Frederick said, his stomach now churning because he knew their savings would be less than she expected. Elizabeth was so much in charge of the household that she also kept close tabs on what projects he was completing. If he could just put her off for a couple months, everything would be fine, he thought. But it did not calm the queasiness in his stomach.

A few months later, the chill of winter once again settled in, the flower garden withered and died, and Frederick struggled to continue his furniture building in the unheated outbuilding. Just outside the building, he would build a small fire using his wood scraps in a small fire pit, and he would squat there to thaw his fingers. The flask of Irish whiskey he kept in his wood bin and the occasional bottle of red wine he stored between the joists of the rickety building also helped him keep the chill away. He made sure to always chew a piece of spruce tree gum before going into the house so Elizabeth wouldn't nag at him about it.

As he worked his lathe turning legs for an expensive display table he was making for Heldman's shop, his mind was grinding on a conversation he had with Frank Hahn as he sat in the saloon the day before.

Hahn owned several acres of the hilly area north of town that Frederick admired. Hahn had thought he might one day have a farm or a vineyard there, but he was realizing that was unlikely, since the saloon supported his family well. He said he wanted to start selling the land off, and he knew Frederick was interested in property.

After the children were quiet and in their rooms reading, studying, or playing, Frederick told Elizabeth about the opportunity to buy five acres of Hahn's property. It was like setting a match to a kerosene lantern. She dashed to grab their ledger books and the metal boxes in which they kept their earnings.

Elizabeth's eyes, as they often did, took on the intensity of a bird of prey. She scanned the pages of their records, quickly scribbling notes on a pad, stopping to count out stacks of bills and making small piles of notes, orders, and receipts. He could do nothing but watch. She had the business acumen of a trained bookkeeper, and her mathematical skills greatly exceeded his. He kept records, as much as he felt he needed to, but he always thought he should focus on his skill as a craftsman, not on ledgers and paperwork.

She moved piles and made notes and counted bills, her eyes darting back and forth with an increasing intensity that made him wish he was sitting in a cheerful bar behind a stiff drink. She sighed—flustered—and muttered, and occasionally shot a glance at him, in a way he thought looked accusatory.

"I am not much of a record keeper, Elizabeth," he said. "You know I have never been good at it."

Elizabeth was well aware that by this time a majority of Greenville's wealthiest homeowners had pieces of furniture and cabinetry crafted by Frederick.

"Nothing about this adds up, Frederick. There are too many orders and too many receipts and not enough profit here. The household money is separate from this. This is our savings. This is our future," she snapped. "Where is all the money?"

His stomach turned and his face flushed. He tried to gather himself up, and said, "There's enough there to afford the five acres, and to begin the house and farm. I don't know why you are acting like I have done something wrong."

"It is your drinking again, isn't it?" Elizabeth said. "You think I don't know about the hours you spend at Hahn's saloon and the other bars? You think I don't smell the liquor on your breath? You think I don't see you stumble? You think I don't see you falling asleep when you should be working?"

Her anger spewed out like a broken water pipe with nothing to stop the flow.

"I am not stupid, Frederick. I keep thinking that you are a grown man and a husband and father, and you will stop your foolish behavior without me having to act like your mother. But I am mistaken. You cannot be trusted!"

Frederick abruptly stood up, leaned over on the table, and said through his gritted teeth, "What's that supposed to mean? I 'can't be trusted?' I am a fully committed husband. I have never looked at another woman. I am a devoted father. Even with all the children we have, I still take care of all of them. I take care of you, Elizabeth. I take care of you, and you dare to say I cannot be trusted?"

She glared at him and said, "I do not wish to talk about you and your irresponsibility anymore. You told me this would not happen again. That was not true, and that means you cannot be trusted. We have enough saved to buy Frank Hahn's property. It will be bought in my name, not yours. It will be Elizabeth Garraux's property. And maybe we will make it a success together—if you can decide that making something of yourself is more important than being a drunk."

Frederick's mind was reeling. He felt like a child being reprimanded by a parent, and he did not like the feeling.

"I don't want to talk with you anymore either," he snapped. "I am going to bed."

Lying in bed staring at the ceiling, he was a combination of angry, humiliated, and hurt. He tried so hard to stay on top of all he needed to for this overwhelming family and this wife with her high expectations and demands. He did not like being chastised.

A very long and restless time later, he felt Elizabeth slide into the bed. He did not speak to her, nor she to him. The next day, their conversations were strained and clipped, so much so that Lucy asked her mother what was wrong.

"Nothing is wrong," Elizabeth said, throwing a stern you-better-say-nothing glare at Frederick. "We are doing important business that we will tell you all about once it is settled. It is good news. It's just a lot of serious business."

With that said, Frederick knew she had made up her mind and there was no stopping her. A week later, in the office of a downtown Greenville attorney, Elizabeth signed a purchase agreement that put five acres of Frank Hahn's hilly property in her name. They went through the motions of celebrating the purchase and giving the children the exciting news, all while both of them knowing, for better or worse, their lives would never be the same from this point forward.

Chapter 3

The property was located across a couple of streams and up a long sloping hill about a quarter mile north of Bucknertown. It was north of where the Main Street ended, about a mile and a half from the courthouse in the center of the downtown.

As soon as the weather began to warm and the early spring rains let up a bit, Frederick and Elizabeth began to work at clearing the land. There was minimal tree growth, which was helpful, but the rockiness that was apparent when they purchased the property was nearly overwhelming as they tried to clear areas where plants could take root.

It meant digging and hauling rocks that would then be used to create stone walls for tiers to hold the soil against the sloped land. The larger rocks and boulders had to be leveraged with pry bars and rolled into place in the stone walls. It was grueling work. Frederick, still working to prove his soberness and worth to his perfectionist wife, took on the task of the wall building with an exhausting intensity.

Whenever he wasn't building furniture, he was at the property, digging, hauling, sweating, and cursing the hundreds of rocks that waited, un-yielding, just below the surface.

One day while he was working in the heavy, humid heat of the South Carolina summer, two men passed by on horseback. They stopped for a moment, watching him struggle against a large boulder, and one called out, "You don't actually think you're going to farm this rock pile, do you? The men laughed loudly and continued on their way, talking about the crazy immigrant and his rock quarry.

Their taunting, along with the questions and often critical comments from others in the town made Frederick even more determined. And for her part, Elizabeth, often with the younger children in tow, spent hours following behind him, tilling, raking, and smoothing this land that she was also determined would provide their livelihood.

The first year of owning the property was a blur of rocks, sweat, exhaus-tion, crushed knuckles, and frustration, but they would soon be ready to begin planting, and starting construction on a home of their own.

As the months passed and Frederick spent less time in downtown saloons and more time working, Elizabeth's attitude toward him softened. She dearly loved her somber-eyed, hardworking, talented husband and she was gratified to see him seem to get past the excessive drinking and wast-ing of money she would never accept as a part of life.

For his part, Frederick often felt overworked and under-appreciated. But then he would occasionally stop working to stand up straight and stretch out the cramps in his lower back, He would look across the property, and invariably see his tiny wife a short distance away, digging, tilling, work-ing as hard as many men, all while looking as clean, pressed, and tidy as a schoolmarm sitting behind a desk. He remained in awe of her energy and drive, and her ability to manage their large brood of children, their household, and everything else she did with such aplomb. Elizabeth was unstoppable, and though he felt less of the romantic love he once felt, he very much respected and admired her. And in some deep, seldom acknowledged corner of his heart, he rather feared her. Her standards and intensity were hard to match. No matter what he did, he feared it might not be enough. Not for her, or for himself.

Frederick had also framed-in the structure that would be the first phase of their new home, and they had a few acres cleared and ready to plant. One afternoon, as Elizabeth worked transplanting some shrubs and flowers from their Buckner Street house while Frederick hammered shingles onto the roof of the small house, they were stopped by someone shouting "Elizabeth, Frederick, hulloh!"

It was George and Matilda Heldman and Fannie in a buckboard wagon pulled by two sleek black horses. The Heldmans usually traveled in a fancy phaeton carriage with a driver, so they were surprised to see George driving a buckboard himself, especially on the bumpy narrow path to their property that barely qualified as a road. The more navigable main street through the town ended a few hundred yards south of where they were working.

"Hulloh," George called again, as his wife and daughter smiled and waved. Mary, Bettie, Rosa, and Lucy, who had been sitting under a nearby tree playing together and tending the youngest children, gathered the young ones up and rushed toward the wagon. Frederick and Elizabeth hurried to the wagon as well, as Fannie clamored down to join the other children.

George explained to Frederick and Elizabeth that he wanted to help them get a head start, so he had brought them some root stock from his vineyard up on Paris Mountain, He said he wished to present the root stock as a gift.

Frederick could hardly believe his eyes. He had planned a trip several hours away to Aiken in the middle of the state to buy starter stock from the grape growers down there. Now, George motioned him over to the wagon, where he showed him dozens of pots containing roots to start grape vines.

"Oh my, this is too much, George," Frederick said. You are too generous."

"I am happy to share my bounty," George said. "Others have helped me along the way. Now, I get to help you."

Then he reached into the wagon and pulled out a pot with a gnarly stump in it.

"This is for you, Elizabeth," he said. "You remember how you told me about the pergola at your home in Bern, and how you loved the vine that grew on it?"

"Yes, I did love those vines," Elizabeth said.

"Well, you know the beautiful wisteria vine you admired on our property?"

She nodded yes. She loved the beautiful lavender blooms, shaped like large bunches of grapes, that hung down from the long vines in early spring.

Handing her the pot, George said, "This is a wisteria vine, just like mine, for you to grow on your new property. It was imported all the way from China. Mind you, it grows very quickly, and it must be tended to keep it under control, like some men." He chuckled, smiling at his wife, Matilda.

The children ran around, giggling and teasing each other and playing tag. George and Matilda smiled lovingly at the sight of their beautiful only child laughing and playing in the sun. They could not have known at the time that one day newspapers would report the amazingly long life of the wisteria vine, and the tragically short life of their daughter.

Despite the lovely gifts and an afternoon spent in pleasant conversation while the children played together, Frederick held onto George's remark about some men needing to be kept under control. He interpreted it as a reference to Elizabeth's hardline nagging about his drinking. When he questioned Elizabeth, she assured him she never discussed their personal life or issues with George. Frederick was not sure he believed her.

Despite George being nearly a decade older than Elizabeth and happily married, Frederick regularly felt jealous of his wife's time spent looking at and talking about flowers with him. George was wealthy, charming, and impeccably groomed, a well-respected businessman and popular Greenville resident. Though he had no reason to distrust either of them, Frederick often felt uncomfortable about their friendship.

At the end of the visit, they both thanked Heldman profusely for his generosity. Elizabeth decided to set the potted wisteria aside to plant after the house was more complete, so the next week became an intense time focused solely on the grape vines. Frederick and Elizabeth dug and tilled and planted dozens of pots of root stock. They would later add dozens more from Frederick's trip to the center of the state. They planted Concord, Clinton, Ives and Catawba grapes, some varietals with which they had some experience in North Carolina, and others that were entirely new to them.

All together, they planted an acre and a half of vines that would one day help make a name and an impressive reputation for the family. At least in the beginning.

Along with the grapes, Elizabeth also began planting seeds and transplanting a huge flower garden. People often talked about her green thumb and her gift for growing things. She would take the compliments humbly, but like any successful gardener, she attributed her success to learning as much as she could about the habits and preferences of the plants she grew, the hard work she invested in preparing the soil and fighting the weeds, and most of all, to unwavering patience.

If there is anyone who knows how to live with hope and patience, it is a gardener, she believed.

With the small, three-room house completed, they began to spend more time at the property, though it was too small for all of them to stay overnight. After the winter of 1878 chilled flower gardens into dormancy and the leaves of the grapevines withered and browned, Frederick and Eliza-

216

beth carefully trimmed the vines, knowing the next summer would be the first that would bring harvestable fruit.

Frederick focused almost solely on furniture building that winter. Elizabeth carried on her usual tasks. The six oldest children were young adults, ranging from sixteen to twenty-four. The youngest four were eight to twelve years old, and the middle two teenage girls vacillated from acting like children to trying too hard to be adults.

Elizabeth spent her time dealing with the youngest children, cooking, baking, sewing, and cleaning, though, by this time, the older children carried out much of the work of the household.

She continued to be the family bookkeeper, and her math and language skills were developing quickly. The family subscribed to the local newspaper, and she would labor over it with the assistance of the older children, and her reading and writing skills improved dramatically during the quieter winter months.

Fred, the oldest son, had finished school, and he spent his time working with both his father and Christian Hahn learning carpentry and cabinet and furniture making. Fred was articulate, accomplished, and self-assured. He had little to no interest in farming of any kind, and he had made that clear. He had been anxious to be on his own for at least the last three years and he began to frequently mention moving out and starting his own life, much to his mother's distress and his father's pleasure.

"I don't need to be taking up space when you try to move to the new house," Fred said. "It's time that the money I make goes to my own life and home. I am twenty-four years old. I want my own space to do with as I please."

Elizabeth knew part of "doing what he pleased" would be entertaining young women. Fred had remained as girl crazy as he had been as a schoolboy. She worried all the time about the trouble it could get him into. Little did she know how right she was to worry.

Frederick, who had felt somewhat smothered by his own mother as a teen, encouraged the children to move into independent adulthood, and as far as he was concerned, it should be as soon as possible. He constantly encouraged both his daughters and sons to figure out how to make their way in the world. Lucy was interested in nursing, and he pushed her to pursue that, helping arrange for her to learn from the wife of a customer of his. The older boys expressed interest in carpentry, machines, and business, and though he wished they had interest in grape growing and developing a wine business, he encouraged them to develop their own interests.

It became a point of contention between Elizabeth and him. She saw her adult children as allies and supporters of the many business opportunities she was constantly developing in her head.

"Maybe they want to have their own lives, Elizabeth," Frederick said one night, as she bemoaned Fred's likely departure from the homestead. "Maybe you should encourage them to move on and find their own way instead of trying to make them future business partners."

Elizabeth, who had her back turned to him as she wiped dinner dishes dry, whirled around and said, "Do you know how many young people are taken advantage of these days? Do you know how badly this world can treat people? If we are in business together, they will be treated fairly and well. They can have their own lives without having to leave their family behind."

"You know you would not be able to stay out of their business, Elizabeth. You know that you think you always know best—not just for yourself, but everyone else," he said, more harshly than he had actually intended.

All the peace and pleasantries of the last few years seemed to burst like a bubble in front of her eyes. Hurt and angry, she blurted out, "If you don't like it, why don't you just go back to your great life sitting in Hahn's bar? Why don't you just leave?"

Glaring at her, Frederick stood up so abruptly; the kitchen chair fell backward, slamming loudly to the floor.

"I will leave. Yes, I will leave," he said as he stormed toward the door. "I can talk to other people anywhere who are more respectful of me than you are."

With that, she heard him stomp through the house and out the front door, slamming it loudly behind him. Lucy, who was twenty-one, came rushing down the stairs, with her sister, Mary. Lucy was a compassionate, strong-minded young woman, generally the first to jump into action. Mary was a kind-hearted, simple girl, who responded to most situations as the loving little girl she had always been.

"Mama, what happened?" Lucy asked. Elizabeth smoothed back her hair and quickly wiped newly fallen tears away with the back of her hand. "What is wrong? We heard loud voices and the door slam."

The fallen chair lay on the floor between Elizabeth and her two daughters.

"It's nothing," Elizabeth said firmly. "Your father and I disagree about your brother moving out. He does not understand what a strong, financially stable life we can build if we all work together. Your father was an unhappy young man who wanted to escape his family, so he thinks everyone must want to. He doesn't understand that I just want to be sure to help you all have good lives. He has his own problems. He is . . ."

Her voice trailed off. She did not believe in cutting her husband down to his own children. It was always a temptation when they disagreed, but she would not do it.

"Oh, Mama, I am sorry," Lucy said, as she moved toward her, setting the chair upright as she passed. She and Mary were immediately at their mother's side, each hugging her supportively.

"Thank you, daughters," Elizabeth said. "It is all fine. You all shall have your own lives. And they will be good ones. And if you want to leave, you shall. And if you stay, we will all work together to make life good. Your father will figure things out. This is nothing. Go back to your sewing. This is not your concern."

She was moved by their empathy, but she sent them away, outwardly dismissing the incident as unimportant. And then she sat in a kitchen chair, stiffly immobile in the flickering light of the gas lantern. She sat perfectly still for hours, until the lamp oil ran out. She listened for any sound of footsteps or a door opening. She continued to sit there, ramrod straight, until dawn crept over the horizon, into the window, and across the table.

Elizabeth was afraid the children would wake up and find her downstairs, so she rushed up to the bedroom. There she sat on the edge of the empty, still made-up bed, as immobile and still as she had downstairs. Her ears strained to hear the sound of the front door opening. There was not a sound until the voices of her awakened children and the creaking of them coming down the stairs.

And for her, she knew, this was the beginning of the end for Frederick and her.

Chapter 4

Frederick had walked into Hahn's bar with barely a thought of where he was, storming along the street with angry, heavy strides. He yanked out a bar stool and slammed himself onto it, holding up two fingers in the direction of the bar keep. The bartender, with the dramatic name Napoleon Bonaparte Freeman, was a congenial thirty-two-year-old local. He went by Bonaparte, Bonny to his friends, and he knew Frederick and his drink preferences well.

"What's going on, Frederick?" he asked, as he set a double Irish whiskey in front of him. "You don't seem yourself. And this is late for you to come in."

Frederick didn't like to divulge his marriage issues, but he was so fed up with Elizabeth's judgmental attitude toward him and the constant spats that he blurted out, "Sometimes I wish I never married. And here I am, with a wife and eleven children. I just get so tired of it all."

Bonny had two young children and a cheerful, much younger wife, and he generally felt his life quite idyllic, so it was awkward to respond to

Frederick. Even though he was younger than Frederick, he had been bar-
tending for long enough to know what he needed to do was to just pour
and listen. And that he did. For hours.

Finally, it became clear that Frederick, who was vacillating between being
furious and weepy, was in no condition to go home. Bonny lived next
door to the Hahn brothers on College Street, so after he closed down
the saloon, he walked Frederick across town with him. Frederick was
in no condition to resist, so he stumbled along, agreeing that he would
stay with Christian Hahn. Christian had a large home and was generally
agreeable about sharing his sofa when needed. He also considered Frederick a friend.

After rousing a bleary-eyed, rumpled Christian from bed and explaining
the situation, the sixty-two-year-old welcomed Frederick into his parlor,
and he brought him a pillow, a blanket, a pitcher of water and a glass.
Frederick did his best to express gratitude with slurred words as the room
spun around him. Christian pulled the drapes closed, shut the doors, and
woke his sleeping wife to warn her of their unexpected guest.

The morning could only be described as awkward at best. Christian and
his wife, Mary, both still spoke German, though they had been in the
country since long before the War. The passion that took Frederick to the
bar was greatly moderated by his throbbing head and the overwhelming
regret he felt about having not gone home the night before. He minimized the crisis as he talked with the Hahns, mostly feeling humiliation
that he had intruded into their home like a pathetic drunk.

It was still early when he walked through the more sophisticated neighborhood of College Street, populated by college professors and admin-
istrators, business owners, and professionals. The glare of the sun and
the glances of those passing by increased the discomfort of knowing the
deserved wrath he would receive upon returning home. This was a mistake, and he knew it. And he knew forgiveness would be hard-earned, if
possible at all.

As expected, the reception at home was as cold as ice. Not only would Elizabeth give him nothing more than a stone-faced glare, even his sweet daughters, Lucy and Mary, were clipped and distant as he passed them on the stairs. The sisters had spread the word among the older siblings, and only Fred and Earnest seemed to show him any warmth at all.

The nearly silent response and the palpable anger continued for days, despite shared meals and the return to normal routine. After several silent nights in the same bed, he reached out to touch Elizabeth's shoulder, her back turned toward him. It was like touching stone. As he had several times over the past week, he again tried to apologize, but his words were cut off mid-sentence by a snapped, "Just go to sleep."

It would be weeks before they could have a civil conversation, and then it would be about the plans for grape growing, the progress on enlarging the new house, or bookkeeping for the furniture business. He was miserable. But she seemed ever more focused on building a life of which he might not be an essential part.

Suddenly one day, Elizabeth said, "I am starting a business downtown. The owner of the Central Hotel has bought bouquets from me in the past, and he is willing for me to have a flower cart in the downstairs of the hotel. Bettie will be my huckster, since she is personable and will be good at selling things. Lucy and she will help me cut and transport the flowers."

It was the first Frederick had heard of any such idea. He knew Elizabeth enjoyed growing and selling flowers, but starting a business of her own was a shock. He was trying to find words to respond when she continued on.

"There is no florist business in the city. I will be the first. And I intend to use whatever profits beyond the needs of the household to buy more land. In my name."

The last statement was perfunctory, as he knew she meant it to be. Mustering what little bit of desire he had left to reconcile their differences, he said, "I am sure you will be a great success."

Her response was a steely eyed look and a terse, "Yes, I am sure I will make it a success."

It did not help their troubled relationship when a couple months later, their oldest son, Fred, announced he was moving to North Carolina, and he would be working on his own as a cabinet maker. Elizabeth knew there was no stopping him, and she did her best to keep her sadness and concerns to herself.

Frederick let his son know he was proud of him moving on and starting his own life, but he was careful to do it outside of Elizabeth's earshot.

Elizabeth continued to manage the household, as she fully threw herself into growing flowers and grapes on the new property. Frederick's furniture business continued to thrive, while he also tended the vines and expanded the house that would allow them to move away from Bucknertown and onto their own land.

The Gower, Cox and Markley Carriage Factory downtown crafted a specialized wooden cart that was soon regularly seen being rolled from the Garraux property to the downtown hotel by Elizabeth and her daughters. The cart had little compartments designed to each hold a small bouquet. The journey was about a mile and a half, including the crossing of two brooks, but as the profits increased, the trip felt easier.

People began to take note of the diligent Swiss family and their business successes, as well as the large, beautiful home Frederick constructed on the property. He had added a long porch and a pergola that wrapped around the side, and by the second spring, much of it was covered with beautiful wisteria vines, all started from the one gnarly stump gifted to Elizabeth by Heldman.

Despite all the success, the relationship between Frederick and Elizabeth remained quite strained. When their son Fred came home to tell them he was marrying a woman he had met in North Carolina, a woman they had not met and knew nothing about, Elizabeth felt like she was about to see her worries become reality. Fred assured them he was ready to settle down. He said he had been offered a good job in the woodworking shop at a machine company in Atlanta, and he and his soon-to-be wife, Pennina Sullivant, would be moving to the big city.

Once again, Elizabeth and Frederick were at odds, with her being concerned about the marriage and the move, and Frederick being glad to see his son get out of the boarding home he had been staying in and into a regular work situation, since Fred had confessed he had been without work for more than a month.

When the father and son went to toast his announcement with an expensive bourbon at Hahn's, he added more information about his fiancé that was troubling, even for his father.

After a second drink had loosened his tongue, Fred said, "I want to tell you about my beautiful Nina, because I know you will understand. But I don't want you to tell Mother."

Complimented that his son saw him as a confidant, Frederick, of course, agreed to keep his confidence.

"Life is not always easy for women who don't have family support. Nina's father was killed in the War and her mother is without means. So, Nina has had to get by however she could. When I met her, I knew she was different from the other women who were making their money that way."

He rambled on, his eyes bright, thinking about the woman he loved, while his father tried to absorb what he was being told.

"Women who made their money what way?" Frederick said. "That sounds like you're speaking of prostitutes."

"Don't ever say that," Fred said. "She is not what you're thinking. She is a good woman, and she loves me. She just had no other way to get by."

225

With that, Frederick ordered another round of doubles and determined he would never mention anything of Pennina Sullivant's background to Elizabeth.

As long as she lived, Elizabeth never knew the 1880 census officially listed her twenty-three-year-old daughter-in-law's occupation as "prostitute."

Chapter 5

Despite her sadness over her oldest son moving away, Elizabeth took solace in continuing to build opportunities and financial security for her family. In 1882, she bought eight more acres of land that adjoined their original five acres. As she promised, the land was again purchased solely in her name. The grape harvest continued to improve year over year, and their new home was ready for them to move into.

All seemed to be going smoothly, despite the distance that remained between her and Frederick.

Then as the family began preparations to leave Bucknertown, Earnest announced to them that he intended to join Fred in Atlanta.

"I know you want me to grow grapes and help with the furniture business, and I don't want to do either," Earnest said. "I want to find my own way in the world. Grapes and flowers and furniture are your ways, not mine," he said defensively, seeing the combination of surprise and hurt in his parents' faces.

As they tried to absorb what Earnest had said, he suddenly blurted out, "And Frank is going with me. He feels the same. He doesn't want to be a farmer or a carpenter, and Fred says there are many opportunities of all different kinds in Atlanta."

"Frank is only seventeen," Elizabeth exclaimed. "He can't know yet what he wants to do. He hasn't even finished his schooling. I will not permit it. Frank is not moving to Atlanta."

She looked desperately to Frederick for support and saw in his eyes immediately that he was not going to stop his sons from making this move.

"Our family is falling apart, and it is your fault," she snapped at Frederick. All the distress she felt was turned into anger and resentment toward her husband. "How can you let this happen?" she said, storming out of the room, tears stinging her eyes and paining her throat.

But Earnest and Frank did move to Atlanta, and Fred helped them find places to live and starter jobs. Elizabeth pushed her sadness over her sons' moving away into a back corner, and she refocused even more effort on her flower business and the vineyard.

The family, minus the three sons, moved into the big house on their beautiful property at the top of the hill. Frederick had built and carved a magnificent mantel and fireplace surround with a Palmetto palm pattern, the symbol of his adopted state. He had also built several special pieces for the home, including an inlaid table for the entry, and a beautifully turned newel post and railing to the second floor.

The flower gardens thrived, and the grapes were healthy and prolific. The family invited their Bucknertown neighbors to visit their new home and grounds. Many neighbors came, including the Buckners—all three generations—the Harrisons, and of course, Arleto, whose loud enthusiasm and excitement over the garden and vineyard were contagious. There was food, singing, and laughter and in the celebration of all they had accomplished, a glow surrounded Frederick and Elizabeth. Together they remembered all the years of love they had shared and the hard work they had invested, and the icy wall between them seemed to melt.

For the next several months, the strain between them lessened, and things went along smoothly, almost as though the blow-up that had nearly severed their relationship had never happened.

One afternoon, Elizabeth hurried to the Central Hotel on the corner of Main and Washington in response to a last-minute request. She needed to be at her floral cart to show some sample bouquets to a prospective bride. The young woman had planned a Charleston wedding but had decided to relocate the service and reception to Greenville. The bride was a member of Augusta Road's high-society, and Elizabeth knew that wedding arrangements for the extravagantly wealthy were often the biggest money makers for florists.

As Elizabeth rushed down the main street, she happened to pass Hahn's corner bar just as her husband, who swore he had ceased drinking, stepped out the door. He straightened his jacket and brushed off his chest before he glanced up and saw her. Elizabeth stopped in her tracks, staring at him.

The color drained from his face as it rose in hers. This was the final straw. She knew what happened when he started drinking again. It would only be a matter of time before customers were once again complaining about furniture orders being delayed, and there would be bookkeeping that did not add up.

Without a word, she turned on her heel, and walked off to her meeting with the bride, knowing that there was no future for her and Frederick. It would be up to her alone to keep the family solvent and well.

Elizabeth and Frederick simply avoided each other and the ugly truth between them for the next few months, as she busied herself determining what help she would have to hire for the grape-tending and winemaking. She and the children could handle much of it, and for the rest, she would arrange whatever was needed. She talked to George Heldman, letting him know she needed the names of any part-workers he had employed and could spare.

"I don't want to discuss the reasons with you, or with anyone, George," she said. "But I will be operating the vineyard, farm, and florist business entirely by myself. Well, with the daughters' help, of course."

Heldman respected her desire to avoid divulging the details, but he was aware, as were many in town, of how much time Frederick spent in the bar and saloons, so he assumed that had something to do with it.

Elizabeth looked for every possible opportunity to help the family financially. She even agreed to give the Hazard Powder company a ten-year lease on a small piece of her land for a gunpowder storage building at a rate of a hundred dollars per year.

She and her daughters quickly formed a millinery business to make mattresses and cushions for most of the furniture manufacturers in Greenville. They were as deft with sewing needles as their mother, and all were talented seamstresses.

Elizabeth's floral business in the hotel became known far and wide, and her flower varieties fetched top dollar. With each passing season, her reputation grew, and Greenville's young gallants knew a bouquet or bud from Elizabeth's cart was a sure way to impress the girls, who were often students at Greenville Baptist Female College.

From the outside looking in, neighbors and residents of Greenville marveled at the amazing Swiss family and what they had created from a rock pile at the edge of a city. The Garrauxs were the model of immigrant success and admired far and wide for succeeding at every endeavor they took on.

Most observing could not see that Frederick's inability to stop drinking had far exceeded Elizabeth's ability to tolerate it.

After the grapes had been harvested, some sold and others made into wine that was bottled and ready for future sale, Elizabeth calculated how much of the profit they could spare, along with some of their savings.

Holding a ledger that laid out the business of the last few years, as well as the amount she had determined they could give up, she told Frederick she wished to speak with him, in private, in his workshop.

Frederick immediately knew it was to be a difficult conversation, because Elizabeth very rarely entered the workspace in the small barn he had built behind their new home.

He offered her a seat in the only chair in the shop, but she said she'd rather stand, and he said he would, too.

Elizabeth took a deep breath, trying to line up the words she had practiced in her head too many times over the last months and years. She had decided to divorce Frederick but had quickly learned that women were not allowed to divorce their husbands in South Carolina. It was literally forbidden by law. There had been a brief window of several years during Reconstruction during which divorce had been legal, but South Carolina lawmakers had since slammed that window shut.

"Frederick, I want you to move out of the house. I cannot divorce you, because of the law, but I cannot live with you. I think you know that it is your behavior that is causing the end of this marriage, so therefore, I will not be the one to move. I will stay here and maintain the lives of our children. They do not deserve to suffer because of your bad choices, so we will stay in the house. I have the grapes, the shop, and the floral and millinery businesses, so we will manage. You have your furniture and cabinetry business, so you will manage too.

As though she feared what would happen if she stopped speaking, she continued on, barely breathing between sentences.

"You can take what you want from the house, and I have come up with what I think is a fair amount of money to share with you from this last

231

grape harvest, as well as from other profits over the past few years. It will help you get settled wherever you decide to go."

Frederick stared at her, pale-faced, mouth slightly opened, not believing what she was saying.

He blurted out, "After all we've accomplished? After all I've done to build you this new home? This grand farm? You think you can throw me out of my home?"

"You had many chances to change your behavior, and you did not," she snapped. "You used to complain about your father being a drunk, and now, you have become one. I don't want you to teach our children your family tradition."

Frederick stepped toward her, fists clenched at his sides, furious at her criticism, wounded by its truth. Leaning toward her face, speaking through his clenched teeth, he snarled, "I'll be happy to leave. I cannot stand being constantly judged by you. I cannot stand never measuring up to your standards. I cannot stand any of this anymore. I will be gone by the end of the week. And you will regret it."

Elizabeth did regret how things had turned out. She had so deeply loved her creative, complicated husband. But she still had eight children at home she felt completely responsible for. Not just for them, but for their futures, and even the children they might one day have. She could not let her husband's weakness hurt their lives. She was determined that any space left by his absence would have to be filled by her strength.

A vague and tearful conversation with the children followed, in which Elizabeth said only, "Father will be gone for a time to sort some things out."

Frederick kept his word. Four days later, he was gone.

The night after he left, Elizabeth, with tears falling and hands shaking, picked up a pen and a small piece of paper. She wrote a few short sentences on the paper. She blew lightly on the paper until the ink dried, and then she carefully folded it in half. She picked up the inlaid wooden box Frederick had given her when they were courting. She opened it and put the folded paper inside. She then opened her bottom dresser drawer, and moved the items of clothing aside, placing the box in the bottom of the drawer. She closed the drawer and dried her tears.

She would never again touch the box, or the piece of paper inside it.

Elizabeth's heartbreak over their failed marriage was a secret she held tightly and did not share. Even those close to her were told Frederick was looking into a business opportunity elsewhere. In truth, for a time after he left, she had no idea where he went or what he was doing. When she eventually found out, it further sealed her determination that he would never be part of her life or influence her remaining children ever again.

Chapter 6

As was her style when under pressure or duress, Elizabeth worked harder, longer, and more intensely than ever.

In late summer of 1884, just before Frederick's departure, she had entered a flower arrangement in the State Grange and Agricultural Society competition in Columbia, an event that recognized the prowess of the best farmers and growers in South Carolina.

The event drew large crowds to its colorful displays, and the outcome was even written up in the newspapers across the state. People would dress for the occasion, and women would fan themselves as they ogled the impressive fruit, vegetable, and flower displays, while men exchanged farming information, and equipment vendors tried to line up customers. In the fruit division, Hugh Buist, who was also from Greenville, won first place for his apples, and Elizabeth's friend, George Heldman, who grew a variety of fruits, won for the best general collection.

When Bettie got a hold of the local edition of the newspaper with the article in it, she ran nearly all the way from downtown Greenville to the house on the hill, stopping only occasionally to point out the item in the paper to anyone who wanted to see.

Bettie was out of breath and red-faced, with hair fallen loose and messy by the time she got the crumpled newspaper into her mother's hands.

"We are famous, Mama! The flowers won!" Bettie shouted, as the other children ran from all over the house to join in the excitement.

Elizabeth, who had worked very hard over the years to master the reading of English, spoke slowly as she read aloud:

> *"A brief and eloquent address from Governor Thompson formally opened the exhibit, and Judge Haskell made a pleasant allusion to the fact that Paris Mountain, from whence came many of the rich exhibits of which the Governor had eloquently spoken, as the place where the Governor himself was born . . ."*

Fannie interrupted the reading, saying, "Come on, Mama, get to the part about your flowers!" as the other children chimed in and urged her on.

Elizabeth scanned through the article with the tip of her finger, then read aloud:

> *"The floral display was excellent beyond description, embracing many of the rarest flowers known to this climate."*

Elizabeth's face flushed, and the children hopped about, clapping, and cheering as though they had watched their team score a homerun in a baseball game.

Elizabeth scanned down the page to the listing of winners, and she read out loud, voice strong at first, and then faltering and fading:

> *"Best display of flowers, Mr. F. Garraux, of Greenville."*

She then realized the display had to be entered in Frederick's name, despite it being her creation. Only men were allowed to enter the contest.

Eleven-year-old Fannie said innocently, "Father won the prize?"

"Mama arranged the flowers, Fannie," Bettie said. "Father never arranged flowers. That is a mistake. The prize should be Mother's."

Elizabeth folded the paper, sat up a little straighter, and said, "No matter. We all know who arranged the flowers. Soon, it will be clear to everyone who is responsible for our businesses and livelihood."

With Frederick gone and her not having to spend time maintaining any of the orders or bookkeeping for the furniture business, Elizabeth could focus solely on the grapes, the flowers, the shop, and the millinery business. Those aware of what she was working at while her husband was "away" were in awe of the tiny woman's energy and determination.

Her skill as both a grower and a businesswoman became clear later in the fall of 1884. And this time, the newspaper coverage got it right, and the story spread all across the state.

The article, headlined "Grapes and Growers" said:

> "Few people, even in Greenville, have any idea of the dimensions reached by the industry of grape growing here, and a still smaller proportion of our citizens realize what an important part of the business will form our commerce and enterprise.
>
> "The figure of the shipments will doubtless be astonishing, especially when we remember the limited capital and means employed. The books at the express office show that 3,061 baskets of grapes were shipped from here during the season, beginning in the latter part of July and virtually ending on the tenth of September, although there were some occasional shipments up to the eighteenth of this month. In pounds, the grape shipments aggregated 37,800.
>
> "The principal shippers were Messrs. Garraux, H.B. Buist, and Marshall. The best market was Charleston, where a very large proportion of the shipments went, but New York and Philadelphia took considerable quantities,

and a few lots went to Cincinnati . . .

"F. Hahn, who has shipped very few grapes this year, it being the 'resting season' for his vines, is satisfied with his experiences, having sold $400 or $500 in grapes from his two acres last year, netting a very comfortable profit.

"Mrs. Garraux has kept a more accurate account of the result of her year's work than any of the others, and her figures may be relied on. The Garraux vineyard of an acre and a quarter was a beautiful sight in the bearing season, the vines being literally loaded and covered with immense bunches of the luscious fruit.

"The acre and a quarter yielded 15,500 pounds of grapes, of which 1,200 pounds were shipped, netting five cents a pound on average; 2,500 pounds of grapes were sold at retail.

"The other thousand pounds was made into thirty gallons of wine, or lost, given away, etc., and some few grapes are still ripening. The $850 on an acre beats cotton, and the grape growers say the yield is better every year. The records at the express office and account sales stand to prove these almost incredible figures."

This time, Elizabeth read the article aloud to the children, then again to herself before bed. Then again when she awoke in the morning.

Each effort of hers in the business world was challenging. Women did not generally buy and sell real estate, open stores, win prizes or outdo male growers. She was often greeted with quizzical, and frequently irritated expressions, partially because she was less than five feet tall, but mostly because she was often the only woman present.

She read the article again, and said out loud to only herself, "I can do this. I can take care of my family."

As time passed, fewer people asked about Frederick, where he was, or when he was coming back. Elizabeth, who by then was fifty-eight, was preoccupied with managing life and family business endeavors, as were the children who still lived at home.

Lucy, the firstborn daughter, and the oldest child remaining at home, had studied nursing along the way, though she most often worked in the family businesses instead of caregiving. She was almost twenty-eight, and never seemed bothered by seeing her friends marrying off one-by-one, or by the occasional whispers about her spinsterhood. She had her mother's icy blue eyes and dark hair, and though she stood several inches taller than her diminutive mother, her demeanor and shyness made her less likely to stand out in a crowd.

Lucy was a gentle soul, known for her quiet, dignified disposition and her deftness with a needle. She loved to create intricate quilts and cross-stich pieces and other things of beauty, but she also found great satisfaction in the millinery business. She remained her mother's staunch supporter, being more keenly aware of her parents' marital issues than most of her siblings. Some neighbors felt as though Lucy limited her chances of marrying with her unceasing loyalty to Elizabeth.

Mary was only a year younger than Lucy, but socially and emotionally, she was much younger. She learned slowly and lagged behind the other children in reading and writing, but she was so dear to all of them, they made up for her deficits. Mary had a kind spirit and was especially fond of animals. She helped with many of the tasks around the farm, particularly caring for the chickens, horses, and cows the family had acquired. The other children were protective of Mary, whose innocent view of life made her seem childlike and delicate, adding to her sweetness.

Bettie, at twenty-five, was her mother's other strongest supporter. She knew her father's absence was because of her mother's standards and her father's failures. She had never told anyone in her life, not even Rosa or her other sisters, of what had happened a few years before their father had left.

Bettie had gotten up during the night and was scurrying to the outhouse, when she bumped into her father as he stumbled around the corner to the backdoor. He was as startled as she was, and they stopped briefly, frozen in the moonlight, until in a cloud of whiskey vapors, he slurred, "Oh, hulloh, Bettie. I am just off to bed. Your mother is sleeping. No need to wake her. No need to bother mother about this, Bettie."

She understood what he meant, and she did keep it to herself. But when his sudden departure took place years later, she was not surprised. And she was proud of her mother for not putting up with his ill behavior. If anything, it caused her to be closer to her mother, and more determined that their family would be a success without her father.

Bettie was a strikingly attractive young woman, with sky-blue eyes, thick dark hair, and a ready smile. She typically wore modest but well-tailored dresses that showed off her buxom figure. Her self-assured, and yet pleasant manner made her attractive to the young men of Greenville, many of whom would find reason to shop in the family market for a chance to interact with her.

Bettie and her two-years-younger sister, Rosa, both in the mid-twenties, were inseparably close. Unlike Lucy and Mary, both Bettie and Rosa were intent on one day marrying and having families of their own. In their mid-twenties, both hoped it would happen sooner than later, but they were also firmly committed to making the family a financial success.

All the older daughters doted on Fannie, now fourteen and the youngest of the clan. Having been born a tiny, premature baby, Fannie remained small through childhood. As a teenager, she was as petite as her tiny mother. She was a cheerful, amusing, popular girl, who made friends readily, and entertained the family with her quick wit and quirky outlook on life.

The three younger teenaged sons, John, Charley, and Willie, all missed their older brothers very much. Willie, at sixteen, was the last to have recently finished his lower-school education.

John had attended Colonel Patrick's Military Academy, where he studied bookkeeping, along with arithmetic, Latin, and other subjects. He was impressed with his mother's skills as a bookkeeper and liked the detail involved.

Willie was tall, like his father, and his face had a strong bone structure, similar to Frederick's. He was well-spoken and impressed most of those with whom he interacted as being older than his age.

John, Charley, and Willie were all good students and pleased their teachers and instructors with their work ethic and diligence.

The three brothers were constantly thinking about what they would do with their adult lives as they looked into various opportunities. Charley helped Bettie out in the confectionery shop, and they all worked hard on the farm and in the vineyard, but they seemed anxious to find their own way and were less interested in the family businesses than their sisters were.

All in all, the family was busy, hardworking, and supportive of one another. Without apparent intent, it did, however, sometimes seem the family fell into two camps: the side that supported their mother, and the side that missed their father and longed for his return. The girls, invariably, sided with their mother, nearly idolizing her. The sons often missed their father's strong, quiet personality, and the furniture crafting skills they were all so proud of.

It had been more than a year since Frederick left, and there had not been a word from him. It had gotten to the point where he was seldom mentioned in conversation, especially when Elizabeth was nearby. She had been surprised, and initially troubled by his complete disappearance, but when she came to learn where he was, she was furious.

Chapter 7

One day, Lucy rushed out into the vineyard where Elizabeth was tending vines. She said, "There is a letter for you, Mama. It is from Fred in Atlanta."

Elizabeth laid down her hoe, took the letter, and walked to a boulder in the shade of a nearby oak tree. She sat down, removed her straw hat, and opened the letter.

Her older sons had been completely out of touch since their father left home. She assumed Frederick had contacted them and they were angry about her forcing him to leave, but she had no way of knowing. She had briefly thought about taking a trip to Atlanta to talk to the three of them, but she had too many responsibilities to leave behind, and she wasn't sure what the reception would be.

Her hands were trembling as she unfolded the letter, not sure what she would find.

Dear Mother,

I am writing to inform you of several things that I think it is only fair you

241

know, since I am still and will always be your oldest son.

I am doing well here and have been promoted to a supervisory position at the Winship Machine Company. I have bought a house for Nina and me. Earnest was staying with us for a while, but he wants you to know he is moving to North Carolina. He has been courting Minnie Blair, whose family is from Charlotte. He plans to marry her.

Elizabeth's heart sank since the tone of the letter already sounded as distant as if it had been written by a stranger. She felt she might be reading between the lines, but she immediately felt that she was not likely to be included in the wedding.

Frank is doing fine. He is boarding with Mr. Gann, a wealthy man who owns a saloon here, and he is working for him now. I am sure you disapprove. But Frank is doing fine and is happy.

Father is currently living with me and Nina, but he will soon be moving to an apartment here in Atlanta, since he has nowhere to go after being thrown out of his own home. Father is a good man, and I do not understand how you could force him to leave for no reason.

I am providing you with this information because Earnest felt you should be told about his move and likely marriage. I will leave it to him to decide if you are to have any further contact from him.

I hope you are all well. Please tell the sisters and brothers that I miss them.

Fred

Tears spilled out of Elizabeth's eyes, running freely down her cheeks. Lucy, who was standing quietly by as her mother read the letter, said, "What it is, Mama? What is wrong?"

"Nothing is wrong. Everything is fine," Elizabeth said, quickly drying her tears on her long gardening apron. "It sounds as if your brother Earnest will be moving to North Carolina and getting married. Your brother Fred has been promoted and your brother Frank has gotten a job."

She cleared her throat and said, "Your father is living in Atlanta. He is living with Fred and his wife. I do not wish to speak about it anymore. You may tell your brothers and sisters where your father is, since I am sure they have wondered."

With that, she stood up, shoved the letter in her apron pocket, grabbed the hoe, and went back into the vineyard. She began hoeing vigorously, nearly violently, around the vines.

So, her son had taken in his useless father, and her other son was working in a saloon, she thought as she slammed the hoe into the reddish clay soil again and again. Clearly, Frederick had not explained what led him to leave their home. His influence and dishonesty were still affecting her children, she thought angrily.

"I am so glad he is gone," she said out loud to no one.

A short time later, in her boldest business effort yet, Elizabeth expanded her flower cart business in the hotel and relocated it to a leased shop space of her own on Main Street. She opened a market there, to be run by Bettie, that, in addition to flowers, grapes, and homemade wine, was stocked with nuts, cigars, canned goods and Swiss-style confections. Because of the high-quality goods and Bettie's charming personality, the shop instantly became one of the most popular in town.

Elizabeth had determined that their farm and vineyard would be even more successful, and she intended to continue to expand it until she owned the whole hilltop. She wanted all the property from Earle Street to the south, to the river in the east, to the brook at the bottom of the ravine in the north, to Townes Street to the west. Townes was one of the few streets north of the city with some homes and businesses on it. It would take her time to make the land purchases needed to buy the more than 150 acres that covered the plateau above the town, but she was determined that one day that property would be hers.

Frank Hahn had grown tired of trying to grow grapes, so he agreed to sell his remaining two acres next to the Garraux farm to Elizabeth. He knew she wanted the property, so he named a price higher than it was worth. Elizabeth was in no mood to haggle with Hahn.

"Since it was your saloon that helped my husband down the wrong path, leaving me to manage my household and children on my own, it would seem a fair price is in order," she said matter-of-factly to Hahn.

Elizabeth never openly acknowledged why her marriage to Frederick had ended, but in this case, she wanted Hahn to know she felt he was a contributor to Frederick's downfall.

Frank Hahn was caught a bit off-guard. As a blind business owner, he had learned to be on guard against those who might take advantage of him. But in this case, he had to admit he understood Elizabeth's feelings.

"You name your price, Madame Garraux," he said.

She did name her price, a bit lower than what he could have sold it for, and it added two more acres to the farm. The businesses grew, the farm expanded, and the vineyard and the wine it produced became known far and wide.

Then would come cause for sadness, followed by a year of disaster.

In October 1886, Elizabeth received a letter postmarked Asheville from her son Earnest. She opened it eagerly, hoping it was an invitation to his wedding. She had been saddened by not being included when her oldest son, Fred, had married. She hoped that Earnest would not follow suit.

Dear Mother,

I am writing to let you know that I married Minnie Blair two weeks ago. She is a wonderful girl from a good family in Charlotte, and I am very fortunate that she would have me. We are living in Asheville, not far from where we lived when we first moved to the States. I am very happy, and I wanted you to know that.

I miss the family and Greenville. I hope to bring Minnie there for a visit someday soon. We hope for children, and if we have them, I would like them to know their grandparents and aunts and uncles. I do not want us to remain separated by anything more than miles.

I did not invite you to the wedding because Fred, who was my best man, insisted that father be included, and I knew it would be uncomfortable for you. I won't put you in any uncomfortable positions with him.

I will be in touch.

Fondly,

Your son Earnest

Elizabeth was again heartbroken to have missed the marriage of one of her children. But at least she felt the closeness she had shared with Earnest remained. He had always been easy-going and quick to reconcile after conflict. She tried to picture his wedding day, and his love for a woman she had never met, and she let her happiness for him temper her sadness over being left out.

Chapter 8

That winter, it seemed the weather had become an enemy of the South. In the same year that an earthquake in August killed dozens of people and destroyed much of the coastal city of Charleston, the winter turned bone-chilling, crop-killing cold. The damage wouldn't be completely clear until spring, but Elizabeth could see that the crowns of many of the grape vines had been damaged. And the cold was only the beginning.

When Spring came, the rain began. It was usually welcome after the dryness of winter, but this Spring, the rains did not stop. Day after day, week after week, it continued, washing away parts of garden beds, leaving the vineyard standing in pools of water. The rain continued unrelentingly for weeks. Elizabeth, the children, and a few part-time helpers she had hired tried to trench water away from the vines, working with hoes and shovels in the pouring rain as they watched the garden tiers wash away through the stone walls, and the property's pathways become shallow streams.

When the deluge finally stopped, and the ground began to dry out, they replanted many of the flower garden beds, and removed the vines that had been killed by winter cold. Unfortunately, the Spring rains led into what turned out to be a wet early summer, with just a few weeks that allowed the ground to dry out between rainstorms.

Finally, the rain stopped in late summer, and many of the flowers were even more prolific than typical. The grapevines were loaded with huge bunches of grapes, and it appeared they had survived the unrelenting rains of the early season. And then, just before harvest, it began to rain again. Elizabeth knew that though vines may tolerate rain, once they are fully leafed-out and grapes formed, the rain was not welcome.

She and the children and workers started checking the grapes several times a day, on the lookout for the black rot she knew could happen with the late rains. They found no indication of rot, and it seemed that all would be well.

Elizabeth dismissed the workers and children, but she continued to check the more than seven hundred vines in their vineyard. On the third day of rain, holding her dress up out of the mud and the handle of the umbrella in one hand, she moved from vine to vine, planted up from five to eight feet apart. She used her free hand to gently move aside the large grape leaves to check on bunches of grapes on each vine.

As she worked her way deep into the vineyard, she lifted a leaf and saw brown lesions on leaves and several shriveled, blackened grapes on one vine. Her heart stopped. She did not want to believe her eyes. She looked at another bunch on the vine. More damaged leaves and more blackened grapes. And as she moved to the next vine, she found even more.

Switzerland was drier and cooler, so rot wasn't nearly as much of a problem. But she knew it could be in the Carolinas. She had heard of one grower who lost his entire year's harvest to it. There were treatments that some people were having success with—sulfur powder and sometimes a copper mixture—but there was no time to get the chemicals. She knew

247

black rot could rip through an entire vineyard within just a few days.

She started walking quickly back to the house. Then she began to run. They could not lose the harvest. The panic she felt was foreign to her nature. But now, on her own, her entire family depending on her success, she could not fail.

"Children!" she shouted, when she was still an unreasonable distance from the house. "Children, come quickly! Lucy! Mary! John! Children! Come quickly!"

She continued to run, slipping up the slope, falling to one knee, the mud covering her always prim dress and apron, her free hand burying in the sloppy mud up to her wrist.

"Children! Lucy!" she shouted as she neared the house. Lucy ran onto the porch, as John and Charles burst out the door behind her.

"What is it, Mama? What's wrong?" Lucy cried out.

Breathlessly, Elizabeth heaved the words out, "Rot. The grapes have black rot! They must be picked now, or we will lose them all! Gather the family and get your rain jackets and come quickly."

The older children were privy to many of the grape discussions their parents had between the two of them and with other growers, and they knew the devastation rot would bring.

The fungus would first cause the grape skins to break, then the grape would turn brown and shrivel, turning into what growers called mummies. At that point, grapes were worthless.

"Charles, go find our workers and see if they can come back today. We must pick all we can as fast as we can," Elizabeth said as she threw down her umbrella. She grabbed the Macintosh raincoat that Frederick had left behind, a waterproof coat that was so long on her short frame it dragged on the ground.

248

Ideally, Elizabeth knew grapes should not be picked in the rain. But without knowing when the rain would end, she also knew they could not let the rot continue unchecked for even a day.

Chapter 9

Elizabeth, the children, and eventually three of the hired workers, swarmed into the acre and a half vineyard where they loaded large baskets with grapes that were then set at the upper ends of the rows of vines. A worker would then load the baskets into a buckboard to be unloaded into large wooden tubs in the barn.

Picking was typically arduous, even on a good day, but in the torrential rain, sliding, slipping, and falling in the mud because of the speed demanded by the urgency, made it exhausting.

The oil-cloth coats helped keep them dry, but they also over-heated them. Eventually, Elizabeth threw the oversized coat aside. She was quickly drenched in rain that covered the tears of frustration on her cheeks, angry that her height diminished her ability to pick, the wet skin of her hands raw from cutting and pulling hundreds of pounds of grapes. And for one of the rare times in her life, the problem she faced felt insurmountable.

She straightened back, uttered a silent prayer, and looked through the vineyard seeing eight of her children and her loyal workers silently, quickly trying to save their harvest, and she once again found the center of her strength.

They worked until it was too dark to see the grapes and returned to the vines when the sun rose the next day. The rain finally stopped by late morning, and by sunset, the vines had been stripped clean.

In the barn, the baskets had been sorted, salvageable grapes into lugs— large wooden bins—and the rotted grapes tossed aside. In the end, one third of the crop was lost, far less than would have been without the family's quick response. The wine made from the grapes was not as good as previous years, since the fungus had led to what vintners referred to as foxiness, a musky animal-smell some thought similar to a wet fur coat.

The 1886 grape season was the first of three consecutive damaged harvests that, along with increasing pressures from the temperance organizations who sought to shut down sales of beer, wine, and liquor, would lead Elizabeth to invest her efforts in a more secure business.

She remembered seeing a grand greenhouse at the University of Bern when she was young, and the idea of being able to control the growing environment had stuck with her. She talked to George Heldman about it, and though he was not aware of any greenhouses in the Greenville area, he was familiar with a heated greenhouse that had been built in Macon, Georgia several years before.

As an officer in the Agricultural Grange, Heldman had many contacts, and he arranged for Elizabeth to meet with Lemuel Jacobson, a man he said could help her plan a greenhouse.

When Jacobson was in Greenville several weeks later, George Heldman brought him to meet Elizabeth. Jacobson was a nattily dressed, very short, intensely groomed, middle-aged man who seemed, to Elizabeth, overly anxious to impress Heldman.

After brief introductions by Heldman, who brought Jacobson to the Garraux property, Heldman left quickly to return to his harness business.

251

It was clear that Jacobson was not pleased that he lost his opportunity to impress the wealthy and well-connected Heldman, and he looked rather miffed about being left at the farm.

Elizabeth pointed out the area of the property on which she wanted to construct a greenhouse. It was a fairly level, cleared area that received several hours of sun every day.

"I have some sketches I can show you of my ideas," Jacobson said. "But shouldn't we wait for your husband?"

Heldman was so used to Frederick's absence and so comfortable and respectful of Elizabeth's business dealings, he obviously neglected to tell Jacobson that he would be dealing with her alone.

"My husband will not be joining us. He will not be part of the planning nor the construction. This project will be managed by me, with assistance from my older children. My sons and my workers will be constructing the greenhouse."

Jacobson looked at her as though she was talking pure nonsense.

"Well, who will pay for my design services?" he sniffed.

Elizabeth, quite used to this condescending treatment from men in the business world, wanted nothing more to do with Jacobson.

"I will pay you five dollars to leave your sketches and get off my property," she said tersely, stressing the word "my." "Otherwise, you can keep your drawings, and I bid you good day."

"Keep the sketches," Jacobson said. "They are of no use to me. They are not design drawings, just some scribbled ideas on paper."

He shoved the sketches into her hands and stormed off down the dirt road in front of the house, headed toward town without ever looking back.

Apparently, Jacobson was, like many men of the day, incapable of conducting business with a woman. She would later tell Heldman about the exchange, and he was embarrassed that he had orchestrated their meeting.

Starting from Jacobson's scribbled ideas and working from memory of what she had seen in Bern, Elizabeth, Lucy, and Charles created a plan of their own for a large greenhouse, more than twelve feet wide and twenty feet long. It would be heated by a piping system that would use steam from wood fires outside to warm the interior in the winter.

Elizabeth could not stop the cold from damaging her vines, or the rain from causing the grapes to rot, but once constructed, the greenhouse would allow her to grow flowers year-round, something no one else in Greenville or the surrounding area was able to do.

The greenhouse would become one of Elizabeth's many claims to fame. People would come from miles around to marvel at the beautiful blooms inside, sometimes walking through snow to peek with amazement at the flowers inside. Elizabeth, her children, and the workers became adept at knowing when to stoke the fires and when to ventilate the greenhouse.

Elizabeth grew roses, fuchsias, coleus, rare geraniums, and many exotics year-round, which made her floral business extremely successful. College commencement was her busiest time of year, and her bouquets would sell for at least thirty cents, sometimes as much as the amazingly high price of a dollar.

As Elizabeth's businesses thrived, so did the city of Greenville. Over these few years, the Paris Mountain Water Company started providing water service from two reservoirs on the small mountain just northwest of town. The gas lamps on Main Street were replaced with electric streetlights, after the first electric plant was built downtown on the Reedy River near Broad Street.

The city was now the third largest in the state with more than six thousand residents. The downtown was booming, with several hotels, banks, druggists, tobacconists, bookstores, clothiers, groceries, a tailor, an opera house, a meat shop, and a newspaper. The horse-drawn streetcar rail system still ran the length of the business district and helped passengers reach depots on main railway systems that could transport them to other major cities. The city had even begun to pave Main Street near the river. There were telephones in many of the downtown homes and businesses, though it would be several more years before that luxury would reach the Garraux homestead.

The bumpy little dirt street where the family lived was now named Swiss Avenue, in honor of the family's heritage. Initially, the general area had been called Germantown, a nod to the Garrauxs, Frank Hahn, and other German-speaking immigrant property owners.

There were several Jewish business proprietors who settled in Greenville after the Civil War, many of whom were Ashkenazi, exiled during the fall of Jerusalem. A few of them were among the most successful downtown business operators.

The city generally dealt with less racial conflict than many Southern cities, but it was not without tragedies associated with the ugly history left by the Civil War. In one case, an opera house had been built on the corner of Main Street and McBee Avenue, the site of an earlier venue that burned down in 1866. In December 1879, after just a few performances in the newly opened opera house, it also burned down. Five black men were charged with arson, and three of them were eventually hanged, though there were many questions about their guilt and about apparent technical errors in the way the trial was conducted.

Greenville largely avoided the terroristic activities of a secret and violent racist club for white men that had been established in Tennessee. In fact, in September 1871, the Southern Enterprise newspaper reported that the Ku Klux Klan was guilty of crimes in other parts of the state, but not in Greenville.

When a Joint Congressional Committee held hearings in South Carolina in the summer of 1871, President Ulysses S. Grant suspended the writ of habeas corpus in nine counties where action was needed to shut down Klan activities, but that wasn't necessary in Greenville.

In 1875, two Klan members, referred to in newspapers as "desperados," were arrested in Newberry and returned for trial and jailing in Greenville. The city was widely acknowledged for controlling and avoiding Klan activity.

As the city progressed, there were multiple colleges and schools, including a few schools for black students, even though there were still some who resisted integration in education, and others who felt black children need not be educated at all.

Conversely, many of the neighbors and friends the Garrauxs had made in Bucknertown played significant roles in the economic development of the city. Black businessmen formed unions for carpenters, blacksmiths, and other trades, and they had literal monopolies in transportation and hacking, as well as in catering, barbering, and blacksmithing. There was a black-owned bank, and the all-black fire station, the Neptune Fire Company, that remained a source of great pride in the black community. John Buckner also continued to be known as a popular civic leader.

As Greenville was finding its stride, so were Elizabeth and her children. She continued to buy property, adding another seventeen acres for a total of more than twenty-five acres, all atop the rocky hillside surrounding their homestead. The shop at 105 North Main Street became a local favorite, since it carried specialty items, such as fresh fruit and flowers, cigars, wine, and confections. Bettie was well-known and highly regarded as one of the most popular downtown shopkeepers.

In the next year, the family experienced the joy of another marriage and the sadness of an unexpected death.

John had recently become a foreman at the Paris Mountain Water Company at just twenty-one years of age. He was small in stature, but widely recognized for his strong character, kindness, and communication skills. He had always seemed older than his age, due to his serious demeanor, so despite being so young, no one was surprised when he announced his intention to marry Metta Hudson, the daughter of a local farmer whom he had been seeing regularly. Metta was the youngest of six children, and daughter of a Greenville farmer who had long been a friend of the family.

John's new position with the water company along with his marriage to Metta, a pleasant and popular young woman, lifted the spirits of Elizabeth and his siblings.

Despite the late season loss of much of the grape crop, the new greenhouse was a huge benefit to Elizabeth's booming floral business. By late fall, she was the sole provider of flowers for Greenville and much of the surrounding area.

Lucy and Mary also continued to work along with their mother in the millinery business, with their sewing equipment and supplies set up in the back room of the house. They ran one of only two shops in the area to make mattresses and furniture cushions, and their work was recognized as being of desirable quality. All in all, the winter of 1888 was quickly taking the edge off the difficult fall they had endured.

Then, shortly before Christmas, Elizabeth received a letter from Earnest.

Chapter 10

The year before, Earnest and his wife, Minnie, had moved from Asheville back to Minnie's hometown of Charlotte. They had stopped in Greenville for a visit while making the move, and Elizabeth had been very glad to see how happy Earnest was, and to be introduced to his lovely wife.

Earnest was a train engineer for the Florida Central and Peninsular Railroad, and at thirty-one years old, he was a tall, solid man with a thick handlebar moustache. His looks reminded Elizabeth of her husband, Frederick, when he was the handsome young man who had stolen her heart. When she saw Earnest with Minnie, the way they looked at each other made her think wistfully of a time when she, too, had been so much in love.

Earnest and Minnie planned to visit during Christmas, so Elizabeth was surprised to hear from him with the holiday just weeks away. Anxious to read the letter, she wondered if perhaps it would bring news of a grand-child on the way. Elizabeth hurried into the parlor and sat on the sofa, ripping open the letter.

Dearest Mother,

*I am so heartbroken I can hardly think of the words to write. My beautiful
Minnie is gone. She now resides in Heaven and all I can do is long for
the day I will see her again. She suffered terribly for several days until she
passed into God's arms Saturday night. I cannot bear the sadness.*

*I will stay here in Charlotte where we made our home and where my
sweet wife is buried. I will not be visiting during the Christmas holiday as
we had planned.*

Your son,

Earnest

Elizabeth could hardly comprehend what Earnest had written. Just
months before she had been so pleased to meet her son's lovely twenty-
eight-year-old wife with the bright eyes, wide smile, and easy laugh. It
seemed impossible that her boy should be a widow at his age. She said a
prayer for him, and for Minnie, and called the children together to share
the terrible news. Together they composed a letter of care and consola-
tion to Earnest, knowing that words would mean little in the face of such
a loss.

The death of someone so youthful and vibrant was a terrible shock to
Elizabeth. She could not have known at the time she would soon be con-
soling a dear friend during a similar, but even more tragic loss.

George and Matilda Heldman had remained close friends of Elizabeth's,
even after Frederick's departure. George and Elizabeth shared a true
passion for flowers, and both delighted in the growing and propagating
of plants—the rarer, the better.

The Heldman's daughter, Fannie, was now an accomplished and beautiful
young woman who had graduated from Greenville Female College. She
had remained friends with Rosa and Bettie since they were young girls
playing under the wisteria vine on the pergola at the Garraux homestead.

The vine was now as big around as a man's waist, and it covered more than fifty feet around the side of the house and out toward the barn. People would come from miles around to admire the vine that had been just a gnarly root stump when George gave it to Elizabeth.

Fannie was twenty-five and engaged to be married, and Elizabeth was planning the floral arrangements for the wedding, which would be a major social affair in Greenville.

Just a week after Minnie's death, Elizabeth was to meet with Fannie and her parents to work out the final details for the floral arrangements. Charley drove his mother down to the Heldman home with a plan to pick her up a short time later.

When Matilda answered her knock on the door, she was sobbing, kerchief held over her face.

"What's wrong, Matilda? What has happened?" Elizabeth asked as they stepped into the foyer. Her immediate thought was that George, who was seventy, might have been taken ill.

"It's Fannie," Matilda sobbed. "It's our dear Fannie." Her voice rose in pitch to nearly a wail as she sobbed, "She has lost her mind. Our Fannie has lost her mind."

Elizabeth was trying to find words to respond, when George came around the corner, also in tears.

"George, what is happening?" Elizabeth said. "What is wrong with Fannie?"

"Oh, it's so awful," George moaned. "The doctor cannot help her. We do not know what has happened. Her mind has turned dark, and she talks constantly about ending her life. She will not listen to us. She will not listen to the doctor."

He was overcome with sobs that shook his whole body and he sat down on a bench, head in hands. "We've had to lock her in her room," he sobbed. "We had to lock our beautiful daughter in her room like an animal."

Matilda threw herself down beside him, and they grabbed each other, clinging and crying uncontrollably.

Elizabeth did not know what to say to them. Fannie was to be married in just a matter of days. Was this all because of her impending marriage? Everyone seemed to think the prominent young attorney to whom she was engaged was a good match. Watching her dear friends in such agony broke Elizabeth's heart.

"I am so sorry," she said, hearing her own words sound feeble against the depths of their distress. "Fannie is such a sweet, smart girl. I am sure she will be all right. Maybe she is just terribly nervous about the upcoming wedding?"

"No, that is not it," George stammered. "She has lost her mind. Our beautiful girl has gone mad."

"I am just so very sorry," Elizabeth said, feeling uncomfortable about being present during such deep and private grief. "I will come back another time when things are better. Is there anything I can do?"

"No," George said. "I am afraid there is nothing anyone can do."

Matilda suddenly stood up and rushed out of the room, sobbing, "I can't . . . I just can't. I don't know what to do."

George apologized and said goodbye to Elizabeth, showing her out the door. She hesitated, feeling she should somehow help, but realizing there was nothing she could do. She sat on a bench by the sidewalk in front of the house until Charley came back for her.

That night she told Rosa and Bettie and the others about Fannie, and they all agreed they would remember her in their prayers. Rosa and Bettie were inclined to rush to the Heldman house, but Elizabeth, having seen the depths of grief Fannie's parents were experiencing, advised them against it.

Days later, their worst fears were realized.

Fannie's death was reported in South Carolina newspapers and in papers as far away as the New York Times. The reports said that on January 1, 1889, weeks after she "suddenly became insane," Fannie managed to slip out of her locked bedroom. Her parents said she had tried to drown herself weeks before, so they immediately organized search parties to look for her.

Her father and several men in one search party went to the C&WC train trestle over the Reedy River near the Main Street bridge. During the frantic hunt for his beloved daughter, George slipped and fell through the wooden railroad ties, breaking his shoulder and several ribs.

As the men carried badly injured George back to his home, they met a second search party carrying Fannie's lifeless body. They had found her drowned in knee-deep water in the Reedy River.

The tragic and inexplicable death of the popular young woman left the Garraux family and the city in mourning.

Elizabeth's dear friend, George, would never fully recover from the loss. It seemed Minnie's death followed so quickly by Fannie's began the weaving of a dark thread into the Garraux family's life.

Despite Elizabeth's unwavering strength, resilience, and ongoing successes, the next decade would hold many more challenges and heartbreaking losses.

Chapter 11

Frank, who was still living in Atlanta, sent word that he was coming to visit the family. It had been years since he had come back to Greenville, and it was as though the prodigal son was returning. When they learned Frank was coming home, his siblings were beside themselves with excitement.

Elizabeth was filled with anticipation as well. She knew Frank would bring news, of not just his own life, but also of her oldest child, Fred, whom she dearly missed.

Frank had stayed in touch through the years, but Fred, who was now in his later thirties, was strongly aligned with his father, and his loyalty kept him at odds with his mother and siblings. Since he had left home nearly a decade before, the letters from Fred were few and far between, and he had never once returned home to visit.

Elizabeth was also cognizant that she would also likely have to hear an update on her long-departed husband. She generally found it more comfortable to avoid thoughts of him. Knowing that Frank was still close to

Frederick and saw him on a nearly daily—or at least weekly—basis, made her feel slightly anxious.

When the dogs barking in front of the Garraux homestead signaled an arrival, Elizabeth, Lucy, Mary, and Fannie all rushed out front to greet Frank. He was in a spritely, two-wheeled gig carriage, pulled by a beautiful, sleek, black horse. He waved as he stepped down from the carriage, looking dapper and impeccably groomed.

Elizabeth noted how much Frank's hair had thinned since she had last seen him. He had sandy-colored hair, lighter than most of his siblings, with her bright blue eyes. He was sporting a stout moustache, similar to what her husband Frederick had always worn. He was no longer the teenage boy Elizabeth held in her mind's eye. Though rather slight in stature, Frank had the appearance of a mature and successful businessman.

After an enthusiastic and affectionate greeting from his mother and sisters, they all went inside the home. Frank commented on how the wisteria had grown and thickened, and how the grounds around the home looked even more beautiful than he had remembered.

Bettie and Lucy updated him on the success of the store and the millinery business, and the sisters all took him on a tour of the greenhouse he had never seen. He was duly impressed with everything he saw, though he was saddened along with them to see the once lush vineyard now clearly failing.

The years of dealing with blight and rot followed by three harsh winters had led Elizabeth to nearly give up on grapes. She grew enough to sell fruit and wine in the store, but there was no more wholesaling to other states.

Nearly all the grape growers around Greenville had given up and planted other crops. Even the renowned French vintner, Messr. Carpin, who at one time had an eighty-acre vineyard with plans for a hundred acres more on Paris Mountain, had realized the struggle against the climate and disease was more than could be handled.

Frank, who had developed a keen business sense, was impressed with his mother and proud of her being such a nimble businesswoman. He was amazed that she had redirected her efforts from grape growing to the floral business, creating nearly a monopoly in the area in just a few years.

Elizabeth had to admit, the more she listened to Frank, the more she realized she had been quite wrong about Frank's mentor, Albert Gann.

A.C. Gann, as he was commonly known, first met Frank when he took him in as a boarder in Atlanta. Impressed with the well-spoken, hard-working young man, Gann then employed him at one of his Marietta Street saloons. It was a position Elizabeth had strongly questioned and immediately disapproved of, after her experiences with Frank's father.

As it turned out, more than just a bar owner, A.C. was a major property owner in Atlanta and Fulton County and was the extremely successful owner of several varied businesses. He was also a city ward councilman and known to be a beneficent supporter of charities.

"He is a remarkable man, and he has made me his partner in business," Frank said. "Because of my partnership with A.C., I have been able to invest in several properties and share ownership of several of the businesses."

Sounding somewhat defensive, he continued, "I know you disapprove of saloons, but Gann's saloon is a profitable, well-run establishment, and I am proud to be involved with it."

Elizabeth had to admit, listening to Frank did make her reconsider her fury over him being involved with a saloon owner. Frank seemed happy, relaxed and proud of what he was accomplishing in business with Gann as a partner.

A little later, John brought along Metta, who was very round and pregnant with their first child, to meet Frank. Charles and Bettie arrived after they closed the Main Street shop for the day. Earnest and William were both planning to come the next day, so Elizabeth was basking in the pleasure of having so many of her adult children together.

The talking and laughing lasted until long after the dinner dishes were washed and put away and the sun had set. Finally, as everyone went their separate ways to bed, Elizabeth slipped her arm through Frank's, and she said, "Come sit with me in the parlor."

The two of them sat side-by-side on a settee in front of the fireplace with its stout, well-oiled mantel and the heavy side frames that Frederick had carved into intricately fashioned Palmetto palms.

It was time to get past the niggling anxiety Elizabeth had felt since she knew Frank was coming.

"How is your brother Fred?" she asked, and after a pause and a repressed sigh, "And how is your father?"

Frank drew a deep breath, knowing that the topics he would prefer not to address could not be avoided.

"They are both in good health," Frank said. "Father is working as a cabinet maker. Fred has done very well with Van Winkle Machine. He started out as a machinist, but he is now a foreman, and even has patents in his name for ginning equipment he designed. He has invested in property and owns several houses. So, he's done well."

"And his wife, Pennina? How is she?" Elizabeth said. "Do they have any children? I am so sad to know nothing of his life."

Frank hesitated, clearly trying to formulate what he would say next.

"No one ever really knows about what goes on in the lives of others, Mother. I do not know the details of Fred's life. He and Pennina do not have children. Fred, well, . . . Fred has always had a bit of a wandering eye. I do not know if there is anything to it, or if I should even repeat it, but

Nina came to my apartment by herself one day, and she made some awful accusations about Fred."

"Oh, no," Elizabeth said. "Do you think he has done something wrong?"

"It is not for me to say, Mother. Fred is living his life the way he wants to. I don't really know Pennina, but there are some who think she also may not have the finest reputation," Fred said.

Then, clearing his throat and looking away, he said, "I have already said too much. Fred is fine. He is well-to-do with an important job and much property. I don't think we should discuss it anymore."

Elizabeth, slightly shaken by the thoughts that now raced through her head, sat silently.

"Before you ask, I will just tell you that father is getting by. He is still renting a small apartment, but he is determined to get back on his feet." And chuckling a little, Frank said, "And he's still tough as nails. Do you know a burglar broke into his apartment last month, and father found him in it when he returned home."

"Oh no," Elizabeth exclaimed. "A burglar?!"

"Yes," Frank said. "The part of Atlanta where he lives has some petty crime issues. Anyway, it was actually written up in the newspaper. They said," chuckling again, "'Anyone should be able to recognize the suspect because of the damage to his face.' Apparently, father gave him a pounding before he ran away."

"Oh, my goodness," Elizabeth exclaimed. So, Frederick, now at nearly sixty years old, could still take on an intruder in his home.

She said, in as kindly sounding voice as possible, "I am glad he was not hurt. I am sorry to hear of the concerns about Fred. We should go to bed now. Earnest will be here by late morning, and I still must deal with the needs of the farm and businesses before we can take time to visit.

Yes, Frank thought to himself. *She's still mother, managing everything, carrying the load, avoiding the conflict, making it all work. She is still the indomitable Elizabeth Garraux.* His feelings were a mixture of respect, slightly tempered with irritation. *No wonder all of us have to work so hard to measure up*, he thought. *And no wonder father never did.*

The next day, Earnest arrived before noon, and he was not alone. Much to everyone's surprise, he was accompanied by an attractive, well-dressed young woman with a round face, pink cheeks, sparkling blue eyes, bouncy blonde hair, and a wide smile.

Earnest helped her step down from the carriage, and as the family rushed out and gathered to greet them, Earnest proudly announced, "This is Ximenia Giles, my betrothed. We are soon to be married."

Elizabeth and Earnest's siblings were caught off guard, but immediately warmly welcomed Ximenia. Elizabeth was so happy to see her son happy again, after being so deeply grieved when his wife Minnie had died. The family had a delightful time talking, catching up, and showing Ximenia the property.

Frederick and his sons had built a large, handsome home for the family, with a sizeable addition off the back, and two outbuildings and a cottage, in addition to the greenhouse. The plantings around the homestead gave it the feel of a European estate, and though the wisteria was not in bloom, the expanse of the vine covering the long pergola was still impressive.

As they walked around the property that had been greatly expanded since her sons moved away, Elizabeth felt a small swell of pride, knowing it was singularly her effort and the effort of the children who remained at home, that had made it happen. It was no small task for a woman to be a major property and business owner, and she was grateful for the opportunities she had and the life this American city was providing her family.

Frank, who was continuing to invest in property with his partner, A.C., was duly impressed with the expansion of the Garraux assets in Greenville. The floral and millinery businesses were great successes and the farm was clearly thriving.

Charles, who was twenty-four, was actively courting Permelia Belle Peden, a young, local woman. Charles had taken over a section of his mother's property and had built a small house surrounded by a cleared, tiered, and well-planted farm of his own.

Pointing at acreage adjacent to the large farm, Elizabeth told Frank of her intent to eventually own the whole hillside along the creek. She always spoke with such assurance about future plans that Frank had no doubt she would accomplish her goals.

When William arrived in the afternoon, he came with news that he had, at just twenty years old, been hired by the Southern Railroad as an assistant engineer. He was jubilant about the opportunity to work with the railroad, and the family was excited that someone so young was rewarded with such an important position. Having her youngest son earn such a job with the railroad delighted Elizabeth.

William was tall like his father, and just as handsome. He had a quiet dignity about him, and most people thought he was older than his years, which probably helped him win the position with the Southern Railroad.

All in all, with John and Metta expecting their first child, Earnest announcing his remarriage, and William his new position, the weekend gathering took on the air of a family celebration. Even learning of Fred's success had lifted Elizabeth's spirits, despite the questions that had been raised about his behavior and marriage.

The family weekend initiated a time of joy that lasted on through the May birth of John and Metta's baby, a son they would name after his father. Elizabeth bought another adjoining acre, bringing the total to fifty-one acres.

Bettie, who was twenty-nine at the time, was being courted by a doctor from Massachusetts who had met her in the store when he was visiting Greenville. Dr. Adelbert Bryson was both a physician and a druggist, and he returned to Greenville several times to see Bettie and constantly wrote her letters. Bettie likewise found him charming. She had always longed to be married and had nearly given up the idea by her age.

Unfortunately, the months of happiness and hope were followed in the next year by great sadness for Elizabeth, with the failing health and passing of her dear friend, George Heldman, in 1892. George was never the same after the tragic death of his daughter, Fannie, three years before, and the injuries he had suffered in the fall.

When Elizabeth would visit him, they would still talk about the flowers and plants he enjoyed, and they would exchange seeds and cuttings as always, but the light had gone out of his eyes. She was deeply saddened, but not shocked when she learned of his death.

Chapter 12

After George's heavily attended funeral in which he was lovingly and respectfully eulogized, he was buried in Springwood Cemetery in the plot alongside his daughter. The cemetery was very old, with the first burial there in 1812 and the cemetery purchased by the city in 1829.

At a cost of a thousand dollars, George had ordered an enormously tall grave marker for Fannie. It had an elaborate carving of an angel with an inscription saying:

> *She was of more than ordinary attractive and promise but she died in the bloom of lovely womanhood leaving her parents in their old age childless and alone. Though parted for a while, they have met again where beyond these voices, there is peace. There fragrant flowers immortal bloom and joys supreme are given. Beyond the narrow tomb appears the dawn of Heaven.*

Heldman's family, always proud of the fact that his father had fought against Napoleon in the Prussian army, included mention of it in the inscription on his monument:

He was the son of Christian Heldman, who fought under Blucher at Waterloo. He came to the United States on October 18, 1840, and lived in the city of Greenville, South Carolina, forty-seven years. He was distinguished for his industry, perseverance, and uprightness of character. He loved the country of his adoption and the city where he labored in his manhood and spent his declining years. He was fond of the delicate and beautiful and gave his leisure time to the cultivation of fruits and flowers.

With a heavy heart, Elizabeth created an elaborate and exceptionally beautiful display of flowers for George's grave. Though his long goodbye had begun with the death of his daughter, Elizabeth did not realize how very much she would miss him until he was gone.

The sadness of that year carried over into 1893, a year of tumult and tragedy for Elizabeth and the family.

The shop and businesses were still stable and successful, and the city was growing in leaps and bounds. Elizabeth had been able to acquire more than seventy-five additional acres around the Garraux homestead in eight separate transactions. Her total land holding, as she had planned all along, was more than a hundred acres.

As she had always hoped, her property now ran from Swiss Avenue—the location of the Garraux homestead, Charles' home and the family's other barns and buildings—west all the way to Townes Street, and north to the creek that meandered through the ravine. Looking out over the property at the orderly fields and lush landscaping, there was no doubt that the family was one of the most successful of Greenville's pioneer families.

It was a brief time of affluence, peace, and healing, until an unexpected and inexplicable tragedy shook the family to the core, setting in motion changes that no one could have predicted.

On the afternoon of February 11, 1893, Gus Haynes, a well-known second baseman for the Greenville baseball team, walked into the Garraux's downtown market. Gus was about the same age as Charles and John, who had known him since grade school.

The newspaper would later report that Gus had been drinking heavily for a couple of days, and he had been talking about killing himself, even asking a friend if he would be a pallbearer. The report said no one he spoke to took him seriously, assuming he had just been drinking too much.

Just before two p.m., Gus walked past Bettie who was working at the front of the store. She smiled and waved a hello to him, but he didn't speak and kept walking. Charles was in the back room unloading fruit, and unaware that Gus was in the store.

A young man who was shopping in the store later said Gus walked up to him and said, "Tell everybody that I love them," before he put a pistol to his temple and fired.

The report said Gus never regained consciousness and died about an hour later.

Bettie and Charles both heard the gunshot. They rushed through the store to find Gus laying in a pool of blood. A young man stood nearby, face ashen, eyes closed, hand over his mouth, muttering "Oh, my God, oh, my God."

Charles told Bettie to run for help, and she was able to find an officer just down the block who whistled up other policemen who then swarmed into the store, pushing back curious bystanders who heard the commotion, and making room for a doctor who ran to the store from his office a block away.

Bettie and Charles were horrified by Gus's suicide, and the store was immediately shut down and draped in black for several days. The sudden, unexpected, violent death left Bettie particularly distraught. Even her closest confidant, her sister Rosa, could not console her. The entire family, including Elizabeth, were shaken by the inexplicable death, and they would forever wonder why Gus had chosen their market as the place to take his life.

Adelbert, who had been actively courting Bettie, began to immediately work at convincing her that with the disruption and distress in the family, she should marry him and move to Fall River, Massachusetts, where he had an established practice and comfortable life.

"I cannot leave Rosa and mother with all the family has just been through, Bert," Rosa said. "I love you, but I have loved my sister and mother longer. I can't abandon them just now."

"Do you want to spend your life just being your mother's daughter, or do you want a life of your own, Bettie? Rosa can move to Fall River too," Adelbert said. "There is nothing to stop her. You said you can't return to the shop, and Rosa would have more opportunities in Fall River. It is time she socializes and finds a life of her own. She would make a lovely wife, and she is not getting any younger."

And that began conversations between Bettie and Rosa that would lead to a major change for the sisters, for the family, and for Elizabeth.

At first, Rosa was resistant to the idea of leaving her home, but the more she and Bettie talked, the more Rosa realized there might be new opportunities for her in a different town. She particularly hoped that she too could find a husband and have a family.

When the sisters sat down with Elizabeth a few days later, she was completely shocked by what they had to say.

"I have agreed to marry Adelbert, Mama, and we are going to be living in Fall River, where he has his practice," Bettie blurted out.

Elizabeth felt strongly opposing emotions that made her heart both soar and then break. She, of course, wanted her daughters to find husbands. But she also wanted very much for her children to stay near her.

"Oh Bettie, I am happy for you," Elizabeth forced herself to say. "Adelbert seems like a good man who will be a good provider. But I will be sad to see you move so very far away."

A second later when the reality sank in, Elizabeth said, "What will happen with the market? You have made it such a success. Who will manage our store now?"

She then seemed to catch herself. "I am sorry. Forget about the market. It is your happiness that matters. We will manage the business."

Bettie said, "I have already talked to Charles, Mama, and he said he will take over the bookkeeping for the market, and we will hire a shopkeeper. We will keep it going. Charles will not let it fail."

There was a pause as Elizabeth tried to absorb this decision that had caught her completely off guard. As she tried to regain her balance, Rosa broke the silence, suddenly saying, "I am going too, Mama. I am going to move to Fall River near Bettie. It is a chance for a new life."

Elizabeth tried to put up a good front and managed to say words of encouragement to her daughters, though her heart was hurting with the thought of them leaving. She would hold her tears and fears inside until she was in the solitary darkness of her bedroom.

When the family gathered to hear the news about Bettie's marriage and move and that Rosa was leaving too, Charles said, "Well, before my sisters leave town, it seems that would be the right time for me to marry Belle!"

Charles and Permelia Belle Peden, who went by Belle, had planned a summer wedding, but they were happy to have an excuse to move up the date.

Even on short notice, Elizabeth created the most beautiful floral wedding arrangements anyone had ever seen. She was overjoyed to finally be participating in the wedding of one of her children, feeling that she had missed out on both Fred's wedding and Earnest's first marriage.

Bettie and Aldelbert's wedding and the small reception that followed at the Garraux homestead were joyous, but also bittersweet, knowing that

Bettie and Rosa would depart for Massachusetts within days.

Seeing her daughters off was terribly difficult for Elizabeth. She still had Lucy, Mary, and Fannie living with her, so she was definitely not alone, but the departure of each child also brought a certain measure of loss and sadness.

Chapter 13

By early spring, Bettie and Rosa were happily settled in Fall River. Bettie was busily redecorating the home she now shared with Adelbert, and Rosa renting a room in a boarding house while working as a dressmaker. The boarding house was run by an affable Scottish woman who was raising her two daughters and son alone. There was a total of eleven lodgers, a nineteen-year-old being the youngest, and a sixty-two-year-old widow being the oldest. A majority of the boarders were Irish, and most worked at retail or labor jobs.

Just about the time the sisters settled in, the news of Fall River's most infamous resident was burning like wildfire across the country in every newspaper, including the newspaper in Greenville. The trial was about to get underway in the case of Lizzie Borden, a woman just a year younger than Bettie, who was accused of brutally hacking her father and step-mother to death.

In August 1892, with only Lizzie and a maid in the house, Andrew Borden, Lizzie's father was killed in what was believed to be an ax attack that left his face and head destroyed. A short time later, a neighbor who Lizzie had called for help, discovered her stepmother, similarly hacked to death in an upstairs bedroom. From the body temperatures, her stepmother had apparently died first, investigators later said.

An intruder had been immediately suspected, but in a very short time, police investigators turned their attention solely to Lizzie, having decided she had opportunity and perhaps, motive. There were some in town who said Lizzie was not terribly fond of her stepmother, even though others who knew her well said there was no evidence of dislike ever shown. Despite the lack of physical evidence against Lizzie, the police, prosecutors, and most of the country believed her to be guilty.

All of America found the story titillating, and many of the letters between Bettie, Rosa, and their family included gossip and theories about the gruesome crimes.

That same spring, the weather once again became a vicious adversary. In June 1893, a violent thunderstorm slammed into Greenville. The lightning increased overnight, and early on the morning on June 13, bolts of lightning repeatedly struck homes and buildings all across the city, injuring several people.

The lightning coursed through telegraph and telephone lines, damaging wires and equipment. As many as sixty telephones in downtown homes and businesses were burned out. A horse was killed in the West End, and a house on Coffee Street was struck and badly damaged. Shortly before the storm finally blew through, a bolt hit a house on Mulberry Street, killing a man named John Brown, who was standing forty yards away at another home.

Elizabeth and her daughters had closed the windows and shutters as the storm rolled in, but just before six a.m., Mary screamed, and they all jumped when a bone-shaking crack of lightning struck very close by.

"That one hit our property," Elizabeth shouted to her daughters, as she bundled up the skirt of her nightshirt and ran up the stairs to see if there was damage or fire in the upper rooms.

The three of them ran about the house, checking each room, and peering out the windows, trying to see what tree or structure might have been hit. When the storm moved on and the thunder was finally rumbling a distance away, they went out to check the property. They found that the bolt had struck their well-house and had blown it into a pile of smoldering pieces.

In the end, they were grateful for damage only having been done to something that could be replaced. On the other hand, the man who was killed during the storm ended up being the brother of a man who regularly worked for them at the farm. They respectfully attended his funeral, along with only a handful of other white residents among a large crowd of black family members and friends.

They soon had the well-house rebuilt, and the farm returned to normal; the new acreage was plowed and producing well, as were the flower gardens. They had hired a shopkeeper and stock boy for the market, and with Charles assisting with the bookkeeping, the shop continued its success.

Lucy and Mary continued the millinery business besides their work on the farm. Elizabeth grew more and more flowers, each year's new contacts in the floral business allowing her to grow rarer and more interesting plants. She often wished she could discuss her new finds with George, and regularly realized she missed him more than she had ever expected to or would ever admit.

She had tried a couple of times to visit George's widow, Matilda, but the loss of her only child and now her husband had left Matilda preferring to live a quiet life of near solitude. Elizabeth understood. She knew better than most that sometimes, quiet aloneness is often the only thing that can help heal your heart.

Chapter 14

One rainy afternoon, in a quiet and pensive moment, sitting alone in her parlor, sixty-five-year-old Elizabeth found herself running through a mental inventory of her children's lives.

She admittedly worried most about Fred, her oldest, who at thirty-seven still had no children. And from what his brother said, it seemed he might have marital problems. But with Fred in Atlanta and not communicating with her directly, it was impossible to keep track of his life. It grieved her, because as her first born, he held a special place in her heart.

She was glad thirty-six-year-old Earnest had survived the loss of his first wife and now seemed to have a happy life with Ximenia and their three-year-old son. He was living in Charlotte and was working for the Florida Central Peninsular Railroad. Like his much younger brother William, who worked for the Southern Railway, Earnest had also become an engineer. Unlike his older brother, Fred, Earnest made a point of staying in touch, and he and Ximenia and their first child, a son they called Earnie, named after him, visited quite often.

Charles and Belle had settled immediately into family life on their farm, with daughters born a year apart in 1894 and '95. Charles had taken on much of the business connected to the shop when Bettie left, and yet he still kept up well with his farming business. He also treated his relationship with Belle with loving commitment and diligence as always, and he was devoted to raising their daughters.

Lucy was both Elizabeth's constant companion and truly, her dear friend. They ate most meals together and sat side-by-side at the first Presbyterian Church most Sundays.

Mary was just as sweet and amiable as she had been as a child, and more often than not, accompanied Elizabeth and Lucy wherever they went. She remained the family's animal lover, and she had a gentle, caregiving rapport with each of the pets as well as with the herd animals. Elizabeth knew it was unlikely either Lucy or Mary would ever marry, so she was grateful they had each other.

She very much missed Bettie, now thirty-two and living in Fall River with her doctor husband. Bettie had an energy level and drive very similar to her own, and she often missed having her to turn to. But Elizabeth was, in the end, glad that Rosa had moved near Bettie and Adelbert and was part of a new social group.

Unlike Mary and Lucy, she knew Rosa wanted a family of her own. She hoped and prayed being in Fall River would help her meet the right man.

Frank had stayed in touch more since his visit, and she had come to feel better about his situation in Atlanta with A.C. Gann's partnership. She still didn't like saloons being part of his life, but she had to admit that at twenty-eight years old, Frank seemed happy and successful. Though he said there was no woman in his life, he didn't seem terribly interested in finding one.

John, at twenty-six, was now the well-respected general foreman of the Water Company, and he was utterly devoted to his work, his wife Metta, their son, and the city of Greenville. John was the one of her children who could always be depended upon, no matter the need or situation. In her heart, she admitted relief that it appeared kind, diligent John would never leave Greenville.

Elizabeth felt very fortunate to have John and Charles nearby, as well as their twenty-three-year-old brother, William, who had been work-ing with the railroad for three years and had already been promoted to engineer.

And then there was Fannie, her beloved last baby. Now twenty-one years old, Fannie still maintained the good humor, delight in life, and energy of a teenager. With her bright attitude and enthusiasm for life, she always buoyed Elizabeth's feelings, no matter what happened in the day.

For all the ups and downs in life, Elizabeth was grateful to have been blessed with these eleven children, all so different, all precious to her. It would forever be a disappointment to her that her husband Frederick could not have remained part of their family and their lives. But it was also a source of pride to her that without him around, she and the chil-dren had forged decent, successful lives.

Once they adjusted to the absence of Bettie and Rosa, life for the family returned to status quo. All was well in Elizabeth's world until a visit from Frank brought a dark cloud of shame and embarrassment to the family.

When Frank arrived from Atlanta in early 1895, she was happy as always to see him. But within moments, it was clear he had troubling news for her.

"Mother, I am sorry to be the bearer of bad news, but I am afraid this news will make its way to you through someone else if I do not inform you," Frank said.

"I am afraid the accusations Pennina made against Fred are now public knowledge. She is divorcing him, and the details have made the newspa-pers."

"Why in the world would the details of a divorce be written up in a newspaper," Elizabeth exclaimed.

Frank pulled out the folded page of a newspaper from the inside breast pocket of his jacket and handed it to her.

Elizabeth unfolded the clipping from the *Atlanta Constitution*, dated January 19, 1895, and read it silently:

> One of the divorces granted was to Mrs. Pennina Garraux, who sought separation from her husband, Fred Garraux. The allegations in the bill for divorce were decidedly lively, and the husband was portrayed in a not very enviable light.
>
> Mrs. Garraux alleged that she married Fred Garraux in 1880 and lived peaceably for some years. About four years ago, according to this petition, the husband began a systematic series of cruel treatment. This was not all; if the petition is to be believed, Frederick was an exceedingly naughty man.
>
> Mrs. Garraux alleged that he had another household, and that the central figure was Jennie Baker, with whom the wife alleges her husband lived. She also claimed that this same Jennie Baker lived in a house which she was informed and believed was owned by her husband, Fred Garraux. The divorce was granted. In the meantime, there has been a suit for alimony dispersed of, and Mrs. Garraux was given a certain amount monthly.

Elizabeth read the clipping a second time, and then said, "Frank, is this true? Is what Pennina said true?"

"Yes, mother, I am afraid it is," Frank said. "Fred came to tell me about what was being said in the divorce hearings, and he was unapologetic about his behavior. He excused himself by saying he no longer cared for Pennina, and that he had loved Jennie Baker for years.

"When I asked why he hadn't just divorced her, he railed against Pennina, saying he knew she would just try to take all his money. It's an exceedingly ugly divorce, and with Frank being well-known for the cotton gin machinery he has patented for Winship, and his position as a foreman and property owner, the newspapers are having a field day writing every salacious detail."

Frank said, "The newspaper also reported that Fred built two houses on Magnolia Street that he deeded to Jennie Baker, who lived in one of them. She lived there until the neighbors complained so much about Fred's affair with her that they drove her out of the neighborhood. Fred admitted to me he owns five houses, and Jennie had lived in one of them for some time."

"Oh, how awful!" Elizabeth cried out. "How shameful! How could a son raised in this family end up behaving this way?"

And in her next breath she said angrily, "It's his father's influence. His drunken father! Fred has always stayed too close to him. Who knows what that man has behaved like over the years!"

Frank took offense, and said, "Mother, you cannot blame our father. Fred is his own person. And I have never known father to have the womanizing issues Fred has. I don't know why Fred behaves the way he does."

Elizabeth found it difficult to absolve her estranged husband of responsibility, but she did have to admit that Frederick had apparently not wrongly influenced Earnest or Frank, who had also stayed in close contact with their father.

"This is terrible, Frank. Oh, I hope this news doesn't make it to Greenville. It will be so humiliating! I will have to let your brothers and sisters know about what has happened."

That night, with her grief cloistered in private as was her way, Elizabeth wept in her bedroom about her oldest, beloved son, and the shame brought to the family by his terrible behavior. She spent most of the next day sniffling, praying and penning letters to Earnest, Bettie, and Rosa. By evening, she had composed herself enough to tell Fred's siblings who lived in Greenville about their brother's embarrassing life.

Elizabeth still loved her son Fred as deeply as ever, but she was terribly ashamed of the choices he had made. When Frank told Elizabeth two years later that Fred had married his paramour, she was glad she didn't have to attend the wedding or ever interact with Jennie Baker.

Chapter 15

Elizabeth was happy, when later that year, a second son was born to Earnest and Ximenia. Earnest had relocated his family to North Carolina to be closer to Ximenia's family in Charlotte, but because of his work as a train engineer, he still visited Greenville quite often, frequently with his family.

After the heartbreaking death of Earnest's first wife, seeing him happily remarried with two sweet sons, Earnie and Willie, brought Elizabeth much relief. And Earnest's brother, William, whom the family also called Willie, was tickled to have a namesake.

That same year, William proposed to Mittie Martin, a local girl who had just turned sixteen. Elizabeth was surprised at the age difference, but Mittie was a level-headed, mature girl, who quickly made a good impression on Elizabeth. After their marriage, William and Mittie lived in Charlotte, but William's position as locomotive engineer also allowed them to visit Greenville frequently before they moved back to the city in early 1898.

William and Mittie's first child was born shortly after their move to Greenville. They named her Lucile, but called her Lucy, after her maiden aunt, who, at forty years old, still shared the house with her mother and sisters.

That same year, John and Metta built a house on Swiss Avenue on the Garraux homestead.

It was still difficult for Elizabeth to adjust to having several of her children living in multiple cities. But at least Lucy, Mary, and Fannie were still with her, and John and Charles, and now William, were still nearby.

Charles and Belle had a third daughter in 1899, and her grandchildren brought much light, love, and laughter to Elizabeth's life. She had a total of eight grandchildren by the century's turn, six of them living near her. When they all gathered together, the sounds of the fun they shared reminded Elizabeth of her happy younger years when they had been a big, boisterous family, especially during the years in Bent Creek.

Often, she would look at her grandchildren, running and playing on the lush acreage of the farm, or telling childhood secrets under the wisteria vine on the pergola, and she would wistfully wish Frederick had a chance to see them all together on the beautiful property. But she would immediately push the thoughts aside, reminding herself that it had been his choice to not make his family his priority. *It was his lack of self-control that prevented him from being part of their lives*, she thought, as she tucked away and hid memories of him, much like she had done with the inlaid wooden box from their courtship.

As the turn of the century approached, Greenville's population had reached more than eight thousand. It was no longer the small town in which the Garrauxs had settled. There were more than half a dozen thriving textile mills built along the Reedy River, employing hundreds of people.

Main Street was crowded with thriving businesses, and some of the city's elite had built magnificent mansions and classic Victorian homes near the business district. Neighborhoods filled with many smaller homes were creeping along side streets out into the hills, woods, and former farms surrounding the city center.

The tiny, outdated post office had been replaced with a grand, large building. Former mayor Tom Gower's wooden bridge over the Reedy River was replaced with an iron bridge, allowing freer transportation and heavier vehicles to cross the river. Off Hampton Avenue, there was a half-mile horse racing track near a railroad depot that regularly drew big crowds.

A good number of Greenville's wealthiest residents had purchased automobiles, and it was becoming more commonplace to see horseless carriages buzzing past, often startling the horses and mules most people still used for transportation.

Gower had been president of Greenville's street railway, with six rail cars and three mules transporting shoppers and business people across the downtown. When he died in 1894, Gower's son, Arthur, who had been superintendent, took over the street railway. By three years later, he was running six railcars with seventeen horses across the city, making thousands of dollars a year. But, by the turn of the century, the Southern Railway, which employed two of Elizabeth's sons, had caused Gower to give up on the street rail business.

Earnest, who was a successful and popular locomotive engineer for the railway, lived in a large home on Buncombe Street, a short distance away from the Garraux homestead, with Ximenia and their two sons.

Charles and Bell had purchased a farm on nearby Townes Street, in addition to working some of the more than 150 acres Elizabeth owned. They had daughters born a year apart in 1894 and 1895, followed by another in '97 and a fourth in '99.

John continued to do well in his work with the Water Company, and he and Metta maintained a close connection to Elizabeth and the other siblings in town. When their son and Charles' daughters got together, the children lined up like five stair steps, from a baby to a five-year-old.

Elizabeth's farm and floral businesses were still thriving, and her boundless energy at seventy-two astounded customers, neighbors, friends, and even her own children. She had given up the shop on Main Street but stayed nearly as busy selling and arranging flowers at the main homestead on Swiss Avenue. The greenhouse continued to give her the opportunity to provide flowers for weddings and funerals year-round, and though there were a few other florists in town, she was proudly referred to as Greenville's first florist.

Elizabeth adored time spent with the grandchildren, and regularly said her flowers and the children kept her young.

Frank had remained in Atlanta and was now the co-owner of a popular saloon on Marietta Street in Atlanta called Gann & Garraux, He and his partner, A.C. Gann, jointly owned many homes and properties in that city.

All in all, the last years leading up to the turn of the century had been productive and relatively peaceful for the family.

The first of several tragedies to strike the family happened in 1900, when Earnest and Ximenia's second son, Willie, contracted tetanus from a cut on his foot. Though some were able to survive tetanus, there was no cure for it, and after several days of unrelenting, agonizing, gruesome, muscle-locking seizures, the child died.

Earnest was terribly traumatized by his son's death, having lost his first wife in a painful passing and now his beloved child. He took time off from the railroad, and he and Ximenia mourned privately while caring for their older son.

Elizabeth fully believed that the death of a child was the most painful loss a human could experience, and she grieved the loss of little Willie for herself, but even more for his inconsolable, heartbroken parents.

Chapter 16

Not long after Willie's death, Elizabeth was extremely shocked one Sunday when Daniel Bull took her aside at church and said he would like to speak to her about her daughter, of whom he had grown extremely fond.

Daniel Hamilton Bull, fifty-four, was a well-to-do widow, with a store on Coffee Street and an extensive farming operation. Bull's wife, Mattie, had died several years before, leaving him with three children, all of whom were now grown and married.

Elizabeth was perplexed by his desire to speak to her about her daughter. He knew Lucy and her other daughters from church dinners and activities, but he was not someone who they had ever brought up in conversation. Caught off guard by his request, she agreed to have him come by for tea the next day. She did not discuss it with her daughters since she could not imagine the true intent of the conversation.

Promptly at two p.m., Bull's carriage pulled up in front of the Garraux house. Elizabeth watched from inside the house as his driver opened the carriage door, and Bull dusted himself down and walked briskly to the front door.

"Hello, Madam Garraux," he said with a slight bow as he removed his hat.

"Please come in, Mr. Bull," Elizabeth said. "I have brewed a pot of tea and there are freshly baked cookies in the parlor."

"You are too kind," Bull said, clearly uncomfortable in this social situation, despite being a man of means and generally of great self-assurance.

After stirring a lump of sugar into his tea while making small talk about their mutual business endeavors, Bull anxiously blurted out, "I would like to speak to you about potentially courting your daughter."

"Courtship?" Elizabeth said, unable to contain her surprise. "Lucy has never even talked about you. I didn't know you actually knew her well enough to be interested in her."

Bull's cheeks flushed, and for a man who usually possessed a calm self-confidence, he looked rather flustered.

"Oh, I have not made myself clear. I apologize," Bull said. "It is your daughter Fannie, whom I hope you will give me permission to court."

"Fannie? My daughter, Fannie?" Elizabeth said, surely looking as flabbergasted as she was. "My daughter Fannie is more than twenty years younger than you! My goodness, Mr. Bull, your son, James, is the same age as Fannie! My youngest daughter has never mentioned any interest in you either!"

"I am sorry, I see you are shocked, Madame Garraux," Bull stammered. "Fannie and I have had several conversations, and she has let me walk her most of the way home from church several times."

Elizabeth thought back and realized there had been many times in the past months that Fannie had told her and her sisters to go ahead after church and she would catch up with them.

Gathering up himself and his confidence, Bull continued, "She is the most charming and delightful human being I have ever met. She makes me laugh, and I feel joy when I am with her that I haven't felt since before I was widowed. I have fallen in love with Fannie. And I know our age difference is great, but I promise you, should I convince her to love me in return and marry me, I will provide her with the life she deserves."

He took a breath and continued, "We were aware that you might have hesitation because of my widowhood and age, so we agreed to keep our interest in each other to ourselves until I spoke with you."

Elizabeth was so taken back by the unexpected conversation, the only words she could muster were, "Well, I will speak with Fannie. I must know her thoughts. But as you can imagine, this is not what I expected for my youngest child. I will have to bid you good day so I can collect my thoughts and then find Fannie to discuss it with her."

Bull looked flustered as well, and he felt somewhat insulted. He might be older than her Fannie, but he felt most mothers would like to know that a well-heeled man could offer their daughter a good lifestyle and a lovely home.

Concealing his feeling of having been insulted, he set down his teacup, picked up his hat and said, "Thank you for your time, madam. Please try to think well of me, as I believe I could provide your lovely daughter with a good life."

"I will let you know what I think after I consult with my daughter, Elizabeth said as she ushered him to the door. "Good day, Mr. Bull."

Elizabeth didn't realize that Fannie had been watching Bull's arrival and departure from around the corner of the house. As Elizabeth prepared to go look for her, Fannie burst into the room, words spewing from her as she ran to her mother, grabbing her arms and looking her in the face.

291

"You talked to Daniel, Mama! He thinks he loves me, and he wants to court me. I think I love him too, Mama! He is a strong, good man, and he has been a good father to his children. I know he is older, but he makes me feel safe and loved whenever we talk. Please, Mama, give him your blessing to court me. I know we will be good together. And we will stay nearby, so I will never have to move away from you."

Fannie's enthusiasm was like getting caught in a whirlwind. Elizabeth was still left off-balance by Bull's intentions, and now even more so by her daughter's desire to be courted by him.

But seeing the pure joy in Fannie's face told her in advance what her decision would be. Elizabeth, more than anything, wanted this youngest and most life-loving child of hers to have the happiness and care she deserved.

Elizabeth called Bull back to the homestead the next morning and told him that she would approve of him courting her dear daughter, Fannie. But she made it clear, almost in the tone of a threat, that she expected him to keep his word that he would provide her with a good life.

Though the idea of their beloved little Fannie having a much older husband took some time for her siblings and mother to adjust to, they eventually found Bull's kind and affectionate treatment of their sister and his affable personality such that the age difference became much less important as time passed.

Daniel and Fannie's wedding was lovely and was attended by more than 100 people. Though she was a second wife, Bull was well-liked in the town, and many people were glad to see him find another woman. Fannie moved into his large home on Bull's Alley near Bucknertown, and immediately settled happily into her new life. Fannie was gregarious and witty, and immediately became extremely popular in the society her marriage to Bull provided.

Meanwhile, Charles and Belle, who had four daughters, were thrilled when Belle gave birth to their first and only son, his father's namesake, in November of 1900.

Charlie was an exceptionally happy, easy baby and Elizabeth loved spending time with the chubby, cheerful boy. He was her ninth grandchild, the others ranging from one to seven years old.

She still awaited news that her oldest, Fred, would be having a child, but none came. Even with his second marriage, it appeared not to be. He had, however, continued to be very successful in business, and in 1901, he left the Van Winkle company to start his own manufacturing plant for cotton gins and ginning machinery.

Frank brought along a newspaper article with him on one of his visits that described Fred's investment of more than $10,000 in the plant on about three and a half acres near the Roseland train station. Elizabeth always knew Fred would find his way in business and was not at all surprised it was a machinery business, since that had always been his greatest interest. Fred was the sole owner and proprietor, with no investors, which was quite an accomplishment.

The first couple years of the new century were a time of joy for Elizabeth and the family, until the happiness was crushed in 1902 by her greatest loss.

Frank, who generally visited about once a month, arrived unexpectedly from Atlanta, and from his demeanor, Elizabeth immediately knew something was very wrong.

"The news is bad, mother," Frank said. "Fred is extremely ill. He has Bright's disease, and he is not doing well."

"Oh, no," Elizabeth cried, her heart sinking and a lump forming in her throat. "What is Bright's disease? Is he in a doctor's care? Will he recover?"

Frank leaned forward and took Elizabeth's hands in his and said, "No, mother, I am sorry. Fred will not be able to recover. It is an incurable disease of the kidneys. There are treatments that have been tried, but all have failed. It is a terrible disease. Doctors could not even save Theodore Roosevelt's first wife who died of it. So did the great poet, Emily Dickinson."

As tears welled up in Elizabeth's eyes, Frank said, "They have tried several treatments—baths, mercuric compounds, and bloodletting—but the doctor says Fred does not have long to live. I intend to return to him immediately."

"Oh, Frank, this is so terrible. I always believed Fred and I would repair our relationship and be close once again. I cannot believe he can be this sick at just forty-five years old. He cannot die so very young."

With that, she bent over, head in hands, and began to weep.

"I am so sorry, mother. I know you love him so much, and I know you hoped to resolve things with him."

She wiped her eyes and nose with a handkerchief, and said, "I will go to Atlanta with you. I must see him."

"I am sorry, Mother. I asked about bringing you to him, and he said he does not want you to come. You know he has stayed close to father, and father is staying by Fred's bedside with Jennie. I am so sorry. Please do not be hurt by that. Too many years have gone by . . ."

Elizabeth's heart was broken. With all that had happened in Fred's life, her first child still held a special place in her heart. To think of him passing without her being able to see him again overwhelmed her with grief.

Two days later, with Frederick, Jennie, and Frank by his side, Fred passed away in his sleep.

Elizabeth, heartbroken and inconsolable, placed a notice in the Greenville newspaper that said,

Fred Garraux, son of Mrs. E. Garraux of North Main street, died at his home in Atlanta on the night of January 13 after a brief illness. He was

a splendid young man and the pride of his mother, who is deeply grieved over his death. He was buried in Atlanta on the following day after his death.

Fred's siblings all mourned his death, especially Mary, who found it impossible to think of her brother as no longer alive. She had been troubled by the years of his absence, but this was nearly impossible for her to fathom. When Mary heard Fred was likely to die, she immediately took the entirety of the cash she had saved over the years and went to Springwood Cemetery and bought a plot for him to be brought home.

Mary was further crushed when she learned that Fred was buried in Atlanta. The idea of him never returning home broke her heart.

Chapter 17

The most deeply affected of all by Fred's death was his father. Watching his oldest son, his namesake, suffer and die nearly destroyed him. He had been living with Fred and Jennie and had grown very close to his son during his illness. At the moment of Fred's death, he very much wished he could accompany him.

Days later, Frederick moved back to his small apartment. He closed the heavy drapes over the tall windows, and for two days, he did not leave his bed. He would awaken, realize his son was gone, and would sob until sleep overcame him again.

Over the next few weeks, he only left his apartment to gather materials to construct a wooden coffin that he placed in his bedroom. He hoped it would not be long before it would be in use, and he could be reunited with his son.

Frederick then returned to the only escape and comfort he had known all his life. Within weeks, he was missing work and destroying friendships as well as his relationship with Frank with his constant drinking. He drank to forget his grief, and then he drank more to forget the loneliness and rejection it caused.

Elizabeth also struggled to get past her feelings of grief and loss, and the now permanent lack of resolution between her son, Fred, and her. But when life became difficult, Elizabeth also did as she had always done. She worked.

By 1902, at seventy-four years old, Elizabeth ran the florist business, the large farm, and the millinery shop, and she continued to own and manage the downtown store.

She was disgusted when Frank told her in passing that Jennie Baker, Fred's second wife, who had inherited his entire estate, had remarried within just months of his passing. Elizabeth tried to put all the negative thoughts about Fred's life and how it ended out of her memories. She tried to remember the kind-hearted, happy child Fred had been, and she tried very hard not to think of his tumultuous life, its tragic end, or his apparently wealthy, merry widow.

As she worked alongside Lucy and Mary, with Charles assisting at the store, she began to find her equilibrium again. Charles was doing well as a truck farmer, wholesaling his corn and vegetables to stores in Greenville and elsewhere, using the city's well-connected railroad system. His wife, Mittie, loved farm life, having been raised on her grandfather's farm, and she thoroughly enjoyed raising their four girls and their little boy, who was now a bright and inquisitive toddler.

John continued his work with the water company and was active in civic affairs and very respected in the city. He and Metta lived in a house they had built on Swiss Avenue, near the original homestead, and they frequently spent time on the family farm, helping out when possible.

Though in quiet, private moments, Elizabeth still deeply grieved the loss of her oldest son, she and the rest of the family focused on building stable, successful lives for the next generation.

Elizabeth was excited when Rosa wrote and surprised her with news she had eloped and married Amos Marvel, a postal clerk she had been dating. Elizabeth was once again disappointed to miss a child's wedding, but she was so glad Rosa finally found a partner. Amos was 12 years older than Rosa, so Elizabeth was not surprised they rushed to start a family. Rosa wrote in early 1903 saying she and Amos, then living in Rhode Island, were expecting a baby. Elizabeth was thrilled since Rosa was already forty years old, and Elizabeth had wondered if she would end up childless. She expected Rosa would do well, just as she had done when she gave birth to Fannie when she was forty-three.

Rosa and Amos named their daughter Bertha, her sister Bettie's given name. Even at this point in life, married and living in different cities, the sisters remained the closest of friends and confidants.

All was well in Elizabeth's world and in the lives of her children until tragedy struck the family once again in the fall of 1903.

Charles and Belle's only son, Charlie, came down with the flu in October. Elizabeth spelled Belle in her constant care of the sick eleven-month-old. She put cold cloths on his feverish forehead and rocked him while his mother took brief catnaps. He seemed to be improving slightly, but then on the night of October 22, as Elizabeth, exhausted, had just laid down on the sofa, a horrible, screaming wail came from Charlie's room. It was Belle, and she screamed repeatedly, "Oh, my God, no! No, no, no!"

Charles and Elizabeth ran into the room, where Belle, face colorless and ghostly, stood in the dark, holding the limp body of her baby boy. The little boy's body, worn out from fever and illness, had just shut down.

Elizabeth had felt losing her son, Fred, caused the greatest sadness she could ever experience, but with the loss of Willie and now Charlie, she realized that seeing her own children suffer this worst of losses caused her even more pain. The sight days later of Charles and Belle weeping over the tiny white casket of their little boy felt like a grief almost too great to bear.

The family supported Charles and Belle in their mourning, and eventually, ever so slowly, life began to return to normal . . . until February 1904, when what should have been a private issue became a public drama and a humiliating tragedy.

At the beginning of the month, Elizabeth received a letter, addressed in shaky but familiar handwriting. She turned over the envelope, and confirmed from the return address on the flap, the letter was from her estranged husband Frederick.

It had literally been nearly two decades since she had any direct communication with him, so just seeing his name written on the envelope made her stomach turn over.

She opened the letter and read it slowly:

> *Dear Elizabeth,*
>
> *I am sure you are surprised to hear from me. Since our son Fred's death, I have realized that I feel little reason to live. I do not want to be separated from my family or the home I built anymore. Without Fred, and with Frank avoiding me, I am too lonely, and I long for the life I once had. I will be packing my possessions to return home in a week. I would like to reconcile our marriage. We are too old to continue to live separately.*
>
> *Sincerely, Your husband, Frederick*

Elizabeth was stunned. After all these years, he thought he could just write a few sentences and return home? Return home to the successful life and businesses she had built on her own? *The man must be mad*, she thought. How dare he believe he could just simply come home!

She got a pen and stationery, and immediately wrote a response. Then she crumpled it up and wrote another. By the fourth attempt, she was satisfied with what she wrote, and she immediately took it to the Post Office.

She would never tell anyone what she had written, or even that he had written to her. Their failed marriage was a private drama that no one else needed to be a part of. The life she had built in Greenville belonged to her and her children. She felt settled and resolute, knowing no one ever needed to know that Frederick had contacted her.

Little did she know that her response, and his reaction to it would be written up in newspapers and discussed in cities across the South, including Greenville.

Chapter 18

Once again, it was Frank who had the unfortunate duty of bringing bad news to his mother the next week. She was already expecting him since he had told her he had business in Greenville. On the day of his anticipated visit, she had busily prepared lunch for the two of them, Lucy, and Mary.

Elizabeth had been watching for Frank, and when his buggy pulled up in front of the house, she dried her hands and pulled off her apron, calling out to her daughters who were stitching mattresses in a back room of the house, "Frank is here. Come join us for lunch."

"Hello, son," she called out cheerfully from the front porch, but she quickly realized Frank was looking serious, even somber.

"What is it, Frank?" she asked, when he hadn't even returned her "Hello."

"Oh, Mother, I am again bringing you bad news. This is going to be a very difficult time for all of us, I am afraid," he said, his eyes sad and dark.

By then, Lucy and Mary had thrown on their coats and had come out to greet him, their cheerful greetings quickly silenced by their brother's serious appearance and their mother's concerned expression.

"Hello Mary. Hello Lucy," Frank said. "I am going to need to talk to Mother before we have lunch. I need to talk to her alone."

His attitude was greatly concerning Elizabeth, and she could not imagine what was wrong.

"I have brought another newspaper article. You are going to be upset by it," he said as they sat down in the parlor. "First, I have to ask, did you respond to a letter from father telling him he could not come back to Greenville?"

She had told no one of the letter, so she knew Frederick had to have told his son.

"Yes, we exchanged letters," she said. "But what are you talking about—a newspaper article?"

Fred, looking serious and sad, said, "Well, you might as well just read it," as he unfolded a newspaper clipping and handed it to her. The article was headlined, "Opened His Veins."

> *Frederick Garraux, a man 70 years of age, is at the Grady Hospital in a dying condition from the loss of blood resulting from his efforts to commit suicide by severing arteries in his left arm.*

"Oh, my God," Elizabeth gasped, to which Frank said, "He is still alive, Mother. Keep reading."

Shaking her head in disbelief at what she was reading, she continued.

> *It is said Garraux recently wrote to his wife, whom he left in Greenville, S.C., nearly twenty years ago, seeking reconciliation. She replied that she did not wish to see him anymore.*

Crying out in her native German, Elizabeth said, "Oh mein Gott, oh mein Gott, nein!" before she continued to read.

Late Saturday afternoon, he went to Oakland Cemetery, and seated on the grave of his eldest son, began hacking his left arm with a knife. He was in a faint, unconscious condition from the loss of blood when found. There is still much doubt about his recovery.

"This is horrible!" Elizabeth said. "Suicide, on my son's grave? And telling strangers the details of our private life? What is wrong with him?"

And then tempering her anger, she said, "Has he survived? Will he live?"

"He is recovering," Frank said. "He is expected to live. People found him in the cemetery having nearly bled to death and called police. He was taken to the hospital in an ambulance and doctors were able to save him."

Frank said, "Unfortunately, this is one of several newspaper articles about his attempt to take his own life. And many of them talk about the letters you exchanged and your refusal to let him return home."

"It has been nearly two decades!" Elizabeth said. "Why would he, or anyone, think he should come home?"

"I understand your feelings, Mother. I know how hard you have worked to make a good life for our family without him. I also understand why you wanted him to leave. The newspapers do not tell that part of the story. In fact, they make him sound like a very good man who was very unfairly treated," Frank said. "There are many other articles, but I don't think you should read them."

The articles did go into gory detail about Frederick stabbing himself. One described him as a "hard-working and honest man, and a respectable citizen by those who know him." That article also mentioned that Frederick had stored his own coffin in his room for about two years.

One article went into detail saying his family "was not treating him right" and that he claimed his children had "deserted him."

"I just can't believe this," Elizabeth said loudly. "I cannot believe that man would bring more public shame on this family! It isn't bad enough that

Fred's affairs had to be made public, now his worthless father has to do this?"

"Mother, the man is so sad he tried to kill himself! This isn't just about the family reputation. Have you no compassion?" Frank said sternly.

Their voices had grown loud enough that Lucy and Mary appeared in the doorway looking concerned.

"What's going on?' Lucy asked. "What are you both upset about?"

As Elizabeth tried quelling her upset to formulate words to explain the whole outrage, Frank said calmly, "There's been an incident with Father, and it has been written about in the newspapers."

"Father has been terribly upset since Fred passed, and in his distress, he attempted to end his life in a public place. He has survived and is being cared for. It is not something Mother should have to deal with, but because of the news coverage, it is likely to become known, even here in Greenville, so she had to be told."

"He tried to kill himself?' Lucy said, as Mary, color drained from her face, grabbed onto her arm.

Despite being in their early forties, it was still disturbing to hear that the man who they remembered from their childhoods had tried to end his own life.

"Yes, but the doctors say he will survive," Frank said.

"Let me finish this conversation with Frank, please," Elizabeth said, dismissing her daughters from the room.

"So, what is happening now, Frank?" she said. "What will become of your father?"

"Well, even though he is a Protestant, he has a group of Catholic friends who have arranged for him to be cared for at the Little Sisters of the Poor Sanitorium in Savannah. An Atlanta city police officer who is his friend—Detective Harry White—has agreed to gather him up when he is well enough recovered and will put him on the train in Union Station to go to Savannah."

Elizabeth just shook her head as tears welled up in her eyes, feeling both shocked and saddened to think of her estranged husband in such a state.

Ending life in a pauper's hospital, Elizabeth thought. She had never wished any such outcome for Frederick. But she also believed strongly that every person is accountable for their choices in life.

For weeks, the notoriety and scandal of Frederick's suicide attempt and move to the sanitorium would surface in Greenville's barbershops, bar rooms and among church-foyer gossipers. As Elizabeth passed by, she could immediately tell what was being discussed by the looks of sympathy tainted with judgment that followed sudden silences. The shame she felt Frederick brought to the family left a dark shadow that would linger for the rest of her days.

She was surprised, and somewhat irritated, when she learned Earnest and Ximenia had moved to Atlanta so he could take over what remained of his father's carpentry business there as well as a position in a woodworking shop. She knew the decision to leave the railroad and make the move to Atlanta was at least in part connected to loyalty to his father and some type of effort to make amends with the past.

Earnest did remain close to his siblings in Greenville, and he and his family visited Elizabeth fairly often, though the tragedy surrounding his father was not addressed. Elizabeth had made it clear it was not something that would be spoken of in her home.

Some of her distress was diminished by news that her beloved Fannie was expecting her and Daniel's first child. The couple had moved to a beautiful new home on one of Daniel's farms in Chick Springs. The home was near a resort hotel that Daniel's son, James, had bought in 1903.

James, who went by J.A., had renovated and expanded the property into the luxurious Chick Springs Resort, with more than 100 guest suites, a ballroom, tennis court, equestrian trails, a golf course, a swimming pond and a bowling alley. James had started out as a clerk in his father's store, and worked his way up in retail, eventually building J. A. Bull & Co., one of the most successful grocers downtown.

For Elizabeth, watching her youngest daughter in the glow of expectant motherhood was a pure joy. They spent many happy hours together as Fannie prepared a nursery in the couple's lovely home on Chick Springs Road, as well as sharing in many happy gatherings at the resort.

In the fall of 1904, Fannie gave birth to a son they named George.

Chick Springs was only a few miles from the Garraux homestead so Daniel would regularly have someone fetch Elizabeth for visits with Fannie and baby George, which delighted her.

Daniel, at fifty-five, was thrilled to have an infant son, but he was also somewhat distracted by the births of three grandchildren in the same year. Daniel's daughter, Miriam, had given birth to twin girls in July, one of whom only survived four days.

Miriam had previously had a three-year-old son die in 1901, and another son who died in 1902, having only lived a few days after birth, so there was much concern about the health and well-being of her surviving baby girl.

Both of Daniel's sons had baby boys born just a couple months after George's birth in September. The almost-identical ages of Fannie and Daniel's son and his grandchildren, as well as their how they were all related, frequently confused others outside the family.

Though she remained bright and energetic, Elizabeth had begun to show her age, and she was relying more and more on Lucy and Mary for help with the floral and millinery business.

As she began to gradually slow down, Elizabeth's troop of grandchildren continued to expand. In 1905, Rosa and Amos had their second child, a son, in Portsmouth, Rhode Island, where Amos was serving as Postmaster. Rosa, at forty-two, was especially delighted that their daughter, Bertha, would not be raised as an only child.

That same year, Charles and Belle added a son, Joe, to their Greenville farm family of four girls, their first child born since the death of their son Charlie in 1903. John and Metta also had a second son they named Thomas.

Of Elizabeth's fourteen surviving grandchildren, ten of them lived nearby, so family gatherings, especially holidays, were joyful, busy times that brought her much happiness.

Chapter 19

Despite being in her late seventies, Elizabeth insisted on doing most of the cooking for the family gatherings, continuing the serving of traditional Swiss holiday dishes. Along with several other favorite dishes, she would usually make filet im teig, a pastry-wrapped pork roast with sausage meat; scalloped potatoes with melted cheese; and her special rich, moist walnut cake that was reserved just for holiday meals. Knowing that her time in the kitchen would end before long, she frequently passed recipes and cooking techniques on to the next generations. The family tended to make their holiday celebrations last for days, especially since they were sensing the aging of their beloved mother.

By the time grandsons Joe and Thomas were added to the family, Elizabeth's daughter, Bettie, had unexpectedly returned home from New England. She came back alone. Her doctor husband had relocated to Boston when she moved back to Greenville. Bettie refused to speak of why she was living separately from Aldelbert, and would not explain her choice to return home, even to her mother. Bettie and Adlebert had no children, but even after they separated, they remained married. The only one in the family who knew the truth behind their separation was her dear sister, Rosa, whom she swore to secrecy.

Bettie's siblings, and even her mother, had various theories about what might have happened, especially since Bettie moved back with several pieces of beautiful furniture, expensive artwork, and clothing, but her unyielding silence would leave them all wondering. She was known as Mrs. Bryson, wife of Dr. Adlebert Bryson, until several years later when Adlebert died. Then she was referred to as his widow, and that was how she would be known for the rest of her life.

Bettie had moved back into the family homestead, joining her mother, Lucy, and Mary. They all quickly learned to leave all references to Adlebert and Bettie's life in New England out of conversations, much as they had done with Frederick, his life in Atlanta and in the Little Sisters of the Poor Sanitorium in Savannah.

Bettie brought her high energy back to Greenville, and she was a great help to Lucy and Mary, who had taken over much of the work involved with the businesses. Elizabeth had established a reputation in Greenville for being hard-working and unstoppable in business, and the sisters, all in their mid-to-late-forties, reinforced the family's standing in the community as resilient and hardworking.

It was a time of general prosperity and peace, with little of the drama or loss they had experienced in many other years. The only unwanted notoriety was a lawsuit brought against Frank and his partner A.C. Gann in Atlanta by a woman who blamed Gann & Garraux for her husband's whiskey-drinking and subsequent lack of employment.

It was the first lawsuit of its kind ever brought in Atlanta, so it garnered coverage in newspapers all across the South. Once again, Frank found himself having to prepare his very private mother for likely public gossip.

"It's a foolish lawsuit, Mother," Frank said. "The woman is unhappy because her husband drinks too much and she's looking for someone to blame."

"I understand her anger," Elizabeth said, and in the voice of a mother scolding a young child, she said. "Do you yet understand why I don't think a saloon is an appropriate business? Drinking ruined my marriage, and it continues to ruin others."

Frank sighed and looked somewhat exasperated. "I knew you would be upset and would connect it to what happened with father. I am sorry about that. But I do not take blame for someone else's choices. I am only telling you about it in case someone in the Greenville gossip grapevine gets wind of it."

The lawsuit was filed by Lottie Spairs, the angry wife. She claimed A.C. and Frank would regularly promise to stop serving her husband, Crawford, whiskey, and would then break their promise, causing him to keep losing his job. She told the court her husband was a capable machinist who made eighteen dollars a week when he was sober. She said Crawford's drunkenness, caused by Gann & Garraux, kept him from providing for her and their two children, and caused her "much misery and shame."

The lawsuit was eventually settled out of court and public interest in it diminished, but it did tarnish Elizabeth's feelings toward her son Frank's considerable business accomplishments.

In the summer of 1907, not long after the lawsuit, Elizabeth received an envelope in the mail with the return address of The Little Sisters of the Poor in Savannah. She put the letter in her apron pocket and handed the rest of the mail to Lucy before she went to her bedroom and closed the door.

Elizabeth sat by a window in the corner of the room, in a rocking chair that had been built and ornately carved by Frederick. She opened the letter. It was what she expected.

Dear Mrs. Garraux:

We regret to inform you that your husband, Frederick Gottlieb Garraux, passed on to his eternal rest on July 7, 1907. Mr. Garraux passed quietly in his sleep, and we do not believe he suffered. He will be interred in the cemetery here in Savannah, should any family members wish to visit in the future to pay their respect.

May the Lord grant eternal rest unto him, and perpetual light shine upon him. May he rest in peace.

Elizabeth read the letter through three times, the gravity and weight of it becoming heavier with each reading. For more than half a century, she had been Frederick's wife and had carried his name. In the early decades, she had been so in love with the man. They had brought eleven children into the world. The depth and importance of what they had shared still existed, though deeply buried under disappointment and shame over their severed relationship.

Elizabeth folded the letter, slipped it back into the envelope and into her pocket.

She leaned back in the chair in the dimly lit room, and said quietly, out loud, "Frederick is gone. It is over. He is gone." And then she wept. Almost imperceptibly at first, but building until quiet, violent sobs shook her tiny, frail body. She cried not just for his passing, but for all that had been lost. She cried for the years of hurt, the struggle, the nights alone, the unshared successes and failures. And she cried for herself, something she never did. She wept decades of tears, crying until she was exhausted and wrung dry.

Then, as was her way, she washed her face, smoothed back her hair, straightened her dress and apron, and went to find her daughters to begin spreading the word that their seventy-seven-year-old father was gone. It was her sons who would feel the loss more keenly, so Bettie agreed to travel to Atlanta to speak with her brothers, Frank and Earnest, in person.

Chapter 20

Within days, the Garraux family from Georgia to Rhode Island was fully informed, each experiencing Frederick's passing in different ways—some with grief, others with near relief, some with residual bitterness. Only Earnest and Frank would make the trip to Savannah to visit their father's grave. Seeing the simplicity of his poor gravesite left them profoundly saddened. It also provided the closure needed to say goodbye to the complicated man who had died so very far removed from his family and his past.

After Frederick's passing, Elizabeth began to disperse property to family members, making sure the homestead and farm would stay in Garraux possession when she would also be gone. She arranged for the bulk of the property along Swiss Avenue to go to Charles, who maintained a large farm, and Lucy and Mary, who lived in the main house. Bettie also lived on the property in a small cottage near the homestead, though she would eventually move into the main house.

The passing of her estranged husband moved Elizabeth into her final chapter, as if his mortality reminded her of her own. Over the next year, she continued to occasionally work with Lucy and Mary on flower arrangements for large events, but she would tire more quickly, and they would often have to finish the work under her direction as she sat nearby. The three of them still attended church together every Sunday, but more often than not, Elizabeth would take a Sunday afternoon nap, something she had never done until her seventy-ninth year.

By the fall of 1908, Elizabeth was limiting her social time to visits from the children and grandchildren, who still brought her great delight. For the first time, she let her daughters and daughters-in-law take over the kitchen for the holiday meals, only insisting that she would still bake the walnut holiday cake.

She was so exhausted that a few days after Christmas when everyone but the three daughters had returned to their own homes, Lucy expressed her concern.

"I think you are doing too much, Mother. You look so pale and tired. Maybe trying to play with the children and all the visiting is too much?"

"Oh, Lucy, don't worry about me," Elizabeth said, patting her hand. "My heart is getting old and tired, but it is also full. To be with my children and grandchildren is my greatest joy. And you have been such a blessing, Lucy. All of you make me so proud and happy, but without you, I could not have managed this life."

Lucy was so touched by the words, her eyes filled with tears. At fifty years old and having never married, her mother and siblings meant everything to her. She knew Elizabeth was nearing the end of her days, and even though her mother had a long and vital life, the thought of the world without her powerful presence still saddened Lucy greatly.

During the next few cold months of winter, Elizabeth spent longer periods of time resting, and less time outside the house. They had moved her bed into a downstairs room, and Elizabeth divided her limited waking hours between her bed and enjoying the warmth of the fireplace. The steps it took to go from the parlor to her bed became more arduous, and she moved very slowly, though with the help of a cane, she could generally make the trip on her own.

One afternoon, Lucy heard her moving about, and peeked into the parlor to see if she needed assistance. She saw Elizabeth stopped, standing near the fireplace, her hand on the beautiful, carved wooden frame around the fireplace hearth. Lucy could not know what Elizabeth was thinking, but the placement of her hand and the faraway look in her eyes told her that a memory of love or of better times must have caused her to stop there. Lucy silently stepped back out of the room, leaving her mother to whatever distant memories or feelings held her there.

Mary, Lucy, and Bettie would bring bits of Elizabeth's favorite foods to her room, but she ate less and less. Having started at less than a hundred pounds, Elizabeth was now a mere wisp of a woman. She seemed terribly frail, though she remained as mentally sharp as ever. She recognized each of the seven children and ten grandchildren who lived in Greenville and called them by name, asking each of the adults and older children about their endeavors and interests. Elizabeth would brighten during the visits, especially when she had a chance to read books to the grandchildren or watch them play nearby. But there was no doubt as the weeks passed, each of their visits seemed to exhaust her more.

Winter loosened its grasp, and the dogwoods began to bloom as the big oak trees dressed themselves in the lacy bright green of spring.

One afternoon, Elizabeth called Lucy, Mary, and Bettie to her room.

"I want to see spring," she said. She spoke in measured tones, without drama or sadness. "I want to smell the air and hear the birds," she said. "I want to say goodbye to our farm."

Her daughters cast sad glances at each other, but would not insult their mother's spirit by being maudlin.

314

"Well, then, let's get some shoes on you and get you out into spring," Bettie said, forcing an air of positivity into her words.

They helped Elizabeth get her thin arms into a coat and slipped shoes onto her tiny feet. Then, with Bettie on one side, Lucy on the other, and Mary ahead to open doors, they slowly and carefully took her through the parlor and out the front door.

They stopped on the porch, as Elizabeth straightened up as best she could and said, "Oh, the wisteria! Look at the wisteria!"

The long, lavender bunches of wisteria blooms hung by the thousands from the vine that wrapped around the porch and many yards down the pergola toward the barn. It gave a fairyland appearance to the house, and it filled her head and heart with decades of memories.

"My dear friend, George," she murmured. "What a gift of beauty this was. And it will long outlive the both of us. Isn't it just something?"

They helped her carefully down the steps, and onto the path that would take them to the largest flower garden, the one that provided a view across the expanse of the lower acreage. Its beautiful English boxwoods, orderly farm fields and gardens, and remnants of the old vineyard made it look like a beautiful quilt laid out across the hillside. Daffodils of several varieties dotted the hillside. Looking down on the tops of pink and white dogwood trees scattered across the property gave the appearance of wondrously fluffy bouquets. All of it viewed under the cobalt blue sky of a clear spring day made it appear truly magical.

"Look at what you created, Mama," Lucy said. "Look at this amazing property and all you accomplished with it."

"It's beautiful, Mama, and you did it," Mary said.

Bettie chimed in and said, "And most of it all on your own, Mother. With no man to take credit for it. This is your farm. This is your business. You built this, and you gave us all good lives because of it."

Elizabeth seemed to stand just a little straighter then, and a hint of color rose in her cheeks. Her eyes brightened, and she smiled broadly.

"It's really something, isn't it? I have a legacy to leave behind," she said.

"Oh, Mama, you are the legacy!" Lucy said. "Your strength, your spirit, your perseverance. It is you and your example that are your legacy to our family."

Bettie and Mary added their agreement, and the three of them bundled their tiny mother into a hug.

"Oh, thank you, girls," Elizabeth said. "You bring me such joy. I am such a blessed woman."

Then, as the end of the moment seemed to let the strength seep out of her body, she said, "I am afraid I need to go lie down for a bit."

They took her back into the house and helped her into bed. Almost instantly, she was asleep. She slept away the rest of the day, only sitting up briefly for a little tea before falling back asleep for the night. The next morning, they found her nearly unable to awaken, and they called the doctor.

Chapter 21

The old physician had known the family for decades, and he was only about ten years younger than Elizabeth. After he examined her, he came out to speak with her daughters.

"I am afraid your mother has reached the end of her days. It is time you call the rest of the family together. Her heart is extremely weak, and her pulse is faint. I do not think there is much time left."

Bettie immediately sent telegrams to Frank and Earnest in Atlanta and to Rosa in Rhode Island. The sons arrived in Greenville the next morning, and Amos and Rosa with their two children arrived three days later. All of Elizabeth's children and the older grandchildren gathered at the main house, and in the other homes on the Garraux property.

By the time Rosa arrived, Elizabeth was only able to awaken for moments at a time just a few times a day. The whole family was grateful during one of those times when their mother rallied enough to see and recognize Rosa, whom she hadn't seen in a couple years.

"Oh, my beautiful Rosa," Elizabeth said. "I am so glad you are here."

Rosa struggled to keep a smile on her face until her mother's eyes closed again.

Lucy brought out a beautiful, intricately embroidered, velvet crazy quilt that all the sisters had worked on years before as a gift to their mother. They had finished it in 1898, and the date, along with the word "Mother" and many of Elizabeth's favorite flowers were embroidered into the quilt pattern. She gently laid it over their beloved mother as she slept.

Each of the children took time sitting with Elizabeth, saying things they wished they had said more often, thanking her for being such as example, telling her how much they loved her. The older of the grandchildren were allowed to see her briefly. The sight of her, barely visible under the bed covers, so pale, frail, and barely breathing, was too disturbing for the younger ones.

With all of her beloved children nearby, and with the same grace and strength of spirit with which she lived her life, eighty-year-old Elizabeth Schar Garraux, widow of Frederick, mother of Fred, Earnest, Lucy, Mary, Bettie, Rosa, Frank, John, Charles, William, and Fannie, took her last breath on March 25, 1909.

The newspaper article about her death said:

> *She was a woman of indomitable energy and was for many years engaged in the florist and gardening business, being an expert in this line of work she made a success of her business.*

Her children, grandchildren, and all those who loved and admired her knew she was much more than her business. She was Elizabeth: strong, singular, unstoppable, undeniable, and yes, indomitable.

She was buried in Springwood cemetery, located on North Main Street between the Garraux homestead and downtown. The old cemetery contained the unmarked graves of more than eighty unidentified Civil

War soldiers, as well as the unmarked graves of hundreds of slaves, all in their final rest alongside her and many of Greenville's other prominent citizens.

Elizabeth's grave lies under a large monument carved to look like a cross-shaped tree trunk, with a banner across it that says "Mother." Standing at her grave, a tall, obelisk-shaped monument with an angel atop it is visible at the top of the hill. That monument stands over the graves of Fannie Heldman and her parents, George and Matilda Heldman.

Each of Elizabeth's daughters had a mourning pin made containing one of the last photographs of their mother. They wore the brooches for a full year after her passing.

On the first anniversary of her death, Fannie, Mary, Lucy and Bettie committed to cleaning out their mother's dresser and closet. It was difficult for them to be among her things, knowing that she was gone, but at the same time, it brought some comfort and familiarity.

They sorted and divided items, keeping many of them, but deciding to let some go to charity. They worked their way down to the bottom drawer of the dresser, and when Fannie picked up the last small pile of nightgowns, there in the bottom of the drawer was the wooden box.

"It is the box Father gave her when they were courting!" Fannie said.

The box, with its dozens of inlaid pieces of different types of wood forming an intricate border of interlocking rings, was the amazing work of a skilled artisan.

"I didn't know she still had it," Lucy exclaimed.

Mary said, "I wonder if there is anything in it."

Fannie lifted the box out of the drawer and set it on top of the dresser.

The four of them just stood still and silent, looking at the box until Bettie said, "Well, of course, we should open it."

They all continued to awkwardly stare at the box, no one moving.

"Mother kept this for more than fifty years, and none of us even knew she still had it," Lucy said. "It must have been important to her."

"Go ahead, Lucy, you open it," Fannie said.

"Yes, open it," Bettie said, as Mary nodded agreement.

Lucy slowly and carefully opened the box, as they all leaned in to see what it held. It was empty except for a folded piece of paper.

She pulled out the paper, and unfolded it, seeing her mother's handwriting inside.

A lump formed in Lucy's throat as she read the words out loud.

I will always love you Frederick.

Always and forever,

Your little mouse, Elizabeth

Acknowledgments

It is a true privilege to tell Elizabeth Garraux's story, and I owe many thanks to those who helped make it possible:

To my earliest consultant, my brilliant daughter, Hannah Corsa, thank you for setting me off in the right direction with this novel.

To the great staff at the South Carolina Room of the Hughes Library in Greenville, as well as Judy Bainbridge, retired Furman University professor emerita and Greenville history expert, I so appreciate your outstanding and inspiring historical input and assistance.

To Tracie Williams, with the Greenville County Register of Deeds Office, thank you for your good-humored, unceasingly patient, and brilliant help.

To my incredibly talented son, Joshua, I can't thank you enough for your enormous artistic contributions.

To my editor, Dr. Charles K. Phillips, thank you for your helpful, professional, and expeditious work.

Big props to the genius resource of Ancestry.com, which ultimately led me to the Garraux's great-great granddaughter, Elizabeth Williams.

Elizabeth, your openness and generosity in sharing family history and memorabilia made the most significant contributions to this novel. I am forever indebted to you, your brother Tommy, and your sister, Adele, for all you have shared with me.

I thank my forever love and my most loyal champion and supporter, Eric Johnson. Thank you for patiently living through hundreds of hours of research and writing, and tolerating long, late night conversations about a tiny woman whose life is forever intertwined with ours. I am so grateful you encouraged me to finally reach a lifelong goal.

Above all else, I thank God for giving me the time in my life, and words that I hope do justice to Elizabeth Garraux's story.

There is no way to adequately thank all of them, and all my countless other supporters -- and especially Elizabeth Garraux, the indomitable, remarkable woman whose story really had to be told.

This book is set in Adobe Caslon Pro. William Caslon introduced his initial typefaces in 1722, which were inspired by Dutch old style designs from the 17th century and gained popularity in England due to their practicality. These typefaces quickly became widely used across Europe and in the American colonies, with Benjamin Franklin, a renowned printer, predominantly employing Caslon's designs. Notably, the American Declaration of Independence and the Constitution were first printed using Caslon. Designer Carol Twombly conducted a thorough study of William Caslon's printed specimen pages from 1734 to 1770 to revive the Caslon typeface.

Made in the USA
Columbia, SC
25 August 2024

41158434R00198